TO HAVE AND
HAVE MORE

TO HAVE AND HAVE MORE

SANIBEL

8th NOTE PRESS

Published by 8th Note Press
Text Copyright © 2025 by Sanibel Lazar
All rights reserved.

ISBN: 9781961795402
eBook ISBN: 9781961795273
Audiobook ISBN: 9781961795419

Cover design by Vi-An Nguyen
Crest illustration by Vi-An Nguyen
Artichoke art based on photograph by
Valentyn Volkov/Shutterstock
Typeset by Typo•glyphix

First, to Tal

Join me in hurting anyone who hurts me

Iliad, Book IX, line 801
Trans. Emily Wilson

PROLOGUE

Show-and-tell at Sward Country Day was not your average show-and-tell. For starters, it was called Share & Enlighten.

"I'm so excited to see what Emery has brought for Share & Enlighten today!" Ms. Brodie's enthusiasm for teaching first grade was inexhaustible. "Everyone please sit Indian style and zip it, lock it, put it in your pocket."

The class mimed zipping their mouths shut as they settled onto the Shaker rug. Emery stood at the front of the room with a mint-colored keepsake box in her hands.

"This is my adoption box," she said.

"I thought you were bringing your hamster!" a towheaded boy interrupted.

"Marina vacuumed him," Emery snapped at Brandon. She lifted the lid gingerly and a mix of photographs, documents, and mementos were revealed. "This is a picture of the orphanage in Korea where—"

"Is your mom bringing those candies again?" Matt W. asked

"I like the purple ones," Callie volunteered. "Not the green ones."

Ms. Brodie used her patient voice: "I know you're all

excited for Emery's presentation, but remember we're supposed to wear our listening caps during Share & Enlighten."

Emery continued, "My parents got me when I was six
months old. This onesie is the only—"

"You shared and enlightened this last time," Brandon complained. "You promised to bring Fruitrollup. You said we
could feed him."

"Stop interrupting!" Emery stomped her foot. "I told you;
Marina vacuumed him."

Marina had accidentally vacuumed Fruitrollup the day
before Share & Enlighten. Emery had pitched a fit. She had
been bragging about her pet hamster for weeks, and she was
so distraught that she let her mom talk her into sharing the
adoption box—again.

Share & Enlighten was always a bore. Moms sent their first
graders with peonies picked fresh from the garden and just-
polished family heirlooms. It was a competition between
mothers in which kids were merely vehicles. When Ms.
Brodie's class had found out that Emery was going to bring a
rodent to the classroom, they'd lost their minds.

"This is called a *hanbok*," Emery said, pulling a garment
out of the box. "Korean people wear—"

"It's just a dumb dress," Brandon said.

Emery invoked the worst insult she had ever heard her dad
use. (It was the only time Emery had witnessed her mother
rebuke him.)

"You're just a public-school moron."

"Emery!" Ms. Brodie exclaimed.

Brandon started crying. Emery smiled innocently. She *was*
innocent—insofar as she had no idea what her words meant.

CHAPTER 1

There's no such thing as a nice rich kid. Some have better manners or sweeter smiles, but none of them are nice. If you're not rich and you manage to slip into their ranks, do not consider yourself accepted. Maybe you're funny or outgoing or willing to be treated like a second-class citizen, but you'll find out (the hard way) that you're not one of them. It might be a sweet sixteen you're excluded from or a summer getaway you're not invited to—and they'll feel no embarrassment discussing it, at length, in your presence.

• • •

Derrymore Academy, a boarding school, was a hotbed of rich kids. And Emery Hooper, one such kid, was about to lose a crucial tennis match to a girl who didn't belong there. Lilah Chang was a chunky public-school kid who had earned her way into Derrymore with good grades, high test scores, and parental pressure. Her dumpy appearance clashed magnificently with the pristine, newly resurfaced Derrymore courts.

Match point. Emery blasted Lilah's patty-cake, spineless serve straight into the net. Before smashing her racquet against the court, she remembered her last cracked frame. Her father had called her behavior "unbecoming"—then handed over a credit card to replace the latest Prince model. Emery restrained herself and sent a dark look toward the bleachers where her best friend was watching. Noah smiled weakly in return.

Good sportsmanship was not Emery's domain. She had taken private lessons since she was nine and was deeply offended that her run to the varsity team had been cut short by a girl wearing cheap running shoes and a surplus fifteen pounds.

The tryout was a boon and she'd blown it. Now freshman year would kick off with the stench of mediocrity and unflattering JV uniforms. Emery could already hear her mother's soothing words: *As long as you tried your best, there's no shame in JV! You should be proud you made it so far in tryouts.*

It was true. Freshmen were rarely considered. But Emery wasn't going to be grateful for something she felt entitled to. It had slipped from her grip so fast. She had already planned a blasé delivery when telling her friends—especially Candace— that she'd made varsity.

Emery approached the coach to report the score.

"Four, six. Two, six," Emery said. "I lost."

She searched the coach's face for surprise. She liked him less when she didn't find it.

"The freshman showdown," he said. "Which one are you?"

"Emery Hooper."

He noted the score on his clipboard. Emery gestured miserably in the direction of the JV courts. "I guess I should go over there?"

"Let's see." Coach Norton examined the score sheet. "The varsity roster is full, but I don't have a single freshman. I'm going to give you and—what's your name?"

Emery hadn't noticed Lilah sidle up beside her, but there she was—breathing through her nose at max volume.

Lilah mumbled her name.

"You two can be alternates if you want," Coach Norton said. "You'll train with the varsity team, but you won't play matches unless someone is sick. And you'll *only* play doubles. If you hate the idea of benchwarming and JV sounds—"

"No," Emery burst out.

"No?"

"Sorry—I mean, I want to be an alternate. I don't want to go to JV."

"Great. And how about … Emery? No"—he checked his clipboard—"the other one. I gotta get that straight. Lily, what about you?"

Lilah had crossed her arms over her stomach. She looked toward Emery, seeking encouragement. Emery avoided the pathetic gaze and willed Lilah to reject the offer.

"A full season of JV singles is nothing to shake a stick at," Coach Norton said.

Lilah stammered, "I want to be an alternate, too."

"Two for two," Coach Norton said, scribbling on his clipboard.

Lilah beamed at Emery who, in return, let just enough disgust leak into her expression to kill Lilah's smile. Emery assumed a placid look before addressing the coach: "So … see you tomorrow?"

Coach Norton nodded. "Congrats."

It didn't feel anything like Emery had fantasized. Splitting her status with Lilah diminished any sense of accomplishment. On top of that, she resented that she would have to work extra hard to distance herself from Lilah so the older girls didn't mix them up.

Why, of all people, did the other freshman have to be another Asian girl? The coach was already struggling to keep them separate in his mind. Emery suspected that he'd offered both of them a spot on the team simply because he could not remember which one had won.

Emery felt Lilah hovering as she zipped up her bag, but she refused to be lured into conversation. She had already sized Lilah up and had nothing to say to her.

The Lilah breed was familiar to Emery. They went to Kumon after school. They made duct tape wallets. They didn't roll their Soffes. Their parents were professors and IT professionals and mid-level managers who cheaped out on cable. Their moms bought the Martha Stewart collection at K-Mart and shopped for bargains at Loehmann's. They gave Ferrero Rocher chocolates as teacher gifts. Their cars didn't have heated seats and their bathrooms didn't have heated floors. They lived a full zip code (or more) away from Emery's side of town, in a different world.

"C'mon, Noah." Emery called to her friend, and dumped the contents of her Propel bottle into the grass violently. Noah scampered over obediently and gave Lilah a once-over without saying hello. Lilah waited expectantly but there was no introduction. Instead, Emery hefted her bag over her shoulder and walked away.

"Let me carry that," Noah said, falling into step with her.

"Noah," Emery complained.

She was too deflated to tussle over the bag so she let him take it. Noah thought carrying it made people think he was an athlete, but Emery thought it made him look like her caddie.

"Did you hear what Coach Norton said?" Emery asked.

Noah had been eavesdropping dutifully. "It's good, right? You got what you wanted."

"Hardly," Emery spat.

"You should've won, obviously," he said. "But that Chinese girl lobbed everything. She was a pusher."

Noah could be such a brownnoser. But he was right about Lilah being a pusher. Emery's coach always said it was a well-known stereotype that Asian and Indian players opted for the wait-it-out strategy. Instead of taking a risk and going for a winner, they'd moonball it into the center of the court and wait for you to make the error. Impatient by nature, Emery had lost matches to pushers by rushing the net too aggressively.

Noah added, "I think she wanted to play JV. But then she just copied you. She was staring at you so hard when the coach was talking."

"That's because she's Asian," Emery said, with a lilt of *duh* in her voice. "They all think that means we're automatic friends."

Emery grumbled, but she hoped the assumption might work in her favor. She was secretly obsessed with the tennis team captain, Ryan Kim. Ryan was ranked top ten in New Jersey and had been Derrymore's first seed since her freshman year. She was all tight racerbacks and high ponytail, and popular. She had a one-handed backhand and cursed in Korean. Her boyfriend was getting recruited by colleges for lacrosse. In between drills, she texted on her BlackBerry and Coach Norton never admonished her for it.

Emery glanced down at her own white tennis skirt. It was

obvious and infantile. Ryan wore tiny black shorts that sat low on her hips and revealed a sliver of midriff each time she struck the ball. Emery made a mental note to start doing Series of Five every day and to buy some black Dri-FIT.

"What counts is that you made varsity," Noah said. "No one will know what 'alternate' means."

Emery rolled her eyes. Noah was all about riding her coattails.

They convinced themselves that Emery had lost the match because she was *better* than Lilah—and they believed it. That was the sort of best friendship they had: the kind that believes dissent is betrayal and pinky promises are contracts.

CHAPTER 2

Lilah wasn't offended by Emery's abrupt departure. In fact, she hadn't picked up on the snub. It made sense that Emery was upset about losing the match. Warming up with her had been thoroughly intimidating: beautiful form, so much pace. Emery looked varsity.

Her pleated skirt and petite figure fit in with the other Derrymore bodies that did Gyrotonic workouts with their mothers and took squash lessons for cardio. The ones whose home gyms were as well-equipped as fitness centers, and whose personal trainers worked with professional athletes and models.

Lilah vowed to cut back on sugar-loaded grass jelly drinks as she returned alone to the freshman dorm. She had been hoping to introduce Emery to her friends, but it could wait. Over the summer, Lilah had pledged to become outgoing— to make new friends and not rely on the handful of girls she knew from middle school. But once she was surrounded by Derrymorians who wore bronzer and talked about grinding, she'd lost her nerve and clung to those she knew.

Her middle school clique totaled eight, of which four had been accepted to Derrymore. Lilah shuddered to think how it would feel to be in the cursed half of the group. Her mom was still consoling her rejected friends' moms with unannounced house calls and bao. Mom was always in a great mood on the days she performed these good deeds.

Her friends were in the quiet study room that no one else ever used. A soft hello to Cassie and Jenny was allowed, but Lilah refrained from interrupting Annie. No one had ever doubted that Annie would get into Derrymore. The rest of their group was a crapshoot, but Annie was considered a certainty. She was effortlessly smart and poured all her energy into accomplishing measurable and praiseworthy things. She was first chair violin in the Derrymore orchestra and the only freshman on the Mathletes team. It was a given that Annie would go to Harvard (which her parents would announce if you happened to make eye contact with them).

But they were equally vocal in drawing attention to what they believed was Annie's greatest flaw. When guests came over, they often gasped and brought their hands to their mouths when Annie appeared.

"So dark," family friends muttered in greeting, shaking their heads sympathetically.

"Hello, Auntie," Annie would say through gritted teeth. "Hello, Uncle."

Annie's mother bought skin bleaching creams from Korea, but they stained Annie's face unevenly and burned her skin. Her mom begged that she use them anyway.

"But you are so dark," her mom would say. "If you use creams, maybe skin like Lilah. So white. So pretty."

Lilah never understood why Annie was hot and cold to her. When Annie came to a stopping point in her bio textbook, Lilah was allowed to speak.

"I made the varsity team," she said. "I'm an alternate so I won't play matches, but I get to train with them."

"Does that even count as varsity?" Annie asked.

"I think so. It just means—"

"If you don't play matches, then how are you on the team?"

Lilah flushed.

"It sounds like you're just a benchwarmer," Annie said, twisting the yellow Livestrong bracelet around her wrist. "Congratulations, though."

Jenny and Cassie chimed in with their congrats.

"Thanks," Lilah said.

"You're gonna make so many friends," Cassie said.

"Are there any other freshmen?" Jenny asked.

"Just one. Emery Hooper."

Annie's head whipped toward Lilah. "The adopted girl?"

Lilah nodded.

"The squash girl?" Cassie asked.

They had known of Emery before they saw the Hooper Squash Center at Derrymore. She was famous in their town as the first daughter of the wealthier neighboring town. Emery was in the local paper often: for selling the most Girl Scout cookies or winning a tennis tournament or giving a kid's perspective on the best books to read this summer. They had seen her once at the mall, loaded down with shopping bags and her parents' undivided attention.

CHAPTER 3

Inside Derrymore's gates, the sunlight is different and so is the air. It smells honey-sweet—the odor of refined hedonism and certain success. Derrymore is home to teenagers who have their eyebrows shaped and their sweet sixteens tented. Their first kisses arrive around the same time as their boating licenses, and they celebrate getting their braces off with Mediterranean jaunts. Despite six-figure donations and hefty tutoring bills, Derrymore acceptance letters are rewarded with diamonds and purebreds. Emery unsealed her letter at a congratulatory party her parents had planned months in advance. Lilah tore hers open while standing in the driveway with her mom breathing raggedly in her ear. Mrs. Chang screamed so loudly that a neighbor opened his front door, concerned.

• • •

The freshman biology curriculum was an unforseen point of contention at the Derrymore Board of Trustees meeting. A perfunctory update about a new, fashionable science unit turned into a heated debate.

"Calculate Your Carbon Footprint" was an exercise where students would tally up their energy usage and confront their impact on the environment. It would be followed by a lecture on ways to decrease carbon emissions and a pledge to reduce waste.

The initiative met huge resistance. It was denounced as political propaganda. What was the educational value? An older board member called it communism.

But the curriculum won out in the end. Headmaster Runciter referenced his notes: "Exeter and Andover have been teaching this for two years already. I don't have to remind you how far our endowment is lagging behind."

The comment was met with sober murmurs. Exeter had just broken a billion. Derrymore was slumming it in the hundred millions.

• • •

Calculate Your Carbon Footprint was a humblebrag bonanza.

"Do yachts count as vehicles?"

"Am I supposed to include my maids as part of my family if they're live-in?"

"For the number of nights per week that I eat meat-slash-seafood—what if you catch the seafood yourself? So there's no bycatch?"

"We have solar panels at our ranch. Doesn't that make my footprint smaller?"

When someone asked about a timeshare, a snicker went around the room. When someone asked about a cruise, there were loud guffaws. Not everyone at Derrymore was the right kind of rich, and if you didn't know how to pretend, ridicule was an efficient teacher. The hapless student who asked about the cruise took heed, and the next time cruises were mentioned in his presence, he would lead the scorn.

Students closed their eyes, imagining their vast, beige homes and estimated square footage.

"Wait," a girl exclaimed. "I can check online. My house was just in *Town & Country*."

Emery peeked at Candace's screen. She'd been to countless sleepovers and swims at Candace's house—it looked just like her own. Deep pantries. Glossy banisters. Built-ins filled with books arranged by decorators. Gratuitous kitchen islands. Everything was designed to hide signs of living: TVs disappeared down into consoles, trashcans were camouflaged among cabinetry, bread garages concealed sourdough batards. It was a veldt of good taste and prosperity, much like the Derrymore campus.

But even Derrymore's sculpted lushness—its well-manicured everywhere and rarified everything—was not enough to take Emery's mind off Lilah Chang. An ugly blight on the surface of Emery's otherwise perfect life, Lilah was a dark spot that Emery's mother would have lasered off during a same-day appointment.

After filling in her carbon footprint data, Emery was slightly surprised to find herself responsible for six times the carbon output of the average individual. Candace clocked in at eight times the average. They both expressed unhappiness and disbelief, but some pride slipped through.

"It's not my fault my dad collects sports cars," Candace said, sipping from a Diet Lemon Snapple.

● ● ●

Emery's parents were older than the median age of her peers' parents, and richer, too. If anyone asked about Emery's ethnic heritage, her parents gave icy responses and declared the offender ill-mannered. They loved her so much as their own that they were blind to her Korean-ness. She was their only child.

With no siblings to hog the bathroom or steal Ella Moss tunics from, Emery was accustomed to getting ready alone. But she was stumped by whether or not to wear the varsity uniform for the first match of the season. Being an alternate made Emery feel like an imposter and she worried that idling on the bleachers in full regalia would scream *poser*. But if she wore class dress, she might be accused of not being a good team player (a familiar, and true, criticism).

Emery decided to risk being classified as a wannabe and wore the uniform. When she exited her room, Lilah was there waiting.

"Ready to head over to the courts?"

Lilah wore an ill-fitting white polo with too-blue jeans and black Converse sneakers. Emery felt instant confidence in her uniform decision.

"Do you think I should change into my uniform, too?" Lilah asked. "I figured since we're not playing we didn't need to, but you're probably right."

Lilah nervous-laughed through her sentences, which made her difficult to understand.

"Huh?" Emery said. "I'm going to the courts."

She slung her tennis bag across her back.

"I'll be really fast, I promise," Lilah said.

"I'm not going to be late for the first match."

"Do you think I should change?'

"No one *told* me to wear it. I made my own decision."

Lilah's face was pained. It was clear she desperately wanted to change but knew Emery would leave without her.

As they walked, Emery dragged her feet and tried to keep her distance. She stared at Lilah's back fat, which was accentuated by a too-tight sports bra. It would not surprise Emery to learn that Lilah didn't own an underwire bra. Lilah's white shirt had been laundered with something red and the result was a pinkish tinge of sloppiness. Her Ashlee Simpson–inspired haircut was atrocious and mullet-like. Pretending to be distracted by her phone, Emery walked even slower, but she hadn't accounted for Lilah's indefatigable patience.

When they came to the Isle, Lilah halted.

"What is it?" Emery asked, though she already knew.

It was rumored that freshmen were not allowed to traverse the well-kept lawn, which was surrounded (and allegedly surveilled) by upperform dormitories. Unfortunately, the Isle happened to be on the shortest route from the freshman dormitory to the courts. For fear of looking gullible, Emery hadn't asked her teammates if the rumor was true. She usually elected to cross the Isle, but her heart always raced as she power walked through.

Emery stepped onto the lawn.

"Wait"—Lilah grasped Emery's arm—"I really think we should go around."

"Go ahead." Emery pulled away from Lilah's grip. "I cross it every day."

"Wait, please," Lilah said, taking a deep breath. "Just give me a second."

Emery made sure no one was watching as Lilah took several loud breaths.

"Can we jog it?" Lilah asked.

"Ew. No."

"But I don't want to get in trouble and Ryan is really scary and if we get on her bad side—"

Lilah was talking faster and higher.

"Fine."

Jogging had the effect of jouncing Emery's enormous bag against her back as they hurried across the Isle. When they reached the bleachers, Ryan's scornful expression was the first thing they saw. Her beauty coupled with her masculine name suggested a physical and spiritual superiority that made her an effective captain. Emery had heard that Ryan's boyfriend had recorded her voicemail message ("You've reached Ryan, bitches") and she'd recorded his—could anything be more romantic?

"Why the hell were you running?"

The back of Emery's neck burned. Ryan had only spoken to her twice before: once to congratulate her flatly for making varsity, and again to remind her to pick up the team's uniforms (a freshman chore). Emery and Lilah spoke at once, cutting each other off:

"I thought we were late—"

"Freshmen aren't allowed—"

Ryan's hands were on her hips and a silver charm bracelet dangled from her left wrist. Her disdain turned into cruel pleasure after her sidekick, Sara, whispered something in her ear. It was undoubtedly a reminder of the Isle rumor that was passed down from generation to generation. Ryan stood in front of Emery and Lilah, her face stony.

"You crossed the Isle?" she asked.

Lilah launched into an apology, but Ryan cut her off with a sharp gesture, charm bracelet clinking softly.

"Are you *insane*? Don't you know what happens if you're caught?"

Supposedly, freshmen who illicitly crossed the Isle had to perform a song and dance at Chapel. Chapel was the daily all-school meeting that could consist of anything from a snooze-inducing presentation on biodiversity in the Korean DMZ to a provocative dance by the senior boys promoting the bonfire. The regular features were student government notices, birthday shoutouts, and expulsion announcements.

Emery swallowed. It couldn't possibly be true. Ryan wouldn't subject them to that level of public humiliation.

"*Hello?*" Ryan snapped.

Both girls nodded.

"You get out of jail free this time, but next time …"

Ryan's voice trailed off threateningly. Sara giggled.

● ● ●

Coach Norton took no notice of Emery's uniform. He took no notice of her whatsoever. He went down the team sheet reminding each player what she was supposed to focus on during her match. For Ryan, he had only one word—"ferocity"—after which he growled. She nodded vigorously, but when he turned his back, Ryan and Sara snickered. They made cat claws with their hands and pretended to scratch at one another.

Emery would have preferred to watch the matches alone, but Lilah sat beside her on the bleachers. The coach was giving a pep talk to the players on the first court and Emery watched the huddle feeling envious and self-conscious.

"I'm gonna go to the bathroom," Lilah said. "Do you want to come?"

"No," Emery said, with more force than she intended.

While Lilah was in the restroom, a Derrymore photographer arrived at the courts.

"Yearbook photos," Ryan called, dabbing on lip gloss. "Seniors only first."

She stood in front of the center net strap and Sara nudged another player out of the way to stand beside her.

"Now everyone, c'mon," Ryan said. "Two rows, by height. Make sure your straps aren't showing. I told you to wear a sports bra, Sara."

Sara had worn her most dramatic push-up bra.

Ryan gestured impatiently at Emery. *C'mon.*

"Me?"

Emery scrambled onto the court and Ryan maneuvered her into the first row. Emery knelt on the hard court and felt Ryan's manicured hand rest on her shoulder.

The photographer got into position.

"Wait," Ryan said.

Emery breathed a sigh of relief. The captain had noticed that Lilah was missing.

"Like me, girls," Ryan instructed. "One hand on the shoulder of the person in front of you."

The team repositioned themselves and the photographer snapped away. Ryan checked the photos and indicated which one she liked most to the photographer. She said something that made him laugh.

Ryan clapped. "Let's win out there today!"

Emery was brushing sandy debris off her knees when she noticed that Lilah had returned. She wasn't sure how much Lilah had seen and didn't ask, but it was hard to ignore Lilah's pitiful expression. It wasn't Emery's fault that Lilah had terrible timing and even worse luck. And it wasn't her job to tell Ryan that Lilah was missing. But then why did Emery keep thinking about Kitty Genovese and the idle bystanders her history class condemned?

They watched Ryan and her opponent go groundstroke to groundstroke until Lilah broke the tense silence.

"Do you think Ryan hates me?" she asked.

Emery's head continued to move back and forth, following the ball.

"She doesn't like or dislike you. We're freshmen. She doesn't think about us."

"Yeah, but ... it seems like she likes you at least a little. But to me—"

"Being liked is overrated. Who cares what other people think."

Ryan warmed up her serve. She grunted loudly each time the racquet pronated into the ball.

"Yeah." Lilah nodded. "You're right."

Emery was relieved to get out of the conversation so easily. Platitudes never worked on Noah. He always demanded his reassurances with a heavy dose of sincerity. His insecurity ran deep, and he had a kindred spirit in the girl warming up on court two, chugging a hot pink Vitaminwater.

Sara was plain in features, ideas, and personality. She identified as a blonde but her hair was mousy brown. Sara craved attention but didn't know what to do when she got it. From time to time she demanded Ryan show her respect, but mostly allowed herself to be abused. She failed to understand that her role was sidekick, and anything more central would pose a challenge to her abilities. Between every point, Sara looked over to Ryan's court, but her best friend never returned the glance.

Emery swallowed guiltily, remembering how Lilah had averted her eyes when she saw the team wrapping up the photo. But Lilah wasn't in uniform. She wouldn't have been allowed to pose anyway.

• • •

At the end of Ryan's first set, a rotund man watching the match caught Emery's eye. She craned her neck to follow him as he walked to his car.

"Is that someone you know?" Lilah asked.

"It's my chef," Emery said, confused.

She went over to his sedan, where he was looking in the backseat for something.

"Chef Eric?"

He stood up with a baseball cap in hand and took a moment to register who she was.

"Oh my—Emery!" he said, smiling. "How good to see you!"

"What are you doing here?"

"My daughter's on the team. Gracie."

"I didn't know you had kids."

Gracie was a forgettable girl who played doubles with another junior. Emery didn't know Chef Eric's last name so she would never have put two and two together. He had worked for the Hoopers for over ten years.

"I thought my mom sent you or something."

"Off duty today," he said. "How are you liking Derrymore? I'm sure you've made plenty of friends already."

Emery shrugged. "It's good. I already knew a bunch of people. You work for the Perkinses, too, right? Candace is my year."

"What court are you on? I'll cheer you on when Gracie's match is over."

"I'm an 'alternate.'" Emery stuck her tongue out. "I practice with the team but I don't play matches. It sucks."

"I'm sure you'll get plenty of matchplay next season. You're only a freshman. Gracie barely made the team as a junior."

"If I don't play singles next year I'll kill myself."

Chef Eric laughed with professional élan. "I'm sure it won't come to that."

"It was nice to see you," Emery said suddenly. "I'll tell my parents you say hi."

She returned to the bleachers and wondered if Gracie was on scholarship. Emery's mom's therapist had a son who'd graduated from Derrymore a few years ago. Her dad's cardiologist had a niece who was also an alum. It was possible for Emery to run into her family's attorney and interior decorator during Parents Weekend, but she hadn't realized she might also run into their chef.

People like the Hoopers were always friendly with their chefs and ski instructors and landscapers. And they claimed great affection for their nannies and maids and tutors. But their real friends were those with whom they shared a pool guy or antiques dealer. Friends were those they'd run into at a showroom for high-end bathroom fixtures, or at the milliner for a new sunhat, or at the farm share for vegetable pickup.

"You have a chef?" Lilah asked.

"Only during the summer," Emery said. "My mom doesn't like to cook when she's on island."

Ryan switched sides of the court with her opponent.

"What does your mom do?" Lilah asked.

Emery turned slowly. It was the first time she had looked at Lilah since the match began.

"She does … being my mom."

Emery's face mingled concern with disbelief—like she couldn't be certain of Lilah's sanity.

"Right." Lilah nodded heartily. She took a big swig from a red Gatorade to cover up her blunder and sloshed it down the front of her shirt.

In one swift movement, Emery pulled a sweatshirt out of her bag and shoved it into Lilah's lap.

"You can give it back to me whenever. After washing it."

It was a knockabout sweatshirt. Emery wore it after matches when she was still sweaty, and only remembered to launder it occasionally. She kept it shoved in the bottom of her tennis bag with her backup iPod.

Knockabout culture was big at Derrymore. Families had knockabout cars for learning how to drive. They had knockabout dinnerware for dining outdoors. They had knockabout computers for LimeWire and the risks that came with pirated MP3s. Everything was expendable.

Emery's knockabout boots were last season's that she no longer liked. She'd worn them in a muddy field for a "photoshoot" with Noah and Candace. Knockabout digital cameras and peacoats and knockabout velour sweat suits to wear while tie-dyeing knockabout white T-shirts—it was a caste system of belongings.

Everything became knockabout eventually. Knockabout sunglasses and ribbon belts and tennis racquets. And friends.

Lilah didn't have knockabout belongings. She pulled Emery's sweatshirt over her head gratefully. It was stifling, but better to sweat than to be seen with an enormous pink splotch on her chest.

• • •

"Where did you get that?"

Annie's forehead creased with contempt when she saw Lilah's borrowed sweatshirt.

"Emery lent it to me," Lilah responded casually. "I was cold."

Her friends were seated in the quiet study room, in the same configuration they always occupied.

"Emery Hooper?" Jenny asked, eyes widening.

She leaned in to scrutinize the faded crewneck. Cassie joined her.

"It's an ugly color," Annie said. "It looks like diluted period blood."

"Rich people like muted colors," Lilah said.

"I like it," Cassie said. "It looks classy."

"So you're an expert on rich people now?" Annie said, talking over Cassie. "And I guess you go to Nantucket, too?"

She indicated the white letters on Lilah's chest.

"We won all our matches," Lilah said stiffly.

"Yay!" Jenny said, clapping her fingertips together.

"Was the captain nicer to you today?" Cassie asked.

"Uh-huh," Lilah said. "She's really cool actually."

Underneath the table, Lilah fiddled with the hem of Emery's sweatshirt.

"It looks like one of those Vail sweatshirts that Emery and all them wear," Annie said, still staring.

"What's Vail?" Cassie asked.

"I think it's a club or something," Jenny said.

"You guys don't know anything," Annie said. "It's where rich people ski. They might as well get sweatshirts that say 'RICH' in capital letters."

Lilah laughed in spite of herself.

CHAPTER 4

Emery and Noah had become official best friends at the beginning of sixth grade—when the phenomenon overtook their lives. Best friends were coupling up everywhere and, not to be left behind, they clung to each other. Emery was secretly jealous of the pairs of girls who belted out "Unwritten" and wore matching necklaces, each donning one half of a golden heart. She and Noah made friendship bracelets from embroidery floss, but they felt like an inadequate display compared to the airbrushed sweatshirts with "BFF" in fluorescent pink that her peers bought at the boardwalk in Cape May.

They'd met in Latin class. Noah was a new kid and Emery's mom, president of the PTA, had made her promise to introduce herself to at least one new student and "make them feel welcome." Noah's narrow shoulders had tensed up when Emery took the seat beside him and asked to borrow a pencil. He passed one over that was covered in bite marks. Emery noticed that Noah's posture was lousy but his handwriting was beautiful—an elegant cursive. She explained that her mom had demanded she be nice to a new kid and he was the first one she had come across. Her frankness made him fear her a little and trust her a lot.

• • •

In eighth grade, Emery told Noah she was going somewhere better for high school—a boarding school. They were eating Nerds Ropes and splitting headphones. Noah turned down the volume on "She Will Be Loved."

Emery didn't know that Derrymore's grounds were designed by Frederick Law Olmsted or that the school was the executor of Thornton Wilder's literary estate or that it had an apiary. She just knew it was revered and respected, and like all things revered and respected, resented.

When Emery toured Derrymore with her parents, her mother said it was the type of school where someone like Emery belonged. The humanities buildings were red sandstone with ivy-choked porticoes. The STEM tower's endless glass reflected Derrymore's shining egotism in all directions. The football stadium was lighted and so were the tennis courts. Students enjoyed open skate every weekend at the ice rink and, upon graduation, were granted lifetime memberships to the golf course.

The grounds embodied the word "campus," with rich brick hues and winding paths and plush grass that whispered echoes of an era when scholarship students were forced to be waitstaff and serve racks of lamb to their classmates. In the school pamphlet, the Derrymore grounds crew said their aim was to "curate a sylvan atmosphere that complements the nourishing intellectual environment." On the cover of the prospectus was a girl reading *The Fountainhead* in the shade of an enormous Osage orange tree whose leaves were every color of autumn.

Emery knew that her place was inside Derrymore's gates and nothing would keep her out—especially not when her father was a trustee. In Mr. Hooper's day, Derrymore didn't have a television studio or a ceramics studio or a Wii in every dormitory. It didn't admit women or Black or Jewish students.

"My dad went there," Emery told Noah. "And my grandfather. It's called Derrymore."

Noah knew the school. It was only a half-hour driving distance from their middle school. He had passed its wrought iron gates many times but never imagined that he might know someone who attended. It seemed unfriendly to him. Everything was so large and formal-looking.

"What's your backup plan?" Noah asked.

"For what?" Emery said.

"For if you don't get in."

Emery frowned. "Why wouldn't I?"

Noah's anxious face split into a smile. "Right."

"Come with me."

Noah gaped.

"My dad can get you in," Emery said, settling the matter.

• • •

"Lilah listens to classical music when she studies," Emery said. "Candace told me. Their rooms are next to each other. It's supposed to make you smarter or something."

"Does it work?" Noah asked through a mouth of saffron rice. "Maybe I should try it."

"No way. It's bullshit. Listen, though"—Emery reached over and flicked a grain of rice that had stuck to Noah's cheek—"she missed the team photo. It was so awkward because she saw us take it without her."

"Did you do it on purpose?"

"*I* didn't do anything. *She* missed it."

A crush of boys wearing pinnies entered the dining hall quoting "Can I Have Your Number" and reeking of sweat. It was the Derrymore soccer team, still ripe from practice.

"Ooh, look," Noah said.

"*Shhh*," Emery scolded. She glanced over at a boy that Noah had almost talked her into poking on Facebook. His name was Scott Wynand. He had smiled at her once.

Noah began, "If you don't get a date to homecoming—"

"Shut up," she said. "I'll have one."

"I was being nice! I was gonna say that if you don't get asked, then *I'll* go with you."

"What an honor."

"But if someone asks you"—Noah stared conspicuously at Scott—"I'll accept my fate. It's my destiny to be lonely forever."

Singleness was one of Noah's many unhealthy fixations. Emery never knew exactly what sort of reassurance he wanted, so she usually deflected. It was not lost on Emery that Noah was the only boy consistently allowed to join all-girls sleepovers. It was as if the parents had tacitly agreed there was nothing to worry about.

"It's not your 'fate,'" she said. "The dance isn't until October anyway. That's forever. Plus, I bet a lot of people won't have dates. For instance, Lilah."

Noah's eyes flashed. "We should get that Chinese guy to ask her out."

"Which one?"

"The one from Latin class."

"Raymon?"

All of the international students at Derrymore selected English names so their teachers wouldn't have to footslog through foreign sounds. It was supposed to be an act of mercy to both parties.

"Raymon," Noah repeated, pronouncing a decisive "n."

"And his best friend Arnol," Emery added.

"Arnold?" Noah feigned confusion.

"Arnol!" Emery insisted.

They cackled. There were a number of botched names like these: a boy named Quince; a girl named Alisor. The registrar was either too polite to correct the foreign students or simply indifferent. The names were sniggered at and always spoken with a hint of skepticism, even by the teachers.

"Raymon's, like, *Chinese* Chinese," Emery said. "From China."

"So?"

"Lilah's from here!"

Noah raised his eyebrow, unconvinced. "What's her real name?"

"Like I know."

Noah sang, "Matchmaker, matchmaker, make me a match."

They giggled malevolently.

"A project." Emery's voice went up, dangerous and innocent at the same time. "Helping a tragic, lonely girl find love."

Noah laughed and Emery was glad to see him emerge from his self-pitying rut. The best way to get him out of his own head was to sic him on someone else.

CHAPTER 5

Lilah's study hall ritual began with filling her Nalgene in the kitchenette at the end of the hall. Next, she hung her Do Not Disturb sign on her doorknob and turned Haydn on. Finally, she pulled on the Nantucket crewneck and stood in front of the mirror. The only possession she and Emery had in common was Havaianas flip-flops—so on the evenings she felt self-indulgent, Lilah would slide the rubber sandals on and imagine how it felt to be Emery Hooper.

It felt good to be rich. It felt good to wear thirty-dollar flip-flops as shower shoes instead of having to argue with a mother who insisted that the Dollar Store ones were perfectly adequate. It felt good to think things like, "Which immaculate tennis outfit should I wear today?" or "I hope Candace Perkins doesn't invite me to another boring tea with her mom." It felt good to pretend that when she got to the dining hall there would be a sea of people who wanted to sit with her.

Lilah sucked in her stomach. She and Emery didn't look that dissimilar. The sweatshirt was oversized so it hid their weight difference. Lilah leaned into her smudged over-the-door mirror and examined her face closely. She turned profile and scanned the pores on the side of her nose. Her blackheads were numerous and dense. No matter how often she squeezed, they came back immediately.

Through the thin dormitory walls, Lilah could hear a bunch of girls in Candace's double. Candace had recently begun taking guitar lessons and the only songs she knew were "Before He Cheats" and "American Pie." Her halting playing was accompanied by bursts of laughter and off-key singing. Lilah thought she could hear Emery's voice above the rest.

She turned her attention back to her clogged pores and wondered if Emery used those creams and serums that were sold on the first floor of department stores. Most likely. Lilah's mom's only splurge was Shiseido sunscreen, which she used to protect that which she was most proud of: her fair skin. Mrs. Chang used it sparingly and spread it assiduously on her face, making sure not to waste any product. Emery used this same sunscreen sloppily on her legs and arms, throwing the bottle away when there was certainly more left inside. Lilah pictured her mother's Shiseido bottle inverted on the bathroom counter to drain every last drop.

After an hour and a half of focused studying, there was a knock at Lilah's door.

"Ready?" Jenny's voice asked.

"Coming."

Lilah took one last glance in the mirror and set her face in a bitchy expression, resuming her Emery impression. But her face returned to its natural, slightly scared position when she opened her door and saw Annie scowling.

"Why are you obsessed with that sweatshirt?"

"I'm cold," Lilah said.

"Aren't you supposed to give it back?"

"I haven't done laundry yet."

"C'mon, guys," Jenny said. "I reserved the big TV and I don't want someone to take it from us again."

Annie left it at a dirty look. Lilah unclenched her fists. She swore to herself that one more rude question from Annie would have elicited an eruption. When they got to the main common room, it smelled like acetone. Candace and Emery were watching *Gossip Girl* and trying to tie cherry stems into knots with their tongues while their nails dried. Lilah hid behind Annie to conceal her crewneck but neither Candace nor Emery looked in their direction.

Lilah and Jenny waited to see what Annie would do.

"Let's just go to the upstairs TV room," Annie mumbled.

They went to the empty bedroom that hadn't been assigned since a girl hanged herself there in the year 2000. Jenny put her DVD of *My Neighbor Totoro* into the player and they crowded together on a sofa that felt damp and smelled like summer garbage.

• • •

Emery and Noah were waiting for Latin to start when a voice in the hallway yelled "Kobe!" and an empty bottle clattered into the trashcan by the classroom door. The voice's owner sat beside Emery and belched. Flyaway hair and loudness were Errol Hewitt's signatures. Errol was the type of boy Noah wished he could be—boisterous, athletic, oblivious. The word "cocksure" was invented for him. Errol was one of a few freshmen boys to have made the varsity soccer team, and once he found out that Emery was a fellow varsity athlete, he was a willing friend.

Noah was already self-conscious about his androgynous build, and next to Errol, he looked even slimmer. Errol played defense and he was built for it. Noah was handsome and well-coiffed, but his neatness was that of someone well-trained by his mother. Errol was taller, smarter, and scruffier than a fourteen-year-old boy should be. Noah was not thrilled that "Errol from Latin" became just "Errol" so quickly.

Noah was frantically reviewing his translation when Errol twisted open a new Arizona Iced Tea.

"Was that due today?" Errol asked, taking a huge gulp.

"Uh-huh," Emery said.

"Shit. I forgot to do it. We stayed up until three playing FIFA."

"Who's we?"

"Me and Scott and—"

Mr. Arthur entered, and Emery thought about how she would never start a list with herself.

Mr. Arthur's accent was unapologetically Bostonian and his humor wicked—fully translatable into both Latin and Greek. Classics masters generally fall into one of two categories: villain or jester. Mr. Arthur was the jester sort.

Though many Derrymore teachers had taught for years at the school, they were mere tenants compared with Mr. Arthur, who had spent the majority of his sixty-eight years in his first-floor classroom teaching the Ancients. Force-fed Virgil is as much a part of boarding school as dress code, Chapel, and Saturday classes.

"We're going to learn something today," he grumbled, voice hoarse from his mid-morning cigar. "For a change. Who's first?"

Emery wanted to raise her hand, but the idea of being thought over-eager kept it at her side.

"Hewitt," Mr. Arthur barked. "Read Catullus 51—and give me some passion."

"The whole thing?" Errol asked.

"Up to Lesbia."

Errol, who had leaned his chair back dangerously far, brought it down to all fours. For their first few lessons he could not contain his laughter at the name Lesbia—but he had gotten over it.

"Alright," Errol said, rubbing his hands together. "Let's see. What page?"

His book looked brand new—spine uncracked—even though it was the third week of the semester. But Errol was not suspected for a moment. His translation was excellent and Mr. Arthur praised his poetic license. Noah was called on next and his prepared translation was stumbling in comparison to Errol's sight-reading.

"Leisure?" Noah hazarded. "No, pleasure. Pleasure destroyed ... cities? Civilizations? Pleasure destroyed civilizations ..."

Noah's voice trailed off and Mr. Arthur moved on to the next student without remark.

When the bell rang at the end of the hour, Noah nudged Emery before clearing his throat.

"Hey, Raymon," he called.

The startled international student looked up from across the Harkness table. Noah had never spoken to him before, let alone addressed him by name.

"Me?" Raymon asked.

"I'm pretty sure you're the only Raymon," Noah sniped.

"Are you asking anyone to homecoming?"

Raymon's mouth opened in confusion, displaying two rows of crooked teeth. Emery looked away in disgust.

Dr. Ancelotti had done beautiful work. Emery's teeth were perfectly straight and her braces had come off before high school (something she had demanded). Looking at Raymon's yellow, overlapping teeth made her think of something the orthodontist had said: Asian teeth are shovel-shaped and thicker than normal teeth. Emery had remained silent and uncomfortable when presented with this information. Her mother had bristled at the comment and decided not to offer Dr. Ancelotti use of their beach house after all.

"No date for the dance?" Noah said.

His voice glittered with malevolence. He gyrated his shoulders.

"Not me," Raymon said. He smiled bashfully and bowed his head. "I don't ask anyone."

"Oh, come on!" Noah said. "You can't go alone. You must have a crush …"

While Noah patronized Raymon, Emery's attention was stolen by a presence in the doorway and Errol's loud greeting.

"Scotty boy!"

Scott Wynand had stopped to tell Errol some gossip about college scouts coming to their game that afternoon. Emery watched Scott as discreetly as she could. His cheeks always had rosy splotches which she found achingly attractive.

"What're you doing in advanced Latin?" Scott asked.

"Well-rounded. What can I say?" Errol answered.

"Latin, though?" Scott made a face. "At least I'll be able to speak another language when we graduate."

"So you can talk to the help?"

"Let's see how you feel when I'm in La Liga and you're in MLS."

"I'd like to see you make the Red Bulls' starting lineup."

Scott scoffed. "I could walk on to that squad today."

"Stupid confidence. This is why you're striker and I'm sweeper."

Scott laughed. "See you at lunch."

He never looked Emery's way. She felt certain he didn't know her name. Ryan had said the only thing more pathetic than going to a formal alone was convincing yourself that someone was going to ask you. Ryan's spiel was in response to Sara's repeated assertion that Jon Shepard was going to invite her to homecoming—that had shut Sara up.

"Wait, Noah," Errol said. "Who are you taking to homecoming?"

Noah spluttered, "I'm taking Emery."

Emery ground her teeth and said nothing. Her mind spiraled into hypotheticals: What if Scott was planning to ask her to the dance, but then Errol mentioned she was going with Noah, so then Scott asked someone else—

Errol, for his part, was not invested in the answer. "Oh. Nice."

Errol drew Emery into conversation as they exited the classroom and deftly, though inadvertently, angled Noah out of it. This was always happening to Noah, and he held it against Emery even though she never meant for it to happen. One minute, he was by her side laughing at something stupid

Lilah did. The next, he was shunted to the conversational
badlands by Errol.

Errol asked if she had ever been to Mont Tremblant. Of
course. Had he ever been to Park City? Duh. They said
"Okemo?" at the same time and shared a laugh.

Noah rolled his eyes.

"We should do a group trip," Errol said. "With Scott and
Candace and whoever."

Emery crossed her fingers and put her hand in her pocket.

"That could be cool," she said.

The Derrymore student body was one of the most well-
traveled populations in the world, but a small number of
places dominated conversation. The Vineyard. The Hamptons.
OBX. Aspen. Kiawah. Big Sky. Provincetown. They shared a
local consciousness, and if you didn't know the candy shop in
the back of the water sports store or what Back Bowls referred
to or what getting stung by a man o' war entailed, you laughed
along and pretended you did.

"East Coast trails are too short," Errol said.

"But you become a better skier in icy conditions," Emery
said.

"Fair. What about you, Noah?" Errol asked. "East or west?
Manifest destiny or the Orient?"

Noah froze. Nothing had indicated that Errol was aware of
Noah trailing behind them.

"Noah can't ski," Emery said.

CHAPTER 6

Lilah would never understand that her clearance tennis shoes (the ones that reeked of sensible-mom) made Emery hate her. And that her outdated ringtone ("SexyBack") was equally detestable. Emery despised Lilah's infantile baubles: a Hello Kitty pull on her tennis bag, a Winnie the Pooh charm dangling off her cell phone. Lilah was sexless and repellant. She was a child without any precociousness. Emery cringed inwardly when Lilah played violin during Chapel and when she finished last—gasping for breath—in the timed mile. Lilah's most egregious offense, though, was interrupting an almost-conversation with Scott.

• • •

Errol and Emery were waiting for the dining hall to open for breakfast when Scott joined them. His hair was uncombed and he was rubbing crust out of his eyes.

Errol mimed tossing long hair back over his shoulder. "Lax flow," he intoned.

Scott tried to smooth his hair down with the heel of his hand.

"How much longer did you play last night?" Errol asked.

"'Til an hour ago," Scott said, yawning. "Penalties."

"FIFA?" Emery asked just as Scott's sour breath reached her nose.

"We had a tournament in Shawn's room. Did you know his dad played football at Notre Dame? He could have gone pro."

"Sucks that he's just a burnout brain surgeon," Errol said.

Emery was saved the trouble of a witty remark by Scott's asking if they had dates for homecoming.

"I'm going stag," Errol boasted as a green monkey brain fell from a tree beside them. He picked it up and punted it into the road. It bounced several times before coming to rest. "It's the *first* dance—why would I want to be stuck with someone?"

"It's not 'stuck' if it's someone cool," Scott said sleepily.

Emery wanted to clarify that she had no date. Noah was only her backup. But she had heard that Scott was planning to ask Candace.

Scott rubbed his eyes again and Emery took the moment to admire his perfectly pink lips.

"Who are you going with, Emery?"

Her name coming from his mouth was heady. She willed herself to be nonchalant. "I don't want to be stuck with someone either. Unless it's … someone cool."

She couldn't tell if Scott was smirking or smiling. Errol looked at her questioningly and she avoided his eyes.

"My sister has that same necklace," Scott said.

He reached out and touched the gold angel pendant. The feeling of his fingertips on her collarbone made her knees weak even as she got a concentrated whiff of unshowered teenage boy.

He continued, "Yeah, it's exactly the same. Even the glass egg thing."

"It's called an amulet," Emery said.

"How fancy." He smirked (she was sure this time). "Maybe you—"

"Good morning!"

The greeting was breathless and intrusive, spewed from Lilah's mouth like hot ash. Her backpack was filled with so many books that she was off balance and her hair was pulled back in a greasy ponytail. Scott turned away. Emery started to sweat.

"Maybe what?" Emery tried. "Scott?"

But he had flipped open his phone and lowered himself onto the steps in front of the dining hall.

Maybe you—Scott had begun. *Maybe you and I could go to the dance together*, Emery imagined. *Maybe you could be my girlfriend. Maybe you'll never worry about having a date again.* Lilah was still standing at Emery's elbow.

The same necklace as Scott's sister—his eyes had brightened with recognition when he noticed it. She had been so close.

"I'm gonna skip breakfast," Emery said to no one. "I'm not hungry."

● ● ●

For the rest of the day, Emery replayed the short exchange over and over in her head. She rewound how Scott had touched her necklace and how his skin had been against hers. She replayed how he went completely cold when Lilah appeared.

Even though he had sat uncomplainingly beside Lilah while computing carbon footprints, Scott clearly expected her to know better than to address him outside of the class-room. Emery wondered how Scott would have treated her if she weren't friends with Errol, if she didn't have the same necklace as his sister. The thought sat unpleasantly in her gut.

• • •

Emery was on the way to tennis practice when she saw Ryan waiting for her at the edge of the Isle.

"Let's go!" the captain beckoned impatiently.

Emery hesitated in stepping onto the grass, wondering if it was a test. When Ryan realized what was happening, she broke into laughter.

"Ohmygod," Ryan said, flipping her two long braids behind her shoulders. "That Isle thing was totally a joke. My captain fucked with me when I was a freshman, too."

Emery laughed weakly.

Ryan's phone rang. "Yoboseyo," she answered. "Hi, Umma … I'm on my way to practice … Yes! … SPF 50!"

Ryan toggled back and forth between Korean and English, her tone the same in both languages. Emery had only heard Korean spoken in real life a few times, mostly at restaurants. But they were written-up restaurants where the waitstaff was required to pass an English exam and the only words spoken in Korean were the names of foods.

Ryan asked her mom to put her little sister on. Emery imagined what it would feel like to have Ryan for a sister. They would share clothes and talk about boys and Ryan would make her promise not to tell their parents that she had shared a bedroom with Eli on the senior overnight in the

Berkshires. They would speak Korean when they wanted to trash-talk people and giggle maliciously. Ryan would show her how to draw eyeliner on Asian eyes, something few magazines elucidated.

"Put Umma back on," Ryan said. "I have to go, but I'll call you during study hall, kay? ... Love you, too."

The BlackBerry got tucked into Ryan's waistband against her hipbone, which jutted out just the right amount. Emery wondered if Ryan participated in the famous Grapes and Air diet that the senior girls swore by.

"I'm Korean, too," Emery blurted.

"No kidding."

"You knew?"

Ryan turned to her incredulously. "The moment I saw you."

"Really?"

"You look like my cousin." It felt like the best compliment in the world to be compared to a relative of Ryan's. "Why's your last name Hooper?"

"I'm adopted." There was a tinge of shame in Emery's voice that had never before accompanied the statement. Usually she was proud to declare that she was adopted—it meant she was above accusations of fobishness. But saying it to Ryan felt like admitting affliction.

"No shit. Do you like your parents?"

"Um—"

There had been a brief phase when the Hoopers sought to acquaint Emery with her heritage, but when it proved as alien to her as to them, the efforts ceased. Instead, they kept to standard American things that little girls enjoyed like FAO Schwarz and tea at the Plaza. At Disneyland, a ride operator lumped Emery into a group of Koreans who were in line ahead of the Hoopers. Emery was separated from her parents and placed in a teacup with a family from Incheon, but before the door was secured, her father rescued her and berated the confused operator.

"That was rude," Ryan laughed, unrepentant. "You don't have to answer. So can you tell what Lilah is?"

Emery considered. "Not Korean."

"What's her last name?"

"Chang."

"I can tell from her face she's not Korean. She must be Chinese. That's also why she's short. And chunky."

"Really?"

"Chinese people are stockier because they're peasants. Historically."

Ryan was a wellspring of wisdom. Emery had an urge to vent about how Lilah had sabotaged her, but Ryan was back on her BlackBerry—probably texting her boyfriend. Scott was sort of a mini-Eli, Emery thought. Ryan would approve. Both boys were athletes and conventionally good-looking.

When they were almost at the courts, Emery put her hair in a bun. Ryan pulled it through to a ponytail with an expert motion and swatted Emery's hand away when she reached up to adjust it.

"Leave it," Ryan said. "The bun makes you look like Mulan. Me too. Hence—"

Ryan gestured at the two French braids blooming from the crown of her head. Her hair was sleek, black, and never greasy. During class, she wore it down, sometimes with the front pieces clipped back to show off her perfect bone structure.

Emery vowed never to wear her hair in a bun, even when she was alone.

Practice flew by. Emery hit distractedly because she was going over Ryan's wisdom. She wanted more one-on-one time. What Ryan could teach her about hair and boys and ethnic profiling was limitless.

• • •

Every practice ended with sprint relays.

"Partner up!" Ryan called.

Ryan rotated partners each day and Emery could sense that today was her day. Her heart beat faster, thinking ahead to how close they would become and how she would sit next to Ryan on the bus to away matches and split a Chewy bar with her.

"Confucius say"—Ryan affected an offensive Chinese accent and the giggles began immediately—"run sprints or get fat."

Ryan had mastered something that Emery had never seen mastered before. The captain told stories about her eemoh's shikhye, trips to Jeju Island, the time her grandma made glue out of rice—she drew attention to her Korean-ness and used it to make herself more interesting. She managed to treat it as an asset rather than a handicap.

Emery's intuition had been right. Ryan picked her and they won the relay race. Lilah and Sara came in last and had to run two suicides as punishment.

CHAPTER 7

Noah was turning red from a combination of choking and embarrassment. Emery and Errol had teased him for not knowing how to eat an artichoke and swallowing the feathery choke fibers. Errol dipped a leaf into melted butter and scraped his bottom teeth across it. Suddenly, he pointed across the room: "Isn't that your sweatshirt, Em?"

Emery glanced across the dining hall.

"What a little freak," she hissed.

Emery strode over to a table on the far side of the room and stared menacingly at Lilah. Her friends' hungry eyes were unblinking and their attention felt grimy.

"Hi, Emery," Lilah said, falteringly.

"Are you planning on giving that back anytime soon?" Emery demanded.

Lilah willed her friends to stop ogling Emery, who was wearing one of those expensive white T-shirts that could be identified by its extreme thinness.

"I was gonna wash it tonight," Lilah stammered.

"Leave it outside my door."

Lilah's cheeks burned as Emery stalked away. Jenny and Cassie resumed eating dutifully but Annie was gaping.

"Wow," Annie said. "She *really* hates you."

"She just wants her sweatshirt back," Lilah said.

"You made it sound like you were friends," Annie scoffed. "I should have known. You always stretch the truth."

Lilah felt the stinging in the back of her throat that preceded tears. She pushed her pasta around the watery marinara sauce.

The stretching Annie was referring to concerned Lilah's Derrymore application. Lilah had reported that she was first chair violin—and it was true. In her summer orchestra, Lilah had been first chair for three years. But Annie was first chair at their middle school. Lilah's mom said to leave it ambiguous. It wasn't a lie.

Annie had seen the application on the Changs' kitchen table. When she found out that Lilah got into Derrymore, she told everyone about the first chair claim. Lilah received dirty looks for days.

In the dormitory, Lilah did a load of laundry for a single piece of clothing. Her mother would have hated to see the waste. She stayed in the basement watching Emery's sweatshirt spin round and round in the soapy water.

Lilah would have bet anything that Emery had never been in the spidery laundry room. Her mom's house manager, Marina, came by twice a week to pick up dirty and drop off clean laundry. Most of the rich kids used a laundry service, but Emery always one-upped the standard.

● ● ●

Lilah had become more than a nuisance—she was a menace. It would be negligent for Emery to stand idly by. Noah tried to hold a grudge about the artichoke shaming but he couldn't resist the thrill of a mean prank. It took little convincing to enlist his help in tricking Lilah into thinking she had been invited to homecoming.

They agreed it should be a handwritten note, slipped under Lilah's door.

"Maybe it's an invitation," Emery suggested. "Like a poem: roses are red, violets are blue, homecoming is soon—"

"Me love you long time!" Noah burst out.

Emery hesitated then joined in his laughter. He repeated it weakly and dissolved into high-pitched giggles. Emery made a low sound in her throat to simulate laughter, but she didn't need to bother. His eyes were squeezed tightly in glee.

"Focus, Noah," she said. "You should write it because your cursive is better than mine."

"Me love you long time?"

He tried to say it with a straight face but doubled over.

"No." Emery raised her voice. "Be serious, Noah. The poem—you have to help me finish it."

Noah gathered himself after a few more bouts and his brow finally furrowed in thought.

"Roses are red, violets are blue," he mumbled. "Home-coming is soon … and I choose you."

"Oh, that's good—"

"I can draw a Pokémon on it!" Noah blurted. "Maybe an Eevee or a Ninetales."

Emery tried to smile, but it came out as a grimace. Noah was already scribbling furiously, drafting the note on a piece of paper.

"What do you think?"

He held up the illustrated poem. Emery snatched it out of his hand.

"It's perfect." Emery attributed her queasiness to adrenaline. She wanted to slide it under Lilah's door before she lost her nerve.

"Wait, it's just a rough draft," Noah said, reaching toward her. "I want to—"

"No, it's good." Emery jerked it away and admired it at arm's length. "You have to sign it, though."

"What's his last name?"

"Wang or Dong probably," Emery said. "Just do his first name. There aren't any other Raymons, right?"

Noah signed it neatly.

After Emery shoved the poem under Lilah's door, she got stuck on a memory and found it impossible to reset her mind to blank. It was one of those memories that's more a feeling than a scene. It started with a soundbite from tennis camp.

"Asian girls have brown nipples and brown lips."

The speaker had stopped short when he realized Emery was there—not like he was ashamed, more like he was embarrassed for her, the way you might start if you walked in on people having sex. *Yikes*—

Emery had a split second to decide how to react. She pouted her lips playfully and puckered like she was blowing a kiss.

"Your lips are pink, Em," someone said magnanimously.

She had laughed her good-sport laugh to show she wasn't offended, to show that she wasn't a tight-ass. Mercifully that had been the last night of camp. She didn't return the next summer.

• • •

Lilah ambushed Raymon in Mr. Arthur's classroom to accept the invitation. In a terrible coincidence, he had brought a bouquet of tired-looking roses to class and she kept reaching toward them. Protectively, he put his arm around them and made a shooing motion at Lilah.

While the chaos played out, Emery gripped both Noah's and Errol's wrists on either side of her. Mr. Arthur was largely unfazed.

After a confused exchange, Lilah produced the handwritten note. Raymon studied it, then turned her down ungracefully in front of the class. She insisted he had asked her, and he dismissed her with a loud, honking "No!" Before quitting the room, Lilah snatched the note back.

"What the fuck?" Errol's eyes were wide with amusement.

Noah giggled nervously and pinched Emery's thigh under the table.

Raymon staggeringly explained that he had not written the note. His gaze and voice were directed at Emery. She nodded understandingly.

"I'm asking someone else," Raymon announced.

Emery's heart dropped. *Please*, she thought, *please not me*.

Raymon didn't speak for the rest of class.

When the bell rang and Raymon made no attempt to talk to her, Emery breathed a sigh of relief.

It wasn't until evening that Emery found out who he had asked.

• • •

Candace Perkins lived one floor above Emery. Candace was an excellent skier, looked natural with a cardigan draped over her shoulders, and considered Bergdorf's lavender her favorite color. Her double was home to a handsome blend of monogrammed linens and crisp blue and white accents. It stood in stark contrast to her roommate's side of the room—which was a hodgepodge of Macy's comforter and Ikea storage bins.

The only thing that looked out of place was a Z100 Jingle Ball poster thumbtacked above her desk alongside a VIP lanyard. It was proof that Candace was still a kid, and burgeoning taste couldn't supersede the juvenile need to show off her dad's corporate box seats.

Competition between Candace and Emery had existed for ages. Emery's father had been a mentor to Candace's father early in his career and the girls were born into friendship. Candace's older brother, July, had been Emery's first crush. Every winter, the Hoopers received a Christmas card of the Perkins clan in matching Fair Isle sweaters. Emery was threatened by perfect Candace's natural lowlights, scuba certification, and enviably sharp collarbones—everyone was—but she never let on.

When introducing Emery, Candace never failed to mention that the Hoopers' primary residence *and* their beach house had been featured in *Architectural Digest*. She wasn't bragging on Emery's behalf—it was more like vouching for her. Candace's endorsement plus *Architectural Digest*'s meant that Emery was to be accepted.

When Emery overheard Candace's voice in the hallway, she called her in.

Candace peeked her head in Emery's doorway. Her fake reading glasses slipped off the top of her head and she repositioned them.

"Cute shirt," Candace teased.

Emery glanced down at the ancient University of Pennsylvania T-shirt she was wearing. "Shut up, it's my dad's. Marina is late with my laundry."

She motioned to come in and close the door.

"What have you heard?" Candace stage-whispered.

Exchanging gossip was a nightly ritual for them.

"You tell me," Emery said. "I heard you were asked to homecoming."

"Oh that"—Candace grimaced theatrically—"I was hoping no one would hear about it. I felt *so bad*."

"How did he ask you?" Emery asked.

Candace sat on Emery's bed, toying with the pompom border on a throw pillow. "The saddest roses you've ever seen. He tried to get me to take them even after I turned him down, but I hate roses. They're such a cliché."

"And they smell bad when they die."

"So true."

"But *why* did he do it?"

"Remember when I sent out an email to the *whole* grade"— Candace was the Community Service Representative for the freshman class—"and I signed it 'Love, Candace'?"

"The blood drive email? Raymon thought you meant—"

They burst into laughter.

"No!" Emery cried. "That is so sad."

Candace placed her hand over her heart sympathetically.

"Are you coming up to my room tonight?" she asked,

examining a pair of gold lamé leggings draped over Emery's footboard.

Candace held court in her room in the evenings. She was assembling a clique and invited two girls every night to drink chinotto sodas and eat frozen Thin Mints and listen to *Continuum* on repeat—and completely ignore her poor roommate, who had (it was rumored) hyperhidrosis. The exercise always concluded with a long Photobooth shoot, replete with costumes and props.

"Am I invited?"

"Shut up, Em. Did you get these at American Apparel? Can I borrow them to take pictures?"

Emery nodded. She was the only one who had a standing invitation to Candace's symposium, but she only attended once a week. Candace wanted to co-host the evening sessions together, but Emery couldn't stand the girls Candace was test-driving. They hung on Candace's every word and lived for her invitations. A girl named Ginny had cried when she was invited two nights in a row and then snubbed on the third.

Candace's approach to friendship boiled down to: Not every companion has to be a consigliere—some are simply foot soldiers.

"I'm not coming tonight," Emery said. "Noah needs me to edit his English essay."

"Can't he just get a tutor?" Candace asked. "July used a lady who basically wrote his papers for him."

"Candace," Emery said seriously, "tutors are *expensive*."

Candace tested a white eyeliner on the back of her hand.

"You help Noah too much," she said. "You know teachers are only allowed to give out a limited number of As."

Emery considered this.

"We're gonna prank-call Scott tonight," Candace volunteered.

"Maybe I can make it," Emery said after a measured pause.

• • •

When Noah got a C on his *Canterbury Tales* paper, Emery told herself it wasn't her fault. Sure, she had rushed through it, but it wasn't salvageable and she had been generous to help him at all. Plus, teachers never seemed to like Noah.

Candace never got around to prank-calling Scott. Instead, she made them look at her family's Bora Bora photos and Ginny complimented how tan or skinny or "sophisticated" (Candace's favorite word) she looked. Emery deleted old contacts from her phone and left Terra Chip crumbs on Candace's carpet.

The slideshow finally concluded when Emery asked if anyone had tried sugaring. Depilatory techniques were one of Candace's favorite topics, and she shut her laptop immediately to describe her most recent waxing experience: *It wasn't exactly a full Brazilian* ...

CHAPTER 8

The perks that came with Candace's friendship were undeniable. She shared her AllSaints jackets and DVF wrap dresses. Her mini-fridge was always stocked with prosciutto and out-of-season fruit. She subscribed to *Cosmopolitan* and had a direct line of upperformer intel through her older brother. But she was unreliable.

You never knew when making a smoothie would turn into cleaning the blender alone. You never knew if she was going to ditch you when a boy wanted her to sing vocals on Rockband.

When a Candace invitation materialized, Emery knew to be suspicious. Chances were, she just needed a plus-one.

Candace was leaning against Emery's dresser complaining that two years was too long to wait for a phone upgrade when her beat-up LG Chocolate buzzed. She made a show of being pleased and flattered.

"You're friends with Ryan Kim, right?" Candace asked.

Emery nodded. "Friends" was a reach, but she wanted Candace to believe it was so.

"She wants me to pick up some of my brother's things," Candace said. "Come with me."

July had graduated from Derrymore the previous May. Emery and Noah had pored over the 2007 *Hapax Legomenon*

(Derrymore's yearbook, *HapLeg* for short) at the library. Candace's brother had been voted Most Typical Derrymorian and Most Likely to Be Elected President Despite a Massive Scandal.

"I bet he has V lines," Noah had said, drawing his hands against his hips provocatively.

"He does," Emery confirmed. "And a happy trail."

July had dated Ryan until he moved into his Georgetown dorm and decided long-distance wouldn't work after all. Ryan had replaced him within a month.

Candace gushed about Ryan on the way to the senior dorm while Emery prayed that showing up unannounced would not constitute overstepping.

"... her room was so *sophisticated* last year. I saw it when I helped move July out. I was really mad when he broke up with her because we got close when she came to the Vineyard, but I sort of get it. College is college. You have to see her four-poster bed (I have no idea how she got permission for it) but I'm gonna do the same thing when—"

Candace stopped suddenly and stared at Emery's face intently.

"What?" Emery asked.

She refused to flinch as Candace studied her. It was an unpleasant and familiar sensation.

"You actually look so much like Ryan," Candace said. "You guys have the *prettiest* eyes."

Weird compliments were familiar territory. They were intended to flatter—something about her shiny hair or fast metabolism—but Emery's strategy was to move past them as quickly as possible.

Candace led the way to Ryan's room with extreme deliberateness. She had made this journey before and wanted it known. The door was open and Ryan waved them in while continuing to talk on the phone in rapid Korean. It was lucky timing because it gave Emery a chance to absorb her surroundings. She took a seat on an upholstered bench at the end of the four-poster next to a stack of SAT prep books.

Ryan's room was texture and muted colors: knit throws and abstract prints and trays in chalky bone and black lacquer, ecru velvet for the pouf and sisal for the rug. In comparison, Candace's room looked twee and unworldly. Her patchwork quilt suddenly appeared Americana in a Pottery Barn way—a chewed-up and spit-out Sister Parish hack job.

Emery thought about her own room and wondered what Ryan would think. It wasn't as catalogue-ready as Candace's, but it was definitely less contrived. Emery's room *could* have ended up exactly like Candace's—scalloped bed skirt, bolster pillow—but she had considered boarding school a new chapter and prevented her mother's interference.

Emery had elected for all white, unadorned linens and a few orange touches in an effort to break away from the French farmhouse bedroom of her childhood. The inspiration came from a hotel she'd stayed at in Cyprus. She liked the simplicity of it. Now she felt vindicated.

Ryan hung up and turned toward them. In a short, hot pink kimono, she was the only splash of color in the otherwise muted room. Typically, Emery avoided all things that smacked of Orientalism: cherry blossoms, dragons, red and yellow colorways. She hated the phrase "gung-ho." In fact, Emery refused to use chopsticks and went out of her way to profess ignorance of Pocky sticks, feng shui, and dim sum. These were calculated lies that often endeared her to peers: *You've never heard of* Dragon Ball Z? *Are you even Asian?* This false cluelessness wasn't that different from pretending to be unfamiliar with Denny's or acting like you'd never heard of DSW. No one wants to be the only person who knows what BOGO means.

"Emery," Ryan said. "What a surprise."

"I hope it's okay," Emery said. "Candace invited me."

"I didn't know you two were friends." Ryan's eyes flickered dangerously and her mouth curved into a smile. "But I should have known."

"July says hi," Candace chirped, eager to be acknowledged.

Ryan made a noise Emery was familiar with—it was a one-note laugh she used to signify a range of reactions. Sometimes mirth. Other times skepticism. It had a touch of derision that unsettled.

"You can tell him I say 'hello' back," she said. "I hear he has a new girlfriend already. True?"

"He wouldn't give me details," Candace answered obediently. "I called him yesterday, but he wouldn't say anything. They're probably just hooking up."

Candace's words tumbled out in a rush. In her eagerness to please Ryan, Candace was discomposed in a way Emery had never witnessed before.

"I heard she's Asian," Ryan said.

"Half-Japanese," Candace confirmed.

"Did I inspire a little Asian fetish in your brother?"

Ryan said it teasingly, but Emery thought there was strain in her voice.

Candace beamed. "That's what I said, too!"

Ryan addressed Emery with tired wisdom: "Asian fetish is a scourge that we're burdened with."

"Only if you're pretty," Candace chimed in.

"Hear, hear," Ryan said with overplayed sincerity. She mocked Candace so subtly that the freshman didn't notice. "Should you be so lucky, Emery."

Emery shared a knowing smile with Ryan. It was the first time she had ever felt that particular connection.

"It's an honor and a privilege," Emery said, parroting one of her dad's favorite lines.

Ryan snorted.

"Can I have a Pellegrino?" Candace asked.

She retrieved a green bottle from the mini-fridge without offering one to Emery.

"I just got these pearls, but I don't know if they're too much," Candace said. She hooked the strand around her thumb and held them out for inspection. "What do you think?"

"I noticed them," Ryan said, her voice sounding like she was talking to a child showing her a crayon drawing. "Since you brought it up, I'd say they're leaning toward too much."

"Yeah, I thought so, too," Candace said. "I was just trying them out but they're stupid."

"I don't think pearls are stupid. It's more the way you put together this whole look. The pink and green and the Jack Rogers—it feels like a costume. It's like, we're all at prep school, we already know that. Your outfit doesn't have to scream it. It's like a pleated skirt for tennis—it's too obvious."

Candace nodded vigorously. "Yeah, it was just, like, a joke."

She was shrinking into herself, but Ryan continued to examine and assess her. She cocked her head to the side and made one last comment: "It looks like you're going to an audition for the role of Boarding School Spoiled Brat."

"Vivian Kensington," Emery said.

"Ha!"

It was an ugly-sounding guffaw that had to be real. Emery didn't dare look at her friend. At least Candace would shut up now.

"Tomorrow I want you to help me set up for the match," Ryan said to Emery. "Meet at the bleachers at 2:30. Kay?"

Setting up for the match was something that Ryan and Sara usually did alone. It was a feat of Ryan-ness to bestow exclusivity on a tedious chore. Before Emery could answer, Sara stepped into Ryan's space from the door that connected their singles.

"What's all this?" Sara said.

"Field trip," Candace said flatly.

"Aw, how cute," Sara said. "Love the pearls."

Candace pursed her lips and didn't reply. Sara undressed to her lace Hanky Pankys and began examining her bikini line with a hand mirror.

"Ry, do you have those ingrown pads?"

"Yes. But you used up all of my last jar. I'm not giving you any more."

"Jon asked me to hang out tonight and I did a terrible job shaving—TMI, sorry. I'll get you an entire new jar."

"Two."

"Fine."

"You know where they are."

"You're so lucky you have no body hair," Sara said. "You too, Emery. I'm like a monkey if I don't shave for two days."

• • •

After Candace received a vinyl Scoop shopping bag with July's bowtie, two Lacoste polos, a rope bracelet, and a JFK biography, the freshmen headed back to their dorm. Emery noticed that Candace had taken the strand of pearls off.

They made fun of Sara Klein's polka-dot room and her pathetic obsession with her best friend. From that day on, calling someone a "Sara" would be the cruelest insult.

"Kill me if I'm ever that much of loser," Candace said. "Are you hungry? Wanna go to the dining hall?"

"I'm sick of Derrymore food. Let's order in."

"Let's get P.F. Chang's! I love their Szechuan beef."

Emery made a face. "You know I hate Chinese. Let's get pizza."

"Fine. But you have to pay. My dad took away my credit card after I got a C on my French test."

"No problem. I think I owe you, like, ninety bucks anyway."

"For what?"

"That Twilly. Remember I told you I'd go halfsies for Ginny's birthday—or was it Riley's?"

"Don't worry about that. You didn't even go to the party. It was so boring."

"Yeah, but my name was on the card, so I've been meaning to pay you back. I never have cash, though."

"You can treat for dinner. My dad doesn't even understand how hard French is. He got to take Latin like you."

Emery couldn't quite read the comment, so she ignored it. They agreed to call in the order after showers.

• • •

Candace blotted grease off of her third slice.

"Are you, like, friends with Lilah?"

"God, never," Emery said.

"She's so pathetic and cute, though. Don't you think she could be pretty? I wanna give her a makeover."

"It would take more than that."

"I feel *so bad* for how much pressure she's under. Maybe that's why she stress-eats."

"What do you mean?"

"Chinese parents force their kids to go to Harvard. And, like, Princeton is considered failure. That's why their suicide rate is so high—my mom read an article about it. Did I tell you Lilah's mom was talking to my mom at the orientation thing? I have no idea how that happened, but my mom mentioned that July goes to Georgetown and Lilah's mom was like, 'Is that a good one?' She had never heard of Georgetown!"

Candace's uncle had been a significant donor at Georgetown for the past fifteen years, and when July was waitlisted, he threatened to sever ties with the school. The apology was hasty—it had been a terrible misunderstanding.

Emery imitated Ryan's Chinese accent: "Ees dat goo-wan?"

Candace laughed so hard she gasped for air.

"My dad also does a really good Chinese accent, but mine is so bad it's offensive." Candace tossed her crust into the empty pizza box. "Do you wanna skip breakfast tomorrow? I want to lose five pounds."

Candace was perfectly skinny, but always believed she was one pound away from obesity. Dysmorphia was as common as boat shoes at Derrymore.

"No way," Emery said. "I need breakfast or I can't function."

"Ugh," Candace said. "I'd kill to have Asian metabolism."

CHAPTER 9

The following afternoon, Emery put on her uniform for another tennis match she wouldn't be playing in. She was crestfallen when she saw Sara jabbering away on the bleachers. Emery climbed up the metal steps and caught the tail end of the conversation.

"I heard he's rounding out his collection with a Chinese collectible," Ryan said.

"Yichen is Chinese *American*," Sara corrected. "What's more valuable? Chinese Chinese or Chinese American?"

"He's definitely a purist," Ryan said. "I bet he prefers if you have a thick accent and cover your mouth when you laugh."

She affected a demure laugh and they exploded.

Then Ryan ordered, "Get ten cans. And a hopper for warm-up."

"Why me?" Sara whined, gesturing to Emery's able body.

"Ohmygod, shut up," Ryan said. "I do it by myself all the time."

Sara sulked off to gather new balls for the match. Ryan rolled her eyes and turned to Emery.

"Come sit," she said, patting the space beside her. "Want some?"

Ryan held out a familiar bright green package.

"HI-CHEWs always stick to my molars," Ryan said, shoving her finger in her mouth.

It was her mom's day to provide snacks for the team. There was a huge assortment of Nature Valley bars, Gatorade, and Korean snacks Emery had never seen: Choco Pies, dduk, Yakult.

"I know I'm gonna get cavities," Ryan said, "but I'm addicted. Wait, so—you're close with Candace's family, right?"

Emery's heart sank. Ryan just wanted to know about her ex.

"Uh-huh. Her dad used to work for mine."

Emery reached for a yellow package with a clear window and examined it. Ryan took it out of Emery's hands and opened it. She handed Emery a circular, white rice cake.

"It's ppeongtwigi—popped rice. I didn't realize you were so"—Ryan outlined Emery's aura—"banana."

"Huh?"

"Yellow on the outside, white on the inside," Ryan explained. "I thought you were friends with Lilah."

"No! We barely talk. I only—"

Ryan smirked. "I was kidding."

"Lilah's, like, the bane of my existence."

Ryan didn't laugh as Emery expected her to. Instead, the captain's eyes narrowed slightly as she regarded Emery and stated: "I know you're good at math."

She said it with aggression, like it was a nasty rumor that had been circulating amongst whispering townspeople.

"I guess?" Emery said, wary.

"You're in Sara's class." Ryan clapped a mosquito right in front of Emery's face. "Killed it. She's a total dumbass."

Emery's eyes flicked to the shed where Sara was retrieving tennis balls.

"She knows it, don't worry," Ryan said. "Do you hide the fact that you're good at math? Because you don't want to be stereotyped?"

"My parents are white," Emery said. "So it's not the same for me. Race just hasn't really been that much of a thing."

Ryan's face became inscrutable.

"It's not about how you feel. People treat you a certain way based on how you look." Ryan's expression hardened. "Did you hear about that Raymon kid?"

Emery's heart sped up. "What about him?"

"He asked Candace to homecoming."

"Oh yeah, that."

"He's so stupid. I also heard that someone sent Lilah a note—"

"I heard about that, too."

"They're both fobs, obviously, but it pisses me off because people mess with us because they assume we're all passive and weak." Ryan smacked another mosquito against her thigh. "Only some of us are."

Us. The word surprised Emery, and it took a moment to process what Ryan had said.

"Raymon's family is insanely rich," Ryan said. "They own all the pig farms or chicken farms or something in China." She smiled to herself. "Maybe dog farms."

"Like, breeders?"

"Haven't you ever been called 'dog-eater' before?"

"No one eats dogs," Emery said, offended.

"Aw," Ryan simpered. "You and your little white life.

Koreans eat dogs. Not all of us—but it is a real thing. It's cultural."

Emery couldn't tell if Ryan was punking her. It felt like she was being tested.

"Alright," Emery said. "Don't be passive. Don't wear buns. Don't be good at math?"

"You didn't hear it from me."

The rest of the team started arriving and Emery's private lesson ended. When Lilah showed up, Emery discreetly observed her. After Raymon's rejection, she didn't seem sadder or quieter or different. Lilah was her usual docile self. She only spoke when spoken to and managed to be deferent without being polite.

Emery's lip curled while watching Lilah try to get water from the Igloo cooler as upperformers kept cutting her in line. Lilah's meekness was an affront.

"This your friend?"

Emery jerked her hand back from the rough pair that had enclosed hers. The voice was tonal and friendly, but the face was strange.

"Mom, stop," Lilah said. "Sorry, Emery."

"You Emery?" Lilah's mom asked from beneath an enormous visor.

Her accented English made it sound like she was saying *Emily*. Emery nodded tightly.

"So nice. So nice," Mrs. Chang continued. "I worry, worry, worry Lilah has no friend—but she say, yes I do! Emery is my friend!"

Lilah's mother laughed suddenly and loudly. Emery recoiled from the sound, but when she caught sight of Lilah's total mortification, Emery released her breath. She smiled kindly and extended her hand to Lilah's mother.

"It's very nice to meet you."

Lilah's mom held on to Emery's hand. Emery let her.

"Lilah say you Korean, but you look Chinese. So beautiful."

She reached out and tucked a piece of Emery's hair behind her ear tenderly. The gesture caught Emery off guard, and she was surprised when Ryan appeared at her side.

"We're Korean," Ryan said, smiling, "but we like Chinese, too."

Lilah's mom laughed and Ryan joined her with a light, tinkling laugh Emery had never heard before.

"It's nice to meet you, Mrs. Chang," Ryan said. "We're so happy to have Lilah on the team."

"You so pretty, too!"

Ryan leaned in when Mrs. Chang moved to cup her cheek, smiling appreciatively at the compliment.

"Thank you for bringing snacks," Ryan said. "My mom brought some too, so we'll be well-fed today. Hopefully I don't get much fatter."

Ryan pinched the skin around her midriff, but Lilah's mom slapped her hand away.

"You so skinny! My Lilah is little piggy. She's not so skinny like you. You *so* skinny and *so* pretty."

Ryan laughed demurely and detached herself gracefully from the conversation, leaving behind an uncomfortable Emery and a horrified Lilah. Emery smiled mechanically at Lilah's mom and skirted away, but not far enough that she couldn't hear the conversation between mother and daughter.

"Huh?" Lilah said. "Speak English, Mom."

"I tell you too fat." Mrs. Chang's voice was completely different. It was no longer girlish and giddy. She jabbed a finger into Lilah's stomach. "Taiwanese is not supposed to be fat. Koreans not fat—you only fat."

"Are you done?"

• • •

Noah was aghast. He momentarily stopped shoveling Lucky Charms into his mouth.

"That's so harsh," he said. "She's not even that fat."

"And her mom was so embarrassing," Emery said. "She could barely speak English."

Emery went on to describe Mrs. Chang's cranberry-colored minivan and the dozen donuts she brought.

"Ew."

"*Dunkin'*"—Emery emphasized the dropped "g"—"Donuts."

"At least get Krispy Kremes, Mrs. Chang."

Adding insult to injury, Ryan's mother had dominated the snack spread. Mrs. Kim drove a silver Mercedes SUV and arrived with staff in tow. Her hair was bobbed and perfectly coiffed. She wore a camellia brooch on the lapel of her lavender bouclé jacket and spoke orders in Korean to an older woman who retrieved refreshments from the trunk of the car.

Ryan's maid emptied berries from a Tupperware into a ceramic serving bowl. She arranged fresh pastries from the local bakery on a tray. It had looked professionally catered when ajumma was done.

Through spoonfuls of cereal, Noah said, "Your tennis team is, like, Asian invasion with Ryan and Lilah and their moms."

"You're not allowed to say that"—with effort, Emery kept her voice playful—"I can, but you can't."

Noah rolled his eyes. "You're whiter than I am."

Emery frowned.

"You play golf," he said. "Your middle name is Kit. You 'summer' in—"

"Fine, but when you say 'Asian invasion' that's offensive."

"I just said you're white!"

"If you knew Ryan, you'd say she was 'white,' too."

"Doesn't her mom have an accent, though?"

"Yeah, but—"

"Then she's not white."

Noah's decisive verdict knocked the wind out of Emery. That he could pass judgment on Ryan was outrageous. He was an insecure wannabe and Ryan was popular. Yet somehow Noah held the power to decide whether she was enough, and he had decided in the negative.

But this was Noah. He deserved the benefit of the doubt. He had stood guard while she peed at Hummock Pond. He squeezed her back zits. He made fun of people who wrote hateful things in her Honesty Box. They'd watched every season of *America's Next Top Model* together. He couldn't be racist. So Emery didn't press.

"I overheard Lilah talking about you," he said. "To the quadruplets."

It was the nickname they'd given Lilah and her three Asian friends.

"Talking shit?" Emery asked. "I don't care."

"No, she was defending you."

"From what?"

"You're haughty. Or snotty. I couldn't really hear. Both are true so it could've been either."

"Shut up. What did they say?"

"The short one that wore flip-flops for chapel dress was saying that you think you're better than them—"

"I am."

"But Lilah said you're just confident and they're jealous."

Emery whistled a high note.

"Do you think she knows we did the homecoming prank?" Noah asked, shredding a napkin into tiny pieces.

"Who cares?" Emery shot back.

She wet her lips with her tongue and snatched the tattered paper out of his hands.

CHAPTER 10

Like any self-important place, Derrymore was obsessed with its own history. It boasted tradition as its doctrine and equated old with good. Tradition's central place in Derrymore's culture equated to sanctioned hazing. It allowed for a number of out-of-touch faculty to hang on to their overstayed positions. When parents complained, the Derrymore administration always defended the degrading traditions and ancient teachers.

Derrymore rituals simply cannot be understood by outsiders, the school explained. And after complaints were brooked, they were dismissed. The school was quick to tell upset parents to withdraw their children. Someone else would take her spot in a heartbeat if little Grier could not get on board with "the Derrymore way."

A large part of the Derrymore way was an unquestioning acceptance of inequality. Some students were treated like royalty, others were lucky to be there. Riley complained that her science teacher "didn't teach," and she was switched into a different section the next day. Cassie, in the same class, made an identical complaint and was chastised. Ian stole a copy of the math test from his teacher's desk—he received detention. Hector wrote a formula on the inside of his wrist—his punishment was a formal letter of reprimand sent to his parents and a note on his permanent record (and detention).

• • •

The humanities curriculum for freshmen included a week-long History of the Eastern World unit. It had been introduced a year prior, to address concerns that the course skewed Western-centric. Mrs. Peiffer covered Japanese internment in a sentence, the Vietnam War in half a lesson, but spent three classes discussing and psychoanalyzing comfort women.

Emery thought she felt eyes on her for the entire week, but rationalized it away as being oversensitive. In middle school, she had learned about the Silk Road, watched *To Live*, and read Amy Tan. She didn't recall feeling observed or singled out in those lessons.

The history teacher was a woman with a PhD from Northwestern who tried to get her students to address her as "doctor." It never stuck. Mrs. Peiffer read aloud a diary entry from a Korean War prostitute who had refused to offer sexual services to African American soldiers.

"Is there anything you want to contribute, Emery? I'd love to hear your take."

"Like a summary?" Emery asked.

She felt a tingling begin on her skin—the same sensation as when she'd gotten sunstroke at training and blacked out in the doubles alley.

"Not a summary," Mrs. Peiffer said. "Maybe your unique perspective could provide some insight about—"

"Emery's adopted," Noah said.

"I'm aware," the teacher said. "But the experience of being Asian in a *predominantly American* setting lends itself to a fascinating viewpoint. Perhaps you can speak to that?"

Five seconds passed in silence.

"Are you asking if I can relate to comfort women?"

"Right. They're a fascinating collection of women." Mrs. Peiffer smiled encouragingly.

"So," Emery reasoned out, "can I relate to a racist whore?"

The smile vanished as the class reacted. Noah clapped a hand to his mouth. Candace *ooh*-ed. Errol hooted. A boy named Shawn nodded in solidarity. Riley squeaked.

"We'll speak after class."

The last ten minutes of class dragged. Emery was filled with dread and regret. It was Ryan's fault. Since that talk on the bleachers, Emery kept noticing things she had been blind to before.

As soon as someone said "ping-pong" or "mahjong," Emery was on high alert for a comment about how she must be good at it. When discussing Halloween costumes, she readied herself for London Tipton or Cho Chang or Gwen Stefani's Harajuku Girls to be suggested. When someone said Ruby Foos or counterfeit goods or massage parlor or "auspicious"— Emery's anxiety shot up.

Em, aren't Asians way more respectful of their elders?

Asian hair is just flat, right? That's just a fact, not a stereotype.

Don't they eat turtles and sharks and stuff?

Emery rarely replied with the truth, which was that she had no idea. Instead she'd adopt an air of authority and invent something based on the same movies and TV shows that her peers' questions derived from, despite the fact that VH1's *The Fabulous Life of …* and *E! True Hollywood Story* were the programs she watched most.

Yeah, we're into communist social structures.

If you have curly hair then you're looked down on.

Also dogs and tigers and lions. They're delicacies.

She fantasized about replying with honesty—*I have no fucking clue*—and how she would bask in the ensuing discomfort. But Emery would never be so brazen, because no one's sympathies would be with her. She would be seen as uptight and humorless. The takeaway would be Emery Hooper is not fun and—more importantly—not one of us. She makes things awkward and plays the race card.

Mrs. Peiffer's question had come at a time when Emery's guard was down. Ryan's insights had helped Emery discover an internal radar that was capable of detecting when an embarrassing question was two or three sentences away. It could recognize the crescendo to a backhanded compliment—and it was improving every day. But usually, class was the one place Emery's radar could go into sleep mode, and she was furious that she couldn't just take notes, just listen to the lecture, just be like every other student. From now on, she would be vigilant even in the classroom.

She should have just answered Mrs. Peiffer's question with a hate smile and a simple *No, I have nothing to add*. But something had made her retaliate.

As class dragged on, she convinced herself to apologize—maybe even refer to the teacher as "doctor." It was a misunderstanding—the woman was ignorant. Peiffer probably used the word "oriental." Emery ground her teeth.

The teacher would apologize for implying that Emery had anything in common with Korean prostitutes and Emery would apologize for being curt—even though she wouldn't mean it. A stupid class like history was not going to tank her GPA.

Noah gathered his books slowly, to delay as long as possible. He squeezed her hand before he finally left. Mrs. Peiffer shut the door and sat beside Emery, who was doing her best to look contrite.

"I'd like to know why you thought it was appropriate to use that language in my class."

In an instant, Emery's anger flared. She stared into her lap and willed her hands not to shake. The teacher continued.

"I know your father is a trustee, I know you *think* you're untouchable—but you will show respect in my classroom. If you think you can behave like that and get away with it, you don't know who you've messed with."

At the tone of threat, Emery looked up. She channeled pure hatred into her gaze and kept her mouth a neutral line as she stared at Mrs. Peiffer's loose neck skin.

"I'm submitting a memo to your advisor and I expect a letter of apology by this evening."

The teacher's breathing grew faster. Silence was provoking the woman, so Emery let it fester.

"I know your type," Mrs. Peiffer said, her voice shaking. "The vicious type."

Emery waited a beat then asked in her most measured voice, "May I be excused?"

She calmly pushed her chair back and collected her things, gently closing the door behind her. When Emery was outside of the building she dialed her mom, and as the familiar voice answered, she burst into sobs.

Eventually, she managed to convey the story.

"She made me feel like a freak," Emery gasped.

"You are perfect," Mrs. Hooper said.

Her voice had evolved from concerned to deathly calm, and Emery felt reassured by the shift into mom action-mode. It was the same switch that had occurred when Emery came home in seventh grade devastated that she'd been passed over for first singles even though she'd beaten the girl who was awarded the spot. The next day Emery was top of the ladder and the tennis coach had been reassigned to the cross-country team.

"Do not think about this for one more second," Mrs. Hooper said. "She is a parochial, dim-witted woman and you are getting out of that class immediately. I'll speak to your father and we'll see what we can do. I'll call you after dinner to check in again, okay?"

I'll see what I can do—it was the most beautiful phrase in the English language. It alluded to loopholes, workarounds, bribes, threats, and blackmail. "What could be done" was only limited by imagination and audacity. Emery had complete faith in the phrase—and her mother. But after hanging up, she was exhausted.

Emery checked her reflection in the screen of her cell phone and saw that her eyes were encircled with dense red freckles from crying so hard. Going back to the dormitory would require explaining the broken blood vessels so she skulked off to the Green, which was only used for special events like Convocation and Commencement.

She sank onto a bench and pulled her knees into her chest. The momentary high of *I'll see what I can do* was fading. Even if her mother came tomorrow, even if she hugged Emery tightly and said Mrs. Peiffer was a Rust Belt idiot, there was still the un-purgeable memory. Emery would rewind it over and over, feeling hate and humiliation on repeat until something worse supplanted it.

Emery wiped snot on the back of her wrist. Her nose was still stuffy so she plugged one nostril with a finger and blasted mucus from the other one. She repeated the procedure on the second side. The Snot Rocket Method was something she had learned from a boy at tennis camp. She heard the footsteps too late.

"Um, hi?"

Emery turned toward the voice.

"What are you doing here?" Lilah asked. "Are you okay?"

Emery's eyes welled up anew.

"No."

"What happened?"

Her voice cracked a couple times, and she needed to take a few deep breaths, but she explained. Emery blinked and looked upward to stem the flow of tears. Only when she snuck a sidelong glance did she see that Lilah was also crying.

"I'm so sorry," Lilah said.

"It's fine. I'm gonna switch out of that class and my mom is coming tomorrow."

"It's not fine."

Lilah was still. Emery spun her bracelet around her wrist.

"What are you doing over here?" Emery asked, indicating the Green.

"I come here when … I need to be alone."

"Something happened?"

"It's stupid," Lilah said. "My friends think we should use our Chinese names."

"Huh?"

"They think that using an American name is 'giving into the system.'"

"What system?" Emery frowned. "What's your real name?"

Lilah said it.

"One more time?" Emery prompted.

Lilah repeated it.

"It's sort of hard to pronounce."

"You physically can't pronounce it," Lilah said. "After ten years old, your mind can't absorb certain sounds, so Americans literally cannot pronounce our names correctly. I read about it in a linguistics book."

The first day of class roll call was the worst. Teachers didn't know nicknames and every foreign name was a concentrated dose of indignity.

"Do you have a Korean name?" Lilah asked.

Emery shook her head no.

"Just so you know, Lilah is my real name. It's on my birth certificate."

"Oh. Sorry."

There was an awkward silence—which was an improvement in the relationship. You can only have awkwardness with someone you have a modicum of respect for. Emery absentmindedly ran her fingers around the small dedication plaque nailed to the bench. The name caught her eye.

"Oh," she said. "My grandfather donated this bench."

What the plaque didn't mention was that the bench had been part of a campaign to pressure Derrymore into abstaining from coeducation.

Lilah offered a faint smile.

"So … did you see my snot rocket?" Emery asked.

Lilah reddened and they both laughed.

• • •

Emery's parents arrived the next morning. Her father took an extremely rare day off and she felt bad for creating such drama.

While the Hoopers had meetings with the headmaster and academic dean, Emery had a normal day of class and lunch and practice. Emery's parents took her and Noah to a steakhouse for dinner and briefly mentioned that the history teacher had been asked to leave and that the Asian history unit would be put on hold. It was a two-minute summary and Emery's father swiftly moved the conversation into happier lands.

Emery's parents had solved the Peiffer problem and left campus. They would throw whatever they had—money, power, influence—to ameliorate their little girl's suffering. It was the same with all of the parents at Derrymore.

Their duty was to provide bubble worlds where the only times their children confronted war or crime or poverty was through literature. Their children would never befriend someone who couldn't speak a Romance language. They would meet other kids who spoke Rich—the parlance of prix fixe menus and tree trails.

They would only come into contact with the accepted dysfunctions: eating disorders, contested wills, functional alcoholism, and divorce. Their self-contained worlds were charmed, gated, and incomplete by design. They allowed their inhabitants to live home theater lives. Clam bake lives. Grandma's pearls and dad's assistant and "my therapist said" lives.

• • •

"Isn't that Peiffer?" Noah said.

He pointed at a dark green hatchback as they walked through the Isle. Noah gave the finger to the back of the car.

"I wish you'd let me tell everyone what happened." He sighed. "We could have given her a real send-off."

Emery made an appreciative sound. She imagined what it would be like if Errol and Candace were there, and maybe Scott, too. If they were jeering and whistling at the departing Subaru, would that make it feel like a victory?

Through the window of the boys' dorm, they could see that the TV in the common room was playing *Entourage* (as always).

"Wanna watch?" Noah asked.

"I'm gonna study for my math test," she said.

"Now? We should celebrate—your dad got the racist fired!"

Emery shook her head.

"Please don't tell anyone about this."

"The firing part?"

Emery sighed impatiently. "Whatever—that's fine. They're

going to announce that Peiffer was 'let go' anyway. But don't spread what happened in class and that my parents came."

"But it's such a good story! Justice was served and you—"

"The whole thing is fucking stupid. I don't want to think about it anymore."

Noah looked disappointed. He had been so excited to tell everyone how Emery's dad pulled strings at Derrymore, and so, too (by proxy) did Emery.

"It makes you look good," he urged.

"It doesn't. This never would have happened to Candace … or you."

Emery had known her parents would get Mrs. Peiffer fired (and she had felt no urge to stop them), but she wasn't happy in the way she'd expected to be.

It wasn't a triumph of Emery over Mrs. Peiffer—it was one of her father over the school, and that battle had nothing to do with her.

CHAPTER 11

On the last day of the tennis season, Coach Norton organized a prize ceremony honoring the seniors. He gave a short speech about Sara and two others, but his final words were reserved for Ryan.

"Last but not least," he said, and opened his arms for a lingering hug.

He presented Ryan with a grocery store bouquet twice the size of those he gave to the other girls. Coach Norton was always touchy-feely with Ryan, and she navigated it gracefully, as she did all of the repugnant things in her life. She was playful back to him, sometimes turning her head quickly so her braids whipped against his face, or snatching his clipboard out of his grip. He was a little in love with her and she knew it.

Coach Norton's dad was a Vietnam veteran and he liked to say that his stepmom was the only souvenir his dad had brought back.

"If you had told me the Ryan Kim you see before you today was the same Ryan Kim I met four years ago"—he shook his head—"I would never have believed you."

Emery's ears perked up. Was it possible that Ryan had not always been Ryan? Coach Norton unfolded a piece of paper from his pocket and gave it a glance before continuing.

"When Ryan came to tryouts she was *scared*. She was this tiny little thing—I know I shouldn't say this but what the hell—she looked like a refugee. But then she got on court and wow—she blew me away. Six oh, six oh. Straight sets every time. She took down my best players without breaking a sweat. I said to her, 'If you want to be the player I know you can be, you've got to have some confidence in yourself.'

"And, Ryan, I've gotta say, watching you come out of your shell that first year was one of the proudest moments of my coaching career. And look at you now: this formidable presence and awesome tennis player—and heartbreaker." He looked at her adoringly then continued, "Here's what makes you a great captain and a great athlete: You're a go-getter. You're never timid. You don't wait for instruction and you don't let anyone get away with a bad line call. Ryan's not robotic the way other—you know what I'm saying. She wears her emotions on her sleeve. That's called heart and you can't win without it."

Coach Norton applauded Ryan for qualities she didn't have and things she didn't do. Ryan's eyes met Emery's for the briefest moment and imparted a micro-smirk.

Coach Norton praised Ryan for becoming what he wanted her to be. She conformed to his version of strength—aggressive and unrelenting, masculine and ruthless. Emery had seen Ryan win Lilah's mom over in a matter of seconds with a totally different set of tactics: deference and gentle smiles. Ryan thanked Coach Norton for four wonderful years, grinning and bearing his off-color compliments for the last time.

• • •

Emery and Noah decided to go to homecoming together. Errol proudly told anyone who asked that he was going alone. No one could confirm who Scott was going with, but he had asked someone. Candace had been invited by a sophomore on the football team. Raymon was going with his third choice—a curly-haired Texan with huge boobs and a heavy drawl.

At the dance, Emery was shocked to see Lilah arrive on someone's arm. Like Candace, Lilah had been invited by a sophomore. Emery felt a prick of envy, followed by a wave of convoluted relief. Convoluted because she figured the blessing of having a date would make Lilah less likely to pursue the origins of the hoax invitation. Lilah had *achieved* a date, which was more than most freshman girls could say.

The date's hair stuck out stiffly from his head. His tie was a barf green hue. Naturally, he was Asian. Lilah had put effort into her look, but it had turned out all wrong. Her hair had been fried with a straightening iron, and red drugstore lipstick veered beyond the edges of her mouth.

She had on her Special Occasion Outfit. It had made an appearance at every formal Derrymore event thus far and homecoming was no exception. The black velvet shift dress hit mid-calf and emphasized Lilah's pear-ness.

When Lilah and her date held up double peace signs for a photo—a gesture that would usually send Emery into a frenzy of contempt—Emery barely winced. She watched them for a few more moments, trying to catch Lilah's eye and smile, but Lilah never looked her way. A quick exchange of goodwill would exonerate her, right? Emery couldn't stop thinking about how Lilah had reclaimed the hoax note after being rejected by Raymon.

Noah and Emery were posing for a group photo when a series of squeals rose above "Stronger." Scott had arrived (wearing shutter shades) with a girl who was campus famous for qualifying for the Junior Olympics in swimming. Her hair was white-blonde from chlorine damage (*Veela*, Noah called it) and her shoulders were broader than Scott's. Emery felt Noah's sympathetic eyes boring a hole in the side of her head and she shot him a fierce look. *Stop*, she mouthed over the music, but his expression remained pitying.

The dance was no fun—a typical teenage ratio of build-up and disappointment. Emery felt self-conscious all night about not having a real date. When the slow songs played, she hammed it up with Noah. He dipped her to the floor during "Collide," but her heart wasn't in it. She felt like the only girl without a date and couldn't resist sneaking glances at Scott and the swimmer.

At the end of the dance, the pairs finally uncoupled and Emery exhaled. Errol and Scott were leaning against a table that had been pushed to the edge of the room. As she approached the boys, a Cheshire cat grin spread across Scott's face. He pretended to take aim at her and fire. She missed a half step in confusion but managed to mask her trip by grabbing someone who was in her path.

Scott yelled something over "Ignition."

"Huh?" she said.

"Miss Firing Squad!"

Emery sent a panicked look at Errol.

"Lay off, Scott," Errol said.

"I meant it as a compliment!" Scott exclaimed. "I'd be scared of you if I were a teacher. If you're mean to Em on

Tuesday, you'll be packing your bags on Wednesday. Daddy Hooper to the rescue!"

Scott let out a raucous laugh and slapped the table. Emery's cheeks stung. Errol mimed tipping something into his mouth. Scott was drunk.

CHAPTER 12

On the first night back from Christmas break, the dormitory was a runway of extravagant presents. There were new iHomes, Free City sweatpants, and nova check as far as the eye could see.

Candace was perched on her bed wearing a silky, off-white kimono. It was short like Ryan's. But it was not striking like Ryan's. In cream, it looked like a hotel robe. Candace's interpretation was flat and prosaic.

"I read *Memoirs of a Geisha*," Candace explained.

How badly Emery wanted to call her a Ryan wannabe. In all likelihood, Candace had not read beyond the back cover of their mothers' book club selection.

Emery was angry at herself for not beating Candace to the punch. She had almost asked her parents for a green kimono at Barneys when they were Christmas shopping, but she hadn't wanted them to feel uncomfortable.

How would they look—the three of them—buying a kimono? Emery imagined a saleswoman piping in hollow compliments, wondering how they were related, or if Emery was an exchange student—an exchange student that the Hoopers had taken to buy a nice American souvenir, and here she was, choosing a kimono. Within seconds, the scene was erumpent in Emery's mind and her enthusiasm for the green kimono evaporated.

Now it was firmly out of the question. There was nothing worse than to appear a Candace copycat—the contingent was already large and growing in the ninth grade.

• • •

Candace had recently started drinking coffee and had left an enormous stain on the front of a pullover she'd borrowed from Emery. Emery was examining the stain under the fluorescent hallway lights when she noticed Lilah watching from her doorway.

"Do you have bleach or something?" Emery snapped.

"Me? Yeah, um, I have a stain remover," Lilah said. "Bleach is only for white-whites."

"Is this considered white-white?"

It was cream with thick maroon stripes. Lilah shook her head.

"Do you think it will come out?" Emery asked.

Lilah rubbed the stain with her fingertips and stretched the fabric.

"I don't think so," she said. "The stain has set. If you treated it right when it happened, you might have been able to get it out. But it's dry now."

"Fucking Candace," Emery said. "She's the one who let it dry."

"Want me to try anyway?"

The stain remover was next to a fish-shaped bottle of L'Oréal Kids shampoo in her shower caddy. Lilah sprayed a viscous fluid on the stain and rubbed the fabric against itself. The stain got darker as it absorbed the fluid.

Emery sighed. "Thanks for trying."

"It might lift a little once you wash it. But even if it comes out, there will be a faint outline."

"Should we wash it now?" At Lilah's perplexed expression, Emery added, "If you're not busy."

"I can help you. Sure."

Lilah grabbed her Ziploc of quarters and laundry detergent. She led the way to the basement and started a cycle. Emery confessed that she had never done laundry.

It wasn't a BS confession like the ones Candace and Emery sometimes swapped: never gone to a water park, never eaten a Hot Pocket, never heard of an outlet mall. These confessions weren't BS in the sense of being false—they were BS in the sense of pretended shame. When they "admitted" they had never been to Costco or didn't know that credit cards other than American Express existed, they were proud of their distance from the average American.

"It'll be done in thirty-five minutes," Lilah said. "I can get you when it's ready, if you want."

"Let's just wait here," Emery said.

She hopped on top of a dryer and banged her heels against it. It took Lilah a moment to process that Emery wanted her to stay, but she eventually sat on top of the machine beside her.

"I know Candace is gonna be looking for me," Emery said. "I said I'd go with her to hang out with that football player who took her to the dance—but who cares. She's probably giving him a blow job now."

"She does that?"

"Have you ever heard of stone face?"

Emery's phone rang. She held it up so Lilah could see Candace was calling.

"Ignore," Emery said, pressing the call end button.

Candace called back. Emery immediately declined it.

"Shouldn't you let it ring?" Lilah said. "Otherwise she'll know you're pressing ignore."

"I want her to know that." Emery offered her most dazzling smile and continued to kick the machine.

Lilah pushed her hair back from her forehead with both hands and chuckled weakly.

"I promise I'm not usually this mean," Emery said. "Only because she pissed me off so much lately and stained my favorite quarter-zip."

Lilah was surprised to hear Emery call it her favorite—everyone knew a cable-knit periwinkle sweater was Emery's signature piece.

"So who was that guy you went to the dance with?" Emery asked.

"No one," Lilah said. "I know him from my summer orchestra."

Emery pressed for more details and was surprised to discover that Lilah had gone with him against her parents' wishes.

"I'm not allowed to date," Lilah said.

"Why not?"

"Chinese parents."

"I thought you were Taiwanese," Emery said. She stopped banging her heels and waited for Lilah to explain herself.

"People always think that means Thailand. It's easier to say Chinese."

"That's stupid. Are you dating him?"

Lilah became shy. "No. But he asked if I wanted to be his girlfriend. I told him I have to think about it."

Emery's jaw dropped as if Lilah had unexpectedly turned a backflip. She snapped it shut.

"Playing hard to get?" Emery teased.

Lilah giggled and covered her mouth embarrassedly.

"He seemed really nice," Emery said, feeling generous.

"Yeah. But I don't like him."

"I guess that's the beauty of boarding school."

"What is?"

"That your parents don't know anything about your life unless you tell them."

Lilah shook her head. "Chinese parents talk to each other. If Annie found out, she would tell her mom. My mom would find out."

"Annie would do that?"

Lilah nodded. "But luckily she didn't go to the dance."

"Which one is Annie again? Is she the one who uses too much self-tanner?"

"She's not tan. That's just the color of her skin."

The closest thing Lilah's mother gave to a compliment was to cut down someone else. Her way of consoling Lilah for losing first chair to Annie had been to say, "First chair will not make her skin any lighter."

"Is she part Mexican or something?" Emery asked.

"No."

"I don't like her," Emery said. "No offense. She was in Peiffer's class with me. She was such a know-it-all and always asking for extra credit."

"She's always like that," Lilah said. "I don't really like her either. She's a …"

"Kiss-ass?"

"A bitch."

They both burst out laughing and Emery squeezed Lilah's wrist. Lilah didn't know what to do so she just kept it still in mid-air. She had seen Emery and Noah and Candace falling over each other laughing, clutching at one another, play slapping each other—but she couldn't figure out how they did it. Emery let go.

"What else?" Emery dug. "Can you shave your legs?"

Lilah hesitated. "It never came up, so I do secretly. But I'm really bad at it."

"What else?"

"What else is there? I don't really know what normal kids are allowed to do."

Lilah was about to bring up how her mom wouldn't let her buy underwear from Victoria's Secret (which hadn't stopped her from tearing a "One Free PINK Panty" coupon out of a dentist-office *Seventeen* and acquiring a cherry-print hipster panty—though she regretted chickening out of her one chance to acquire a thong), but Emery asked, "Like sleepovers and R-rated movies? Is that why you didn't come to Ryan's house for that tennis retreat?"

"That was because I had a violin thing. I really wanted to go. Was it fun?"

Emery began nodding enthusiastically but toned it down out of regard for Lilah's feelings.

"It was cool. But, like, nothing special. We just hung out."

"I wanted to see Ryan's house," Lilah said in a whisper.

It was the first time Emery had ever heard Lilah express nosiness or anything that didn't adhere to her insipid, model-minority image.

"It was just normal. You didn't miss anything."

"Was there Korean stuff?"

"Like what?"

"Like furniture or pottery? Or food."

"Korean pottery?" Emery considered. "I don't think so. But I don't know what that would look like. Maybe upstairs? We were mostly just out by the pool. The kitchen was normal. Her mom got California Pizza Kitchen."

"What does your house look like?"

"Like anyone else's."

"What's it like to be rich?" Lilah pursed her lips right after she asked, realizing that she'd said too much. Annie said their peers had Make-A-Wish lives—a pool (and a hot tub) in the backyard, a new car at sixteen, orchestra tickets to *Spring Awakening*—and Lilah's curiosity had gotten the better of her.

Emery was no stranger to the "How rich are you?" question. Kids pried after they overheard their parents gossiping about the Hoopers' wealth.

But Lilah was asking about something beyond wealth. Her question prodded at the particular circumstances of Emery's wealth—what was it like to be white-rich?

The Hoopers talked around money like they talked around race. These were self-explanatory topics, they held. There was nothing to probe deeper, and if you possessed the urge to delve, you were gauche. So not only did Emery not know how to answer Lilah, she had never considered the question seriously herself.

"It's … um"—Emery dabbed rosebud salve onto her lips with her ring finger. "Honestly, I don't know how to answer that. I don't want to be rude, but it's a weird question."

"Sorry. I didn't mean to offend you."

"It's not offensive. It's just … weird. Asking someone what it's like to be rich? That's weird, Lilah."

Lilah nodded, chastised.

Emery's phone rang again and she let it go to voicemail.

"By the way, sorry for getting mad about that Nantucket crewneck. I don't know why I flipped out. I was probably on my period or something."

• • •

Over the next few days, Emery continued to think about Lilah's question: *What's it like to be rich?* It stumped her. To be rich meant different things in different places. At tennis camp, it didn't matter that she was rich. It was something that fascinated other kids for a short time, but it didn't factor in on the court, so after the initial discovery, it was uninteresting. Being rich at Derrymore was a more complex animal.

Rich was the default at Derrymore. If anything, Emery should have asked Lilah what it was like to not be rich. But she already knew. She had secondhand access to not being rich through Noah, and it didn't look fun.

Noah never commented on wealth. When the Hoopers took him on vacation he never said the suite was beautiful or the view was to die for. When Emery got an Hervé Léger bandage dress or piece of jewelry, he never acknowledged it. When the Hoopers' backyard was re-landscaped and the pool moved from one side of the yard to the other, he acted like he hadn't noticed.

But Noah always wanted to hang out at Emery's house and not his own. And he never refused an invite to go on island with the Hoopers. He was polite and always said thank you, but he went out of his way to appear unfazed by the trappings of their lives. It was as if complimenting Emery somehow translated into debasing himself.

Before Derrymore, there had been little flare-ups of impatience and annoyance between them, but never outright meanness. But lately, underhanded comments were becoming commonplace. As tension grew, Emery had remained silent when Noah made several comments assuming he would be invited to stay at her beach house as he had in past summers.

Then he'd stolen a pen from Emery. Noah claimed to have taken it for the sole purpose of testing whether she would miss it. It was a Montblanc that her father had given her as a First Day of Derrymore gift. It had been a very sweet gesture, and she appreciated the thought, but she did not prize it and failed to notice that it was gone. Noah said this meant she was spoiled.

"If you don't realize a two-hundred-dollar pen disappeared then you shouldn't own one."

"Fine. I shouldn't own it."

"But you do, so you should keep track of it."

"I didn't ask for it. My dad gave it to me as a gift."

"Then you should take extra-good care of it because it's from your *dad*." He said the last word in a mocking tone.

"What's your problem? Did I lose something you gave me?"

Noah's cheeks flushed. "You said it would never happen to me."

"What wouldn't?" Emery asked.

"That my dad would never swoop in and solve my problems and get Mrs. Peiffer fired or whatever."

"What are you talking about?"

"You said, 'This would never happen to Candace or you,' because her dad isn't on the board and my dad abandoned me."

"Are you shitting me, Noah?"

Noah didn't answer.

"Tell me you're joking," Emery said. "You must be joking."

"This is such classic Emery. You're so selfish that you can't see—"

"That would never happen *because you're white!*" Emery yelled.

Noah stared at her venomously.

"You're a joke," she said. "Keep the pen."

CHAPTER 13

Though they didn't spend meals or daylight hours together, Emery requested Lilah's company every evening after check-in. But as they bonded, a lump of guilt was calcifying in her chest. Emery was not a procrastinator—she hated the weight of things on her mind.

"I have to tell you something," she said.

It was the fourth consecutive night that Lilah was seated on the area rug in Emery's room. In her lap was a blazer lined with grey rabbit fur. Lilah was stroking the fur gently.

Emery was seated at her desk, waiting for coral nail polish to dry. She looked Lilah dead in the eye: "I have no excuses. It was atrocious behavior"—a phrase her mother used when the occasion called for it—"but it's best to be honest. I wrote the Raymon note with Noah, but it was mostly me."

Emery blew on her fingernails.

Lilah looked startled, then she said, "I know."

"But how—" Emery's eyes bugged. "It doesn't matter. I'm really sorry. It was a gross thing to do and there's no defense."

Emery savored apologizing like this. She liked to be repentant, to not shift blame, and to take full responsibility, because it always caught the victim off-guard. This had been the case when she apologized to Casey Wingfield in fifth grade for calling her outfit (two piqué polos layered on top of each other) fugly. Emery had held eye contact for as long as Casey would allow, and Casey had accepted her peace offering of a gummy Krabby Patty. There was power in admitting that one had behaved rottenly. No one expected a young woman to be unflinchingly sorry.

Emery kept her face taut and made sure not to let it slip into a sympathetic, insulting simper. She told herself that the next line belonged to Lilah and she would wait silently until it came.

"It's odd," Lilah said finally. Her shoulders dropped and the tension left her body. She continued petting the rabbit fur. "I realized it was you and Noah, but I wasn't even mad. I can see how it was funny."

"It really wasn't. You don't have to say that."

"I'm not just saying it. I mean, for Noah it's sort of pathetic because he's just—so insecure. You know what I mean?"

Usually this kind of comment would have sent Emery into a defensive rage, but Lilah wasn't wrong. The anonymous note was a shield Noah could hide behind, but that confidence didn't translate to real life.

"And for you—well, what I thought at the time was that you're just oblivious to hurting people. And you thought it was harmless and you probably didn't even think twice about it."

Emery turned a wince into a slight twitch in the corner of her mouth. "And now?"

"I guess you're not oblivious. That probably makes it worse, though."

Emery decided that if Lilah used the opportunity to flay her, she would humbly accept the lashing. But Lilah said she was forgiven and Emery believed her.

"I don't forgive Noah, though."

"Why not?"

"I think he enjoys being mean."

"And I don't?"

"I think you do it for protection. He does it for … sport."

"If you knew him—" Emery stopped. She kicked off her Ugg slippers, trying to think of an example that proved Noah was not one who took pleasure in hurting others. She came up short. "So, um, what did you do with the note?"

"It's somewhere in my room," Lilah said. "But I'll throw it away."

Emery nodded. The incriminating note wasn't going to dispose of itself, but she let it go for the time being.

"You should wear this," Lilah said. She was using both hands to stroke the fur interior of the blazer—the softness was unlike anything she had ever felt. "You already bought it. Not wearing it doesn't reverse the bunnies that got skinned."

"The damage has already been done."

"Right." Lilah yawned. "You know, Noah is the only person who writes in cursive."

• • •

In the lead-up to Valentine's Day, the senior girls sold daisy-grams by the stem. It was a slick, floral front for what the fundraiser really was: an information laundering racket. While they took orders for white, pink, and red daisies, they separately made note of hesitations and second thoughts. They witnessed an order of a dozen reds hastily amended to six whites. They picked up on which recipients were afterthoughts.

They also took the liberty of sending out a few anonymous daisies to stoke controversy because they could.

When Lilah received a dozen daisies (a mixture of red, white, and pink) from Emery, her friends couldn't have been more jealous if a senior boy had asked her to prom.

• • •

"So, you're a quadruplet now?" Noah said.

"Quintuplet," Emery fired back.

How Noah had caught wind of Emery's burgeoning friendship with Lilah was a mystery. Emery never spoke about Lilah and Lilah never intruded on her social life in public. The only way Noah could tell was by the intimacy that had sprung up between the two girls, the type of intimacy that was evident even in passing hellos—or Candace was spying.

"Why are you so threatened?" Emery asked.

Noah made an incredulous noise, which prompted Emery to say, "Is it because I'm your only friend?"

Her tone was half-joking, but Noah went into a tailspin of defensiveness. He listed friends and acquaintances recklessly.

"… and the twins from Lucerne who said they're scared of you. And Marissa, the sophomore whose dad donated the new health center—"

"You only know Marissa through me and—"

"You only know her—"

"I was about to say that I know *her* through Candace. But you're only friends with Candace because I've known the Perkinses since before I could walk, so let's not play this game."

They hadn't resolved the pen stealing episode and bad blood was still flowing.

"Is it like a pity thing?" Noah asked.

"Huh?" Emery was still tallying the roster of people she had introduced to Noah.

"Is it because you feel guilty about the homecoming note? It's not like it affected her. She had a date anyway."

The last comment felt like an express jab at the fact that Emery had not had a date.

"Lilah's smart," she said, noticing Noah's breakout and staring at an angry pustule on his chin. "And I desperately crave someone smart to talk to every once in a while."

"So I'm stupid because I'm not Asian? Or because my dad didn't go to Penn? Real nice, Em. Instead of feeling guilty about Lilah you should feel guilty about getting a teacher fired. You ended someone's *career.*"

Emery speed-walked away from Noah. She didn't hold the door and she didn't look back. He would arrive at Latin just a few seconds after her, but she couldn't bear to be near him. At least she had removed herself before reminding him that Proactiv didn't work unless he did *all three* steps. *Never insult someone's appearance* was one of Emery's mother's golden rules.

"Everything alright?" Mr. Arthur asked after she entered the room stormily.

"It's fine," Emery answered in an unnatural voice.

Mr. Arthur registered a disruption, but he returned to grading papers and allowed Emery to stew. She uttered a half syllable, but it died on her tongue. A false start. He pretended not to notice.

"Do you know why Mrs. Peiffer got fired?" she said finally.

Mr. Arthur looked up as if he had just noticed Emery was there.

"It was me," Emery said, swallowing the last word.

"You have such power?"

Emery nodded grimly.

Mr. Arthur chuckled. "Dear"—he turned the papers over—"you overestimate your agency."

Even though he lived in his own bubble of opera, wine, classical music, and Ancient Greek, Mr. Arthur transcended the out-of-touchness the school specialized in. If asked, Mr. Arthur would have said it was because he was a Jew, and to be a Jew among gentiles at a prep school where integrity and bigotry were often conflated made him fluent in underdog.

Emery was a nontraditional underdog, and those were Mr. Arthur's strong suit. His disciples were misfits who discovered their powers at Derrymore. Mr. Arthur's protégés were rarely peaceable—they took from their Classical education the realpolitik exemplified in the Melian Dialogue.

In Emery, Mr. Arthur recognized a worldview being formed by rapidly collecting chips-on-shoulder. He would do what he could to delay the internalization process, but he already sensed that Emery's greatest triumphs would come from her "the world is against me" mentality. The softness that kept her from wondering *what does this person want from me* in response to any act of kindness was hardening.

"It wasn't my fault?" she asked.

"Is it your fault that the strong do what they're able to do and the weak suffer what they must?"

Emery swallowed nervously at the comparison of her actions to those of the amoral Athenians.

"Let's say"—Mr. Arthur gave a meaningful look—"she was on her way out."

Mrs. Peiffer had been on probation. Sure, she had a doctorate, but she also had a boyfriend who'd stolen a Derrymore maintenance van to go back to his ex-wife. Then Peiffer's dog had bitten another teacher's child, and then there was the time that she drove over the new plantings outside of the admissions building and ripped the Belgian block from the pavement. It was never discovered whether she was intoxicated or not. She claimed to have been texting.

CHAPTER 14

Lilah was sitting on Emery's bed, crocheting a scarf (maroon to match Emery's pullover) that she was excited to give to her. They never met in Lilah's room after once catching Candace with her ear pressed against the door. When discovered, Candace explained she had tripped and landed in front of Lilah's room. Emery had let her stumble through the ridiculous excuse and never broke eye contact.

"Are you still fighting with the quadruplets about the Chinese name stuff?" Emery asked.

"The who?"

Emery bit her lip. "Like you and Annie and them. It's just a nickname that Noah made up."

"Because we all look the same?"

Emery shrugged. "I dunno. I think just because you're always together."

Lilah had stopped knitting.

"Don't take it personally," Emery said. "The nickname was harmless—I swear. He didn't mean anything by it."

Lilah nodded slowly.

"Oh—" Emery stood up and went to her closet. She felt around the corners and found what she was looking for, crumpled in the dark. "I've been meaning to give this to you. I never wear it and I think you liked it."

Emery held out the Nantucket crewneck to Lilah.

"Are you sure?"

"Totally. I have, like, ten of them."

Emery opened the bottom drawer of her dresser with her foot and there was a faded rainbow of sweatshirts.

She made an "it's nothing" gesture when Lilah thanked her.

"Do you mind if I play music?"

The playlist was called "Dad." While the Eagles, Blues Traveler, and Jackson Browne sang, Emery made flashcards for deponent verbs and thought about Mr. Arthur's question: Was it her fault that she was herself and Noah was Noah? Or Lilah was Lilah? Was she supposed to handicap herself to create an artificially even footing?

Lilah sang along softly when "American Pie" came on, and Emery turned the volume up. Soon they were both singing the chorus in full throat.

"I wouldn't have expected you to like my lame dad music."

"Oh, I just know it because—" Lilah stopped abruptly. "It's embarrassing. I shouldn't have brought it up."

Emery suspected that eavesdropping during Candace's guitar phase might have something to do with it. She waited for an explanation.

"It's nothing weird," Lilah said. "It's—I know it from CTY. They play it at the end of every dance. It's a tradition."

Center for Talented Youth was a scam that Asian parents fell for year after year: an academic summer program that required test scores to apply (for a false sense of exclusivity).

"You take *classes*? In the *summer*?"

"It's fun—I mean, it's lame. But the dance is usually fun. It's our version of sleepaway camp."

"There's a dance? With boys?"

Emery was about to ask more questions about this bizarre camp but her phone vibrated.

"Wait, sorry," she said. "Riley and Candace want to show me some blog thing they want me to do. Do you mind?"

"No. Not at all."

Lilah scooted to the corner of the area rug to make more space. Emery watched her for a moment and added, "I just think they'd feel less self-conscious with fewer people. It's just this stupid fashion thing—it'll be fast."

"Oh. Yeah. Of course."

Lilah gathered her hooks and yarn in a pile. Emery placed the Nantucket crewneck in Lilah's arms.

"I'll text you when they're gone."

Lilah nodded and managed a smile. She waited for a text inviting her back, but it never came.

• • •

Hooper. Humbird. Assigned seating for Chapel meant that Noah sat next to her. They had reconciled without solving anything, and like many friendships that carry one from childhood to young adulthood, theirs would become peppered with taboo subjects and unresolved spats.

Dean Andrews announced that two juniors had been caught drinking alcohol on campus. One was expelled and the other was allowed to stay but would be on probation indefinitely. Noah and Emery knocked their knees against each other meaningfully—the probation recipient was a star athlete and therefore untouchable.

Down the pew, Lilah stood up and made her way to the front of the chapel. She was performing a piano solo for the first time thanks to Emery, who had talked her out of roping her friends into a quartet performance.

Dean Andrews finished his comments and two boys moved the lectern to the side. A grand piano was rolled to the center. Lilah waited for a signal to walk up the stairs, but no one was cueing her.

"Go, go, go," Emery said under her breath.

It was uncomfortably silent when Lilah finally took the stage in her go-to velvet dress. She had altered it (against Emery's advice) and made it shorter, using scotch tape to hide the raw edge. It was a sloppy job and inappropriately short. Lilah wasn't taking her seat on the piano bench. Instead, she stood at the front edge of the stage, looking out into the pews.

"What is she doing?" Emery whispered.

Lilah almost curtsied then decided against it. The effect was an ungraceful herky-jerky movement that caused some snickers. She started apologizing and then turned so quickly toward the piano that she stumbled. She caught herself on the piano keys and the discordant sound set off widespread giggles.

Emery dug her fingers into Noah's thigh and he elbowed her in the ribs.

The heavy velvet of Lilah's dress escaped the scotch tape and the uneven hem was on full display. The shoddy workmanship was hardly noticed, however, because Lilah's cherry-print underwear with the words SWEET CHEEKS printed on the seat stared into the audience.

While the giggles were still in full force, Lilah started her performance. She played at a breakneck pace and the sonata lasted half the length it was supposed to. While playing the last measure, she stood up and bowed in one movement before running off the stage.

The dean dismissed the seniors and the juniors first. Emery glanced at the side door Lilah had fled out of before heading in the opposite direction. She pretended to rummage through her bag with her head down so she could lose Noah while pushing through the crowd.

"It honestly wasn't even that bad," Noah said straight into her ear, stepping on the back of her ballet flat in his haste to keep up.

"Careful, Noah! Miu Miu."

"Sorry. I swear it wasn't that bad," he baited again.

"What wasn't?" Emery played dumb.

"Sweet cheeks."

Emery dropped a shoulder to get around a beefy lacrosse player. "Okay … why are you telling me?"

"I mean, like, in case you were worried."

"Why would I be worried? I wasn't the one up there."

"But you're close and—"

"That's just Lilah." Emery forced a laugh. "That's how she is."

"It was painfully awkward," Noah said.

"If you knew Lilah like I do, you'd expect this kind of thing. Honestly, it's not a big deal."

Noah wouldn't drop it. He wanted to recount every mortifying detail and he needed Emery to react. He required it. Each time Emery tried to downplay the incident, he dug in deeper.

"Even if you expected it, c'mon, Em. That was *crazy*. Her underwear—I was dying. How were you not *dying*?"

"Honestly, I thought it was going to be way worse."

Emery's voice was tight with the effort of controlling her irritation.

"How could it have been—"

"Who cares?"

Emery lost her composure. Noah's attack on Lilah felt like an attack on herself. He wanted to embarrass her. He wanted her to regret being friends with Lilah. He wanted her to admit she had blundered and to pick him as first choice.

"Jeez, Em," Noah said. He did a lousy job of hiding a smile. "Chill out."

• • •

Usually when Lilah said something self-conscious—about her not-quite thigh gap or her forgettable face or her inability to articulate herself in class—Emery got irritated.

"Stop being insecure," she'd say. "No one else thinks that."

It took Lilah a few of these exchanges to realize Emery really meant it.

"Ohmygod, shut up. Everyone knows you're the smartest one in our class."

These shutdowns were better than a pep talk because a pep talk was false positivity—lies. Emery's frustration was the most validating response because it meant Lilah deserved to be chastised for underrating herself. Emery never gave credit where it was not due.

On the evening of the piano debacle, Lilah gathered her in-progress scarf and entered Emery's room tentatively.

"Heyyy," Lilah said.

"Hello," Emery said, looking up just long enough to meet the criteria for good manners before returning to her laptop, where she was scrutinizing Warhol-effect Photobooth images.

"This color will look really nice on you," Lilah said, holding up the skein of yarn.

"I'm not really a maroon person."

Lilah nodded. It wasn't the right time to bring up the maroon stripes on Emery's (alleged) favorite pullover. She could give the scarf to her mom for Mother's Day. Or to Annie for her birthday. Maybe "favorite" meant as little to Emery as "best" (as in, best friend)—not a descriptor to be taken at face value. Lilah was becoming conversant in Emery's tempers. Often a bad mood was just a bad mood—but there was something different about this polite coldness.

"Today was"—Lilah shuddered involuntarily—"really bad."

A tight-lipped *hmm* was all Emery offered. No rebuttal.

Lilah continued: "I know everyone will forget about it in a week—and it's not a big deal—but I wanted to die."

Emery was occupied fishing an eyelash out of her eye and didn't respond. Lilah started to get prickly armpit sweat standing in the middle of Emery's room.

"Do you think I should try to, like, redeem myself? And maybe redo the performance next week?"

"No." Emery shut her laptop firmly and crossed her legs as she turned to give Lilah her full attention. "I think—for you—the best thing would be to lie low for a while."

Emery's mouth was turned upward in the shape of a smile but there was no warmth. More concerning, her eyes looked at Lilah like a stranger. The attentive but expectant gaze made Lilah feel unwelcome and rushed, like when she had entreated her parents to have dinner at the farm-to-table restaurant in Emery's town. "Is there anything else we can get you?" the waiter kept asking until they got the check forty-five minutes after being seated.

Lilah was about to make an excuse to leave when Emery asked, "Are you mad at me for telling you not to do the violin quartet?"

It had never occurred to her to blame Emery for the solo disaster.

"Of course not," Lilah said. "I always wanted to play piano in front of people. Even though it went horribly I'm grateful that you made me—not made me, but you know. Like, encouraged me to go up there alone."

"Yeah." Emery was squinting slightly and nodding thoughtfully, like Lilah had just made a breakthrough in therapy. "It is a good thing that you had the confidence to go on stage by yourself and try something new."

"For sure. And I'll do it again—"

"After lying low for a bit."

"Right. Obviously."

"Well." Emery toyed with the diamond stud in her lobe.

Lilah was still clutching her unfinished scarf. Even as she was deeply wounded, she could appreciate Emery's deft communication skills. How did she manage to convey *it was nice knowin' ya* without ever dismissing Lilah directly? Everything was body language and tone, and the message was crystal clear: *Bye.*

CHAPTER 15

Lilah had known it was too good to last. Nevertheless, she held on to the notion that if a single one of Emery's dresses had fit her, it wouldn't be over already. Sharing clothing was the pinnacle of friendship, and the night before the disaster, Emery had given Lilah full access to her closet. "Borrow whatever you want," Emery had said. "Not just tomorrow. Anytime."

Lilah had sucked her stomach in, held her breath, and pulled her shoulder blades together, but she couldn't zip any of the size zeroes over her ribcage. Had she managed to squeeze into any of them—preferably the BCBG bubble hem dress—everything would have been different. Or at least it would've lasted longer.

Study hall was agony. She was both hoping against hope for Emery to knock on her door and, simultaneously, convincing herself Emery would never speak to her again. On top of everything, Lilah needed a new dress. It had taken ages to convince her mother to buy the overpriced velvet thing, and Lilah had sworn up and down that she'd wear it for every formal function through senior year.

Lilah didn't blame Emery. Emery had put herself on the line to befriend Lilah and Lilah had betrayed her. Unintentionally, of course, but publicly and in spectacular fashion.

Even if Emery never spoke to her again, it had been worth it. Lilah couldn't be bothered to miss Annie and the others, but she would miss Emery and fantasize about what could have been, though it had been fated from the start.

Emery went to Wimbledon and received pears wrapped in gold foil from her godmother. Lilah used dry cleaner hangers and the only passport stamp she had was Taiwan. Emery went on mother-daughter retreats where breakfast was a handful of almonds, lunch was a frisée salad, and dinner was a deep, cleansing breath. Lilah and Mrs. Chang loved the Cinnastix from Domino's.

There were footsteps in the hall. Lilah strained to listen. A neighboring door opened to a burst of laughter and an overlapping exchange of words. The door slammed shut.

• • •

Mrs. Chang bought Lilah two new formal dresses and delivered them on a Saturday afternoon. Lilah searched for the TJ Maxx discount tags but she couldn't find them.

"They're from Bloomingdale's," her mother insisted. "AQUA."

One was a black shift dress with lace detailing. The other was strawberry ice cream pink with a black ribbon around the waist.

"They were on sale?" Lilah asked.

"No!"

"It's fine if they were, I was just wondering. You shouldn't have spent so much."

"I can tell that you need it."

"Need what?"

"I hear you're sad. On the phone after bad recital."

"I'm fine, Mom. I'm just stressed out because of a test."

Her mother shrugged, skeptical, and straightened out the comforter.

"You're not mad about the velvet dress?" Lilah asked.

"It's so ugly. I'm glad you cut it."

After her mom left, Lilah examined the new dresses. She had only shared that her first time playing the piano for an audience didn't go so well—she said nothing of the wardrobe malfunction. Her mom had said to focus on violin: "You shouldn't split your practice time—homework and violin is already enough." Ignoring the velvet mutilation was the closest Mrs. Chang could get to actually consoling her daughter.

The new dresses were typical Lilah—neither offensive nor memorable. They would be fine on a twelve-year-old or a thirty-year-old.

While she had always admired nice things, Lilah had never craved them until she got to know Emery. Emery wouldn't be Emery without her cactus silk pillows and amulet necklace and periwinkle sweater.

Emery's room was a treasure cave. Every nook contained something Lilah had never known existed: scented drawer liners, cedar blocks, slate coasters. Even if Lilah won the lottery she wouldn't know where to find a scrimshaw box. Where did one buy a silver bookmark?

Last week—which felt like years ago—Lilah had watched Emery try on outfits. They weren't for any special occasion, just class. Emery was always talkative while trying on clothes and gave Lilah lessons about which silhouettes were flattering and what pieces were timeless. She'd pulled on a houndstooth blouse (borrowed from Candace) then French-tucked it and rubbed the fabric between her fingers. Emery's nose had wrinkled. She'd taken the blouse off and turned it inside out, looking for the care label.

"I knew it," Emery had said triumphantly. "*Seventy* percent polyester. Synthetics will make your sweat smell like BO even if you don't have BO. And Asians don't have BO."

The smell that came from Lilah's dad after he had mowed the lawn or loaded the car with Costco purchases was ripe, but Lilah hadn't corrected her friend.

She checked the labels on her new dresses: one hundred percent polyester. Lilah sniffed her armpit. Inconclusive.

CHAPTER 16

Freshman year wound down and Emery slipped into auto-pilot. Mrs. Peiffer was forgotten. The Sweet Cheeks incident was more or less forgotten. Emery embarked on the fashion blog with Candace and Riley. They batted around different names: Bronzer and Bandage Skirts (too trashy). Closet Prep (muddled meaning). East Coast PCA (required knowledge of *Zoey 101*). Real Fur & Faux Friends (cheesy). It wasn't until Riley asked whether end-of-semester banquets were chapel dress that Emery thought of the perfect name.

"Chapel dress" was Derrymore language for formal attire. Boys wore coat and tie and girls wore dresses. But on most days, only collared shirts or blouses were required (no ripped jeans, no T-shirts). This attire was called—

"*Class Dress*," Emery said. "It's perfect."

"What if people don't know what 'class dress' means?" Riley asked.

"If you don't get it, our blog's not for you," Candace said.

• • •

HapLeg distribution was the final signal that the school year was over. The yearbook superlatives were loaded with esti-mates of future wealth, fame, and indiscretion: Most Likely to

Become a Trustee, Most Likely to Get Arrested (white-collar crime was the implicit meaning), Most Likely to Get Divorced Three Times, Most Callipygian. Candace mentioned—for the hundredth time—that her brother had won Most Typical Derrymorian. Emery pretended not to hear.

"Oh look," Emery said, flipping to the tennis team photo. "There's me."

Her own face peered back at her from the page.

"Uh-huh," Candace grunted.

The smile was just right. Not too toothy, not self-conscious. She looked genuinely happy. Emery scrutinized her own appearance for a few seconds before examining her teammates. The photographer had managed to catch everyone's good side. There were no awkward angles or forced expressions—Lilah was missing. Emery closed the cover abruptly.

CHAPTER 17

It was a beautiful June—mindless and unchallenging. Emery checked out *Freakonomics* from the Atheneum and biked to 'Sconset. She walked Tupancy Links with her parents and watched *Super Size Me* with her neighbor. Nothing varied in her routine. Summers were always the same and the feeling of predictability was cozy, if anesthetizing.

Even though most of her friends had gone to sleepaway camp when they were younger, Emery never did. When she was ten, her mother had explained the concept. There were cabins, a lake, mail call—she was won over in a matter of seconds. It sounded so much better than tennis and golf clinics at the Rosewall Club.

Mrs. Hooper was thrilled that Emery would go to Tawpoot, the same camp she had attended when she was growing up. Emery's father had gone to the brother camp, Nonantum, but only for one summer. He hadn't liked it.

The idea of archery and canoeing and a camp uniform was so exciting that Emery couldn't fall asleep. After being tucked in, she tossed and turned for thirty minutes before getting up to cross-examine her mother about Tawpoot's famous trail mix.

She padded down the long hallway to the master bedroom but stopped outside the doorway when she heard low, tense voices. It wasn't the sound of arguing, but of pleading.

"Ten is so young," Mr. Hooper said. "At least send her with Candace or someone she knows."

"She'll make friends easily. She's never had trouble before."

"But this is different—there's less supervision. Children can be nasty."

"Honey, camp is a bonding experience. I don't see why you're so concerned."

"I'm not worried about her making friends," he said. "She's a great kid. But at camp, she'll be … alone."

"Alone? What are you talking about? There are—"

"It's very white"—Mr. Hooper's voice was clipped—"is what I'm trying to say. It's utterly white."

Emery's mother was silent.

"I don't want to discourage Emery from doing normal things, but we have to *ease* her into the world. You know how these Tawpoot kids are. They balk at anything different."

"People like your father."

"Sure," he said. "But remember yourself at age ten. Had you ever met an Asian girl? Would you have befriended her?"

"Stan, stop."

"I'm serious! I love you, honey, but let's not pretend you weren't one of the very—"

"Don't be cruel."

"I'm not being cruel. Being sheltered isn't a sin. But I'm trying to make you see what I'm afraid of." The duvet rustled. His voice was gentler when he spoke again. "Emmy will have to face so many things alone—no matter how much we try to protect her. As long as it's in my power to keep her safe, I want to exercise that right … I'll tell her that camp is out of the question tomorrow. I'll take the blame."

Emery tiptoed back to her bedroom.

At breakfast, all of her favorite things were served: popovers with strawberry preserves, Rainier cherries, and chilly monkey smoothies. She told her parents that after sleeping on it, she didn't want to go to camp after all. Their relief was visible and no follow-up questions were asked.

• • •

The renovations on the Hoopers' beach house were finally done and guests were scheduled for every other week of the season. Noah came first. As much as Emery wanted to withhold the invitation and make him pay for the pen incident, he still occupied best friend status.

He wasn't a strong swimmer and refused to go in the ocean. In the past, Emery had been more sympathetic, but it felt like a fake excuse now. After a growth spurt, he was taller than Errol. When Candace arrived on Fourth of July, she also put a damper on Emery's beach time, preferring to lounge by the Hoopers' pool, sunbathing and texting boys.

"Ian and Jake are coming!" Candace announced. "Their ferry just left Hyannis."

Emery ignored her. Candace always found some way to add boys to the equation, and when boys were around Candace was more of an attention hoarder than usual. Emery could already imagine Candace using her favorite flirtatious line: *You were in my dream last night.*

"We should invite them over, Em," Candace said. "They're only here for the weekend."

"But Errol's arriving tonight," Emery said.

"That's perfect!" Candace said. "Come on, Em. Please. It'll
be fun, won't it, Noah?"

Noah hesitated.

"Noah!" Candace bleated. "You just told me you're so
bored. Let's invite them. Don't be antisocial."

As always, Candace got her way. Ian and Jake played soccer
at Derrymore. They were one grade older. Errol was thrilled
to see his teammates at the Hoopers' and barely said hello to
Emery. When Ian complimented Candace's bathing suit—
which she had borrowed from Emery—she said thanks and
did a spin without mentioning who it belonged to. Emery
added it to her meticulously maintained list of slights.

• • •

Candace pulled a bottle of Sun-In out of her "I'm Not a
Plastic Bag" tote.

"Who's first?" Candace shook the bottle.

"What's that?" Emery reached toward it.

Candace withdrew it sharply. "It looks really bad on
black hair."

"I know," Emery snapped. "I just want to see the bottle."

Emery snatched it out of Candace's hand and glared at it.
Sun-In was a hair lightener. Spray, sit in the sun, become
blonde. It was that easy.

"If *you* use it," Candace said, "your hair will turn orange,
not blonde."

Emery didn't reply.

"You'll look like *Yu-Gi-Oh!*," Jake said.

Ian and Errol laughed.

"What's you-gay-oh?" Candace asked.

"Anime," Ian said.

"Ew, only creeps watch anime," she said, spraying Sun-In into her roots. "My hair was so blonde when I was little."

"Mine, too," Errol said.

"My mom called mine white-blond," Jake said.

Ian was the only current blond in the group.

"Should I use it, too?" he asked.

Candace ran her fingers through his hair. "No, your natural color is so pretty. That's good genes."

• • •

When Ian and Jake were about to leave, Mrs. Hooper invited them to stay for dinner. The night lasted and lasted until finally, around 2 a.m., Jake's older sister picked the boys up.

The next morning, Candace invited them over again. Before Emery could refuse, they were on their way. Once they arrived, Candace never stopped giggling and screaming and finding implausible ways to sit in Ian's lap. Noah fawned equally over Jake. Errol showed off, doing flips into the pool, and only spoke to Emery when he wanted her to film a video of him. The weekend spun out of Emery's control and she felt like the butler: in charge of swapping out Kings of Leon for Vampire Weekend and mopping up wet footprints.

• • •

"Where's Jon?" Candace asked innocently.

Jon was Ian's older brother and a rising senior at Derrymore. He was all but guaranteed to win Most Typical Derrymorian.

"Meeting with his essay tutor," Ian answered. "This dude is hilarious. And jacked—no homo. You have to see his eight-pack."

Most Derrymore kids had three separate tutors for college applications. One to help write their essays, one to advise on where to apply, and another for SATs. And that didn't include the school-assigned college counselor that was included with their astronomical tuition (because parents would never trust the fate of their little darlings to a salaried Derrymore stooge).

Jon's tutor, George, was living with the Shepards all summer. George was gay, which Ian found hysterical.

"We've been wearing the tightest swim trunks—from like four years ago—just to fuck with George."

"What's Jon's essay about?" Candace asked.

"George is still deciding. It's so hard to come up with 'a challenge that you've overcome.'"

Ian's comment spawned murmurs of agreement and started a discussion about the essays they'd have to concoct in a few years' time.

"Are you gonna write about that time we went to soccer camp and there was no AC?" Jake asked.

"No," Ian said. "I think I'm gonna talk about how I was planning to have surgery, then decided not to."

Candace gasped. "What kind of surgery?"

Ian and Jake exchanged a grave look.

"Leg lengthening," Ian said.

Ian was 5'7". He thought he deserved to be six foot.

"Isn't that supposed to be so painful?" Noah said.

"Plus, I'd be out for a whole season, so I decided not to. But the essay would be more about how I overcame my insecurity about being short. Martin Sheen is the same height as me. I already talked to George about it."

"Candace, you should write about the time they served you *sweetened* iced tea," Noah said.

"That was horrible!" Candace said. She was aware of her princess reputation and laid it on thick. "I think I'll write about doing charity work with intercity kids."

"*Inter*city kids?" Emery repeated.

"That's a really good topic," Ian said. "Schools love that stuff. Where did you volunteer?"

"I haven't yet," Candace said. "And I don't know how I'll fit it in with sailing and field hockey. Maybe I can do it over spring break or something."

Emery couldn't stop herself: "What if you write about how the airline lost your skis and you had to wear rentals?"

Jake and Ian didn't laugh. They looked stricken.

"Your boots, too?" Ian asked.

"It was so ghetto," Candace said, nodding.

Emery looked to see if Noah was getting this, but he was fishing for something under his chaise. He adjusted the reclining angle to more upright and opened *The Great Gatsby*.

"Are you doing the summer reading?" Candace asked.

"I'm almost halfway through," Noah said. "I like it. Did you guys finish yet?"

Noah always said he "liked" things when he didn't understand them: uni, poker, *The Big Lebowski*.

"I read the SparkNotes," Errol said. "American dream and green light and bootlegging. Done in twenty minutes."

Candace added, "July said it's about how rich people are mean and poor people are sad."

"Amen to that," Ian called.

"It's not that rich people are mean," Emery said. "It's that they never deal with consequences."

"The Yale guy killed that lady," Jake said.

"Hey!" Noah said. "I didn't get that far."

"Right," Emery said. "And nothing happened."

"Gatsby's rich and he got shot," Ian said.

Noah pouted. "Just ruin the whole thing."

"It's not rich versus poor," Emery said. "It's old money versus new money. The dead lady is poor and Gatsby is new money so they don't matter. The only people who are okay at the end are Tom and Daisy."

"Daisy really loved Gatsby, though," Candace said. "I wanted her to leave her husband so badly. I was so sure she would."

"She never intended to," Emery said. "That's the point."

"But she was considering it," Candace said.

"But never seriously. That's why it's so fucked-up. She led him on while it was fun but she was never going to leave Tom for someone who didn't have the status—"

"You know who's new money?" Ian interrupted. "That Iraq girl. The one with the Rolls. And the driver. Do you know her?"

"She's so sweet," Candace said. "I forget her name. Her dad makes car batteries."

"Sure, he makes 'car batteries,'" Jake said suggestively.

Ian and Errol made machine gun noises. Ian groaned when he accidentally ripped a scab off his finger in zealousness. It wasn't bleeding but he cradled it like it was. He had hurt himself using scissors and started to rant about being left-handed in a right-hand world.

• • •

Emery retreated indoors. She was reading at the kitchen table when her mother came in with gardening gloves in hand.

"Are you okay, sweetie? Why aren't you playing badminton with your friends?"

Candace shrieked, then there was a splash. Male laughter followed.

"Overheated," Emery said, her gaze returning to her book.

"Do you want Marina to make lemonade?"

"No, we're fine."

"Brownies?"

Emery didn't reply. Mrs. Hooper sat down at the table beside her daughter.

"Noah and Candace have been here a long time, haven't they?"

Emery closed her book. "Yeah."

"It can be very exhausting to host people for so long. Maybe you're feeling a little fatigued."

"Yeah …" Emery stretched the syllable in the way she did when she was deciding whether to say more. "It's not just that, though. I'm tired of *them*. They all SparkNoted the summer reading and didn't even understand it. The 'obstacles' they're using for their college essays are a joke. And Noah is just like—"

Her mother was nodding understandingly and it made Emery feel pitiful. She swallowed. "He's being weird."

"He's trying to fit in with the other boys?"

"He's going along with whatever they want to do. Even things I know he hates—" Emery stopped herself. If her mom knew the boys were dipping, she would step in and Emery would look like a snitch. "None of them are capable of having an actual conversation, including Noah. I just want to go home."

Emery's voice broke and her mom's arms encircled her.

"I'm so exhausted," Emery said, wiping her eyes.

"It's just one more day." Mrs. Hooper took Emery's hands in hers. "I know how draining it is to play hostess to overnight guests. I always reached a breaking point when your grandparents visited, and I'd tell your dad to make them leave—now!" She laughed. "But he always calmed me down and I managed to get through the visit with a smile on. Why don't you go out there and have fun? It's their last day and you'll regret it if you spend it inside moping."

With dead eyes, Emery looked at her mom. Was she not listening? After this weekend Emery would no longer be friends with Candace or Noah or Errol. They had behaved reprehensibly and used her house as a playground.

CHAPTER 18

When Emery was young, her parents had debated whether to sign her up for music lessons. They asked if she wanted to take piano or violin. She said neither. They asked if she'd consider guitar or maybe drums. She said no and they dropped it. When they'd dreamed of having children, they imagined Tchaikovsky and Handel filling the house, and tartan dresses at Christmas recitals. One of their first purchases as a married couple had been a baby grand Steinway. But they'd never thought they might have difficulty conceiving or undergo five failed rounds of in vitro. They'd never planned to adopt a baby girl who had been abandoned on the stoop of a convenience store in Hongdae. Perhaps classical music was too much hewing to type. It would be better to let Emery discover her own interests.

So Emery took ice skating and ballet and played lacrosse and squash and was on the sailing and swim and volleyball teams. She did ceramics and horseback riding and jewelry making. It was at skating lessons in first grade that Emery made her first best friend—Eunice. (Koreans like names like Eunice, Euna, and Eugene because they sound the tiniest bit like Korean sounds. The immigrant instinct to cling to crumbs is strong.)

Emery's parents spoke with Eunice's parents in the

warming room as they watched their daughters shoot the
duck and hockey stop. They talked about adopting Emery
and what a challenge, what an important challenge, it was to
retain the adopted child's cultural heritage. The Parks were
impressed by the Hoopers and couldn't picture a more loving
family for a little girl to be adopted into.

Weekly playdates, Baby Bottle Pops, and Radio Disney
with Eunice became routine. The Parks were invited to the
Hoopers' for dinner. But when Emery only wanted to see
Eunice, when she resisted seeing other friends and gave attitude about going to birthday parties, the Parks were phased
out. When Emery asked for her friend to come over, the Parks
were busy. They were out of town. They had family commit-
ments. Skating ended in the spring and Emery never ran into
Eunice again. Eunice didn't play tennis and she went to
public school, so she was eventually forgotten.

Mrs. Hooper facilitated a new friendship with Courteney,
who had a trampoline and an overgroomed Lhasa Apso.

• • •

Sophomore year began with tennis preseason. Emery had
decided that "arms-length friendly" was going to be her official Lilah stance. She complimented Lilah's new tennis shoes
and asked about her summer. When Coach Norton made a
huge fuss about Lilah's weight loss and embarrassed her in
front of the whole team, Emery found Lilah after practice to
say that Norton was a dumbass.

"I noticed, too, of course," she said. "You do really look great.
But everyone knows you're not supposed to *say* anything."

Lilah said it was awkward, but she was happy that he'd noticed her. Last year, he could never remember her name without the assistance of his clipboard. Emery offered an understanding smile that was very un-Emery. Then she apologized for rushing off (Noah was waiting for her) and left the courts before Lilah had time to pack up her bag.

• • •

Emery forgave Candace's rotten behavior in Nantucket because they'd had a joint tenth birthday party that started at Dylan's Candy Bar and ended at Mars 2112. Because they had matching enamel bangles and knew that a tablespoon of cinnamon had nineteen calories. Because they both loved Freds, omakase, and Liberty prints. Because their mothers attended book club and Canyon Ranch together. Candace and Emery were bound by history and social mores, and even though Candace's behavior in Nantucket had been unacceptable, it was impossible to eliminate Candace from her life.

It didn't hurt that Candace promised to play matchmaker between Emery and Scott. Candace reluctantly agreed that Scott was cute but swore she could never think of him like that. They'd grown up together and she thought of him as a brother. Candace was happy to bring him to a tennis match— what were friends for?

"You're still an alternate, right?" Candace asked.

"No," Emery said, snapping the hair tie on her wrist. "Well, not really. Lilah and I switch off being alternate, so I play every other match."

"I'm only asking to see if you can hang out," Candace said. "Scott won't want to watch you actually *play*."

"Obviously," Emery said. "But I'm not playing today. It's Lilah's match. So you guys should come."

When Emery got to the courts, Coach Norton sent her down to the first doubles court to fill in for Gracie, who hadn't shown up.

Fuming, Emery warmed up with Gracie's doubles partner. Lilah, who wouldn't play until another match ended, sat beside Candace on the bleachers. Candace rudely twisted her trunk toward Scott so her back was facing Lilah.

Lilah glanced toward the Isle to see if her friends were coming. Annie insisted that studying was more important but had agreed to come today with Cassie and Jenny after missing the first three matches.

"Their family is *four* generations deep," Lilah overheard Scott say. "Ian's great-grandfather's yearbook is in black and white."

Candace said, "They're all black and white until, like, ten years ago."

"Whatever," Scott said. "My point is they're legit."

"Emery's dad went here," Candace said. "I think her grand-father did, too."

"Yeah, but it's not *really* her dad."

"True."

Lilah couldn't believe it. Scott's accusation was beyond insulting. And Candace had agreed. They were whispering now and Lilah couldn't make it out.

"Scott!" Candace exclaimed in pretend outrage.

She slapped his arm and giggled.

In straining to hear, Lilah had leaned into Candace's personal space, and Candace responded by scooting toward Scott emphatically.

While Emery double-faulted repeatedly, Candace and Scott jumped from casu martzu, to whether hibachi restaurants were tacky, to who had worse poison ivy on the Perkins-Wynand camping trip last summer.

Emery and her partner lost their match. They were the only losers on the whole Derrymore team. But Emery came off the court with a fixed grin. Her voice was forced and upbeat when she greeted Candace and Scott.

"Who cares?" Emery said. "It was a pointless match. I didn't even know I was gonna play until I got here."

Scott was texting.

"Did I miss anything?" Emery asked.

"Scott's gonna be *Top Gun* for Halloween," Candace said.

"That's so funny," Emery said.

"Have you seen it?" Scott asked.

"No," Emery said.

"Me either," he said. "Halloween is stupid. The costume is Ian's. I'm just borrowing it."

"Did you tell him about our costume, Caddie?" Emery asked.

Candace looked uncomfortable. "Uh, yeah."

"I'm gonna be Nicole, right?" Emery said. "Since you're taller, you can be Paris."

"Actually," Candace began, "I sort of asked Riley to do it with me. Sorry, but … it just made more sense."

Emery was the one who had come up with the *Simple Life* idea. She had already bought a dirty blonde wig and a shade of bronzer three shades deeper than her natural skin tone. Candace had called the costume "genius." Plus, Riley was supposed to be TOO BIG TO FAIL. She'd gone home over the weekend to get one of her dad's Lehman Brothers baseball caps.

"More sense?" Emery asked. "How?"

"Just, like ... for pictures. Riley's mom said she couldn't go as the bailout because it's 'insensitive' or something."

"I'm hungry," Scott said, and left without looking up from his phone.

"So what am I supposed to be?" Emery asked flatly.

She glanced over at Lilah, who had done a poor job of concealing that she was listening.

"There's lots of time," Candace said. "I'll help you come up with something else."

"Scott's right. Halloween is stupid. We should boycott it."

"No! I'll tell Riley you want to be Nicole Richie."

Candace had purchased a risqué midriff-bearing shirt that could only be worn without being called an attention whore on Halloween, and she was determined to show off her nascent abs.

"Then she'll hate *me*," Emery said. "I'd rather boycott it."

"You can be Nicole. Really."

Emery knew she would never be able to boycott Halloween successfully. Their friends were too invested in their costumes. Errol had been growing his hair out for two months to be more convincing as Bob Dylan. Noah was going as Maxwell Derrymore—the school's lionized first headmaster—and had spent weeks finding just the right stick-on muttonchops.

But scaring Candace was an important exercise. Emery's

empty threat had caused a reaction, and that's all she needed to see.

"I don't want to do *The Simple Life*," Emery said. "No one is even going to know what it is. We're the only ones who've watched it. Has Riley even seen it?"

"No, but she's heard of it."

Candace's second thoughts were plastered on her face.

"I'd rather just be devils or something that's not trying so hard," Emery said.

"Um." Candace chewed her thumbnail. "Yeah, maybe."

"Plus, my mom can't stand Paris Hilton. She thinks she's so trashy."

"My mom said the same thing."

"I don't care if you do the Paris/Nicole thing," Emery said. "I'm over it."

Candace picked at a zit by the corner of her mouth. "Me too."

• • •

After Candace and Emery left, Lilah remained on the bleachers, wondering why her friends never came.

She had texted them at the start of the match—emphasizing that Scott Wynand and Candace Perkins were sitting beside her and she could hear everything they were saying. Lilah thought Annie wouldn't be able to resist, but the sun was setting and her friends still hadn't replied.

Lilah stopped by the dining hall to pick up something she could take back to the dormitory for dinner. Her friends were sitting right by the entrance near the silverware and trays. They looked alarmed to see her.

"Did you guys get my texts?" Lilah asked. "I was waiting at the courts. I won my match."

No response. Lilah continued hovering over the table, confused.

"What's wrong?"

Annie set her fork down and wiped her mouth with exaggerated dignity.

"We all think you've been stuck up since becoming friends with Emery Hooper."

Jenny and Cassie were silent. They didn't look up from their plates.

"She's not even my friend anymore," Lilah said. "You know we haven't hung out since last year."

"That doesn't matter," Annie said. "You think being on the varsity team makes you better than us. You're pretending to be friends with Candace Perkins and Scott Wynand—"

"I didn't say that," Lilah said, still standing. "I just said they were sitting next to me. You're the one who said you'd give your firstborn child to see inside Candace Perkins' closet."

"I was joking, obviously."

Lilah didn't know how to counter Annie's cheap retraction.

"Okay, whatever. I'm sorry if I've been acting stuck-up. I'm still just an alternate."

"We thought of a way you can prove you're not stuck-up."

Jenny and Cassie still refused to make eye contact with Lilah.

"What is it?" Lilah asked hesitantly.

"We've decided to start going by our Chinese names—"

"Not this again."

Annie talked over her. "It's disrespectful to our parents—"

"What are you talking about? Your mom didn't give you a Chinese name until sixth grade. *Annie* is your legal name."

Annie glanced at Cassie and Jenny and they shared a knowing look.

"This is exactly what we mean by stuck-up," Annie said.

"I'm not being stuck-up," Lilah said. "Our Chinese names are embarrassing—"

"I told you! I told you she wouldn't do it. Lilah thinks she can be white if she plays tennis and hangs out with Emery Hooper. And wears a Nantucket sweatshirt."

"Why are you so obsessed with being Chinese?" Lilah asked.

"I'm not obsessed," Annie said. "I'm just proud. Unlike you."

"How am I not proud?" Lilah's voice was rising. "I'm being Princess Mononoke with you for Halloween even though—"

"That's *Japanese*, not Chinese."

"Same difference. It's a fobby, embarrassing costume."

Annie's nostrils flared.

"Fob" was an insult batted around frequently. It was snickered and muttered and sneered. It meant "fresh off the boat" and was always directed at Asian students. It was used when they slurped soup or wore a Disney World T-shirt or mispronounced Dartmouth or didn't know how to play cornhole. When they chewed with their mouths open or threw up peace signs in a photo, the accusation of "fob" was leveled just quietly enough so teachers could claim to have not heard it.

The "fob rule" had been coined when a Korean student stored kimchi her grandma had made in the dormitory fridge.

The next morning, another girl opened the fridge and ran into the common room holding her nose pinched shut, declaring that something reeked. From then on, the fob rule banned any kind of foreign food from being stored in the communal fridge.

"Don't dress up with us then," Annie said. "I was just letting you because I know you don't have anyone else to dress up with."

The lap staring continued for Jenny and Cassie.

Lilah left the dining hall with a growling stomach thinking about what Emery would have done. She would have bowed ostentatiously and said xie-xie ("thank you" in Chinese) sarcastically. But then it would have escalated. Maybe it was better if she didn't behave like Emery.

• • •

"How did your Halloween costume go over, sweetie?" Mr. Hooper asked. "That Parisian thing you were trying to explain to me."

Emery's parents called every Sunday and Wednesday evening to check in.

"I didn't end up doing that," Emery said. "A bunch of us just wore flannel shirts and jeans."

"Cowgirls?" Mrs. Hooper asked.

The idea was actually Jessica Simpson in "These Boots Are Made For Walkin'," but Emery knew her parents wouldn't approve, so she said yes, cowgirls. It was the same lying-by-omission as when she'd shared a photo of herself and Candace posing sweetly before a country-club-themed dance. The official event title was "Golf Pros and Tennis Nice Young Ladies," but everyone referred to it as "Golf Pros and Tennis Hos." Riley had snapped the photo pre-waistband rolling, which shrunk their skirts to hip-bone-flashing mini length.

"What happened to the costume you were going to do with Candace?" Mrs. Hooper asked.

"Mom," Emery said sharply, "it didn't work out."

"It's unlike you, Emmy," Mrs. Hooper said equally sharply. "Halloween is your favorite. I'm only being an observant mother. Did something happen?"

"Sorry," Emery grumbled. "Yeah. Sort of. But it's not a big deal and we figured it out."

"I thought this might happen." Mrs. Hooper's voice became inaudible as she made an aside to her husband. "Candace and you have always been competitive, but Derrymore amplifies it. Are you fighting over a boy?"

"No," Emery said. "Everything's fine."

"What is it?"

"Mom, can we not talk about this now? I have a test tomorrow and I barely have time to talk."

Mrs. Hooper was about to argue, but Mr. Hooper cut in.

"You're right, Emmy. This is not the appropriate time." He prompted his wife, "Honey, didn't you want to ask Emmy about Chef Eric?"

"Oh yes—do you know what happened to Gracie?"

"No. What happened?"

"Is she still on your tennis team?"

"She missed a match and, now that I think about it, she hasn't been to any practices this week. She's really quiet. I completely forgot about her."

"I was hoping you'd know. I called Chef Eric to book him for June but he was quite curt and said he wasn't working for Derrymore families anymore. He implied something happened to Gracie."

"I haven't heard anything," Emery said. "Like bullying or something?"

"I'm really not sure. It's such a shame. He made the best chicken tikka."

CHAPTER 19

 TO: All School (Students and Faculty)
FROM: Phillip Heyst

SUBJECT: Derrymore's First Annual Hug-An-Asian Day!

November 8, 2008

Konichiwa, y'all!! In the spirit of homecoming I've taken the liberty of launching a new school tradition. I'm psyched to announce the inaugural Hug-An-Asian Day. Attached you'll find a list of every Asian at Derrymore. Print it out and get to hugging! You need to get each Asian's signature in order to qualify for the grand prize: A GIANT BOX OF POCKY!!!!!

Kung Fu Fightingly yours,
Phillip (Cal) Heyst IV
Student Body President

• • •

Neither Emery nor Lilah checked their inboxes before practice, so it was bizarre when Scott beelined for them and hugged Lilah in the Isle. It was stiff and invasive, followed by a request for her signature on a form.

"Can you sign this? Quickly?"

He thrust a sheet of paper in Lilah's face. On the alphabet-ical list, she was flanked by Chang, Albert and Chang, Zoelle. At Scott's urging, she scribbled her initials next to her name.

"What is that?" Emery asked.

Scott was already jogging toward a new target, but he called over his shoulder, "Hug-An-Asian!"

"What did he just say?" Emery asked.

"Maybe I shouldn't have—"

Lilah was upset, but before she could finish her sentence, Jake and Ian stormed up to them. They were laughing and breathless, also clutching checklists and pencils.

"Can we hug you?" Ian demanded.

"Wait, is Emery on it?" Jake asked.

Ian scanned the list. "Nope."

Jake turned to Lilah: "Are you Tabitha or Jenny?"

He was trying to force the pencil into Lilah's grip, but she was hugging herself and refusing to take it. Emery stepped in front of Lilah.

"Get away," she said. "She doesn't want to hug you."

"It's for Hug-An-Asian day," Jake said. "We need to get every name."

"It's for what?"

"Check your email," Ian said. "The list is attached there. I think you can participate, too, since you're not on it."

"She should be," Jake said, out of the side of his mouth.

"Yeah," Ian agreed. "But can we hug her or what? We only have until check-in."

Emery was still standing between Lilah and the boys.

"C'mon, Emery," Jake said. "You let Scott hug her and we can't win unless we have all the names."

"Shit—he's getting that whole group of international kids."

Emery looked over to where Ian was pointing. Scott was methodically hugging a confused group of Japanese students who were on their way to the dining hall.

"Hug it out, bitch," Jake screamed in Scott's direction.

Emery felt Lilah tug the back of her T-shirt. It was what Emery had done when she was little and her mom was talking to another mom for too long.

"Go hug them then," Emery said.

"But—" Jake protested.

"Leave us alone," Emery said firmly.

"Why do you have such a stick up your ass?" Jake asked.

"Bitch," Ian fake-coughed.

The two boys laughed and started to walk away. After a few paces Ian turned back and said, "Emery, I think there's something in my eye."

He slowly extended his middle finger and used it to pull the corner of his eye so it became a long slit. Jake slapped Ian's arm down and whispered something fiercely—something about Mrs. Peiffer and Emery's dad no doubt. They jogged to intercept the international students.

Emery shepherded Lilah in the opposite direction and kept her eyes peeled for would-be huggers. Lilah was stoic as Emery led her to the library.

Emery logged into her email and dragged Lilah's rolly chair closer to her own. When they finished reading, Lilah's face was strangled by disgust.

"Did you vote for him?"

"Cal?"

In last year's election, Cal had run against an Indian girl

who never had a chance. Cal was captain of the squash team. He was good-looking with a droll sense of humor. His best friend was the vice president (and swim captain). Of course Emery had voted for Cal.

"I did, too," Lilah said.

• • •

It was agreed that they would hide out in Emery's room to steer clear of signature seekers. Lilah did homework with headphones in, which she usually only did when she was studying for final exams. Emery was so upset that she couldn't focus, but she didn't know how to ask if Lilah was okay. Caesar's *Gallic Wars* was open in front of Emery but she was staring into space, replaying the afternoon's events over and over. She glanced over at Lilah to see if she was suffering the same lack of focus, but Lilah was doing her Chinese workbook at a swift pace. Her hand flew across the page and produced a neat line of characters that Emery couldn't read.

CHAPTER 20

When the trip of Emery's dreams materialized, she said yes without thinking. Candace's parents allowed her older brother (and his girlfriend) to rent a house in Vail—but there's no such thing as a free ski trip. The catch was that July had to babysit Candace and her friends.

On paper, only Riley and Emery were invited. In actuality, Candace was smuggling Scott, Errol, Ian, Jake, and another soccer player named Shawn.

"July won't tell," Candace said. "I always lie for him."

"That's five extra people, though," Emery said.

"It's a four-bedroom chalet." Candace counted off on her fingers. "We'll cram into one bedroom (Riley can sleep on the pullout sofa) and the boys will get two rooms. July and his girlfriend will take the master (my mom thinks they're sleeping in separate bedrooms because she's basically retarded). It'll be tight, but July said college kids always do it."

It was only recently that Emery had stopped fantasizing about this exact trip. Last year, she would have slept on the floor at the foot of Candace's bed if it meant going on an overnight trip with Scott. A month had passed since Hug-An-Asian and Emery had been avoiding him since. It was pure reflex that had made her agree to the trip and lie to her parents. "It's the perfect chance for you and Dad to have a second honeymoon," Emery had coaxed.

Mr. and Mrs. Perkins were staying at a ski-in ski-out resort twenty minutes away from the chalet. Emery had omitted this last detail, and when her mother texted Candace's mom to thank her for chaperoning the girls, Mrs. Perkins responded with a simple:

> My pleasure!

Emery knew she was in the clear when her mom began looking up flights to the Lesser Antilles.

• • •

The trip started poorly and got worse. Their flight was delayed six hours, and by the time they reached the rental car office in Colorado, Mr. Perkins was in a foul mood. En route to the house, they were driving behind a dark green car with Yale, Oberlin, and Harvard Medical School stickers.

"What good is Yale if you're still driving a Kia?" Mr. Perkins said.

"Can you turn on the radio?" Candace asked.

Her father ignored the request and sped up to pass the Kia, crossing the double yellow as snow fell thickly onto the already-slick roads. Mrs. Perkins was staring out the window into complete darkness.

They were now behind a white Range Rover with a Bennington sticker.

"Now *that's* success, girls," Mr. Perkins said. "If any of my kids goes to Bennington, I'll wonder why I've busted my ass all these years. But if my grandkids go to Bennington, I'll take that as a sign that July is so successful they don't have to participate in the rat race. Caddie, too. She could be successful."

"Thanks a lot, Dad," Candace said.

"What's Bennington?" Emery whispered to Riley.

Riley shrugged, white-knuckling the door handle as Mr. Perkins accelerated to ride the bumper of the Range Rover.

"It's an artsy-fartsy college," Mr. Perkins said. "The missus went there."

Mrs. Perkins made no comment.

Mr. Perkins didn't even put the car in park when he pulled up to the rental house. July ran out in his socks to say hello to his parents but didn't help the girls with their luggage.

The "chalet" smelled like a locker room. July's girlfriend was smoking in the living room and *The Boondock Saints* was playing on the television. Suddenly, there were masculine shouts from above.

"They're here already?" Candace asked July.

July was loading beers into the fridge and said something they couldn't make out.

Candace finger-combed her hair.

"C'mon!" she said, leading Riley and Emery toward the staircase.

They followed the noise, and the smell. A rank odor was coming from the too-thick carpet.

"*Hiii,*" Candace said, leaning against the doorframe.

Four boys were intensely focused on the small television screen between two sets of bunk beds.

"No," Scott said.

"Yes," Errol said.

"No, no, no," Scott said.

"Oh," Shawn said.

"No!" Jake yelled.

"YES!" Scott bellowed.

Jake threw his controller down on the mattress and it bounced back and hit Scott in the side of his face.

"What the fuck?"

Scott launched himself at Jake and they wrestled while the other boys egged them on. Emery noticed the white controller was stained brown where dirty fingers had death-gripped it.

"Where's Ian?" Candace asked.

Scott caught Jake in a headlock. "Say you're a bitch."

"I'm a bitch," Jake gasped.

Errol groaned. "Do the countermove I showed you. Don't give in."

"You're a bitch, too," Scott said.

"*Hello*," Candace said. "Where is Ian? Actually?"

"He decided to go on college tours with his club team," Jake said, breathless.

Candace turned on her heel and locked herself in a bedroom.

● ● ●

After confirming there was nothing to eat in the kitchen, Emery and Riley brought their stuff to a dingy bedroom. The boys had ordered pizza and polished it off.

"I guess it's good Ian didn't come," Riley said, unzipping

her suitcase and placing her ski socks in a drawer that smelled like mothballs. "At least Candace can have her own room."

Emery hadn't taken off her shoes or her coat. She was standing by the bed, thinking furiously.

"No offense," Riley continued. "This house isn't as nice as what my family usually gets, but—"

"This is not"—Emery grasped for the right word—"acceptable. I *cannot* stay here for a week. There aren't any groceries. The towels smell like mildew. What are we supposed to do?"

"It's not that bad," Riley said. "One time, when—"

"Do you smell that? How can we sleep when it smells like sweaty hockey gear?"

"It's already fading for me. You'll get used to it."

Emery was trying to hold back tears. Riley noticed and stopped mopping up the Bliss body butter that had exploded in her suitcase to put her arm around Emery.

"I'm just tired and hungry," Emery said. "I can't believe they didn't save us any pizza."

"It's just the first day," Riley said. "It will get better. I promise."

Emery nodded, tears streaming silently. She wiped snot off of her Cupid's bow with the sleeve of her periwinkle sweater.

"I'm going to get something to drink."

Emery mentally prepared herself to drink unfiltered tap water.

The door to the master bedroom was closed and Emery felt certain July and his girlfriend were having sex. The boys were still playing video games and Candace was pouting. Emery felt like a child lost in a fraternity house.

The kitchen cabinets were sticky and the laminate was

peeling off. Emery filled a glass at the faucet and almost took a sip when she noticed dirty lip prints on the rim. She examined three more glasses and they were equally filthy. Her first instinct was to cry. But there was no one to see her and no one to help her. She was so thirsty.

The fridge was empty except for two shelves of beer. There was no dish soap or sponge.

She dialed her home phone. No answer. She dialed her mom's cell. No answer. She dialed her dad's cell. No answer. She opened a can of beer and took a tentative sip. Gross. She dumped it down the sink and refilled the can with tap water. She tried all three numbers again.

Then she had an epiphany.

Ten minutes later, Riley came downstairs in her pajamas and moccasin slippers.

"Emery? Are you okay?"

Emery nodded and held her finger to her lips—she was on the phone.

Riley filled one of the dirty cups and sat down beside Emery at the dining room table.

"There's nothing tonight?" Emery asked. "Yeah, sure … it's not like I have any choice … What about a taxi or something? Can you send someone to bring me to the airport?"

Riley frowned and pulled on Emery's sleeve.

"Who are you talking to?" she whispered.

Emery tapped her American Express, which was face down on the table. She thanked the agent and hung up.

"Are you leaving?" Riley asked.

Emery slumped in her chair and took a sip of beer-water.

"Thank god," she said, "for the platinum concierge."

"What are you gonna tell Candace?" Riley said, immediately understanding Emery's exit plan.

"I have a family emergency."

"Is that what you're gonna tell her or, like, do you really have one?"

"I have a family emergency," Emery repeated.

"That sucks," Riley said, credulously. "Did your dad have a heart attack? I feel like that's what it always is."

"No, but my parents need me to come home immediately. The earliest flight I could get is tomorrow morning."

A lie was significantly better than the truth—which was that she couldn't imagine a world in which she survived this week. During sleepover parties in lower school, there was always one kid whose mom would be called to pick up their little crybaby at midnight. It was never Emery. But she understood how that kid felt now.

"Why are you guys in *here*?" Candace said, clomping down the staircase. "Are you drinking beer?"

Emery drained the last of her can. "Are you gonna tell on me, Sara?"

They had been tossing around the insult more frequently since learning that Sara had hooked up with someone in their year over the summer, despite being on her way to college.

Candace responded by getting three more beers from the fridge. She opened them and handed them out.

Emery took a big gulp and swallowed without making a face.

"It's my dad's business," Emery said to Riley. "But you can't tell because it could affect the stock market."

Riley nodded solemnly.

"What are you talking about?" Candace said.

When Emery caught her up, Candace wasn't as upset as Emery expected her to be. She wasn't upset at all. She finished her entire beer during Emery's monologue.

"Anyone else want another?" Candace asked.

At that moment, Shawn, the boy they knew least well, came downstairs.

"Just getting a few beers," Shawn said.

"Sit with us, Shawn," Emery said.

She hiccupped.

"Emery's drunk!" Candace said.

The girls giggled. Shawn pulled up a chair. In ten minutes, the rest of the boys had trickled downstairs.

"Let's pull an all-nighter," Emery said around 2 a.m. She would do anything to avoid sleeping in the musty sheets upstairs. Riley cheered.

"Not fair. You're not skiing tomorrow," Candace slurred.

"Why not?" Shawn asked.

"I have a family emergency. I'm taking a flight back in"— she checked her phone—"eight hours."

"Boo," Scott bellowed and belched.

Emery knew that "boo" didn't mean anything. On a rational level she recognized that "boo" was far from a plea for her to stay and barely an acknowledgment of her departure. But she was searching for more in that "boo," and the act of searching made her feel pathetic. The solution was sitting right in front of her.

Shawn hadn't taken his eyes off Emery since she'd invited him to sit down. A boyfriend would force her to let go of the idea of Scott—because that's all she really liked about him. Scott the person was repulsive.

Candace didn't appreciate that Emery was receiving so much attention for jumping ship, and killed the all-nighter idea swiftly. That was fine with Emery, who spent the hours before sunrise practicing what she'd say to her parents when they called her back.

They were docked that night in Pointe-à-Pitre, and powerless to stop her, but her father hated an "ask forgiveness, not permission" attitude. This had nothing to do with being brazen, she imagined herself saying. It was an emergency situation. If necessary, she would tell them that Candace and Riley were drinking. If really necessary, she would reveal that July was their only chaperone. If really truly necessary, she'd explain that Derrymore boys ran freely through the halls.

Emery went over possible dialogues until it was 6:30 a.m. back home. Lilah was religious about her 7 a.m. runs and Emery wanted to catch her before she left the house.

Lilah picked up on the first ring. "Hi! Are you okay?"

"Are you busy later today?" Emery asked.

CHAPTER 21

When Lilah made her laugh, Emery sprayed buttery particles onto the Chang's kitchen table. She unwrapped a second pineapple cake and swept crumbs into a napkin.

"Right, but it wasn't just that the 'chalet' was filthy," Emery said, mimicking Lilah's French accent. "I'm sick of all of them. Like, Candace is just boy crazy. We already know Jake and Ian are racists. Scott is a douchebag. Riley is fine—I just don't like her. She's such a follower. And they're all so vapid."

Emery regaled Lilah with corroborating tidbits from the Nantucket trip: how Candace had laughed at everything Ian said regardless of how offensive it was, how Jake kept yelling *This is Sparta!*, how Errol wouldn't shut up about nihilism, how Noah was tripping over himself to get their approval. Emery left out how embarrassed she felt to be on the social fringes and that she felt abandoned by Noah and threatened by Candace.

"No offense, because I know she's your best friend," Lilah said, "but Candace seems like the type of girl who would choose a boy over a friend—even a best friend."

"She's not my best friend."

For a moment, Emery thought about how she had almost called Noah instead of Lilah. But things were still prickly between them, and after one day with the Changs, Emery knew she had made the correct decision.

"That's probably good," Lilah said. "You can't rely on her."

"Exactly. She uses people. They all do. Every friendship is like, what can *I* get out of this? They're just leeches."

"Maybe you're outgrowing them," Lilah said. "That can happen."

Emery nodded. She reached for the tray of individually wrapped cakes and opened a third. They were crumbly but rich, with a gooey pineapple filling that was somewhere between jam and custard.

"No thanks—" Lilah refused the cake Emery held out to her.

"These are so good," Emery said. "Where did you get them?"

"My grandma brings them from Taiwan whenever she visits. They're called ong lai so."

"Ooh," Emery said—and before she considered who she was talking to, "Do you have a house there?"

"We have an apartment," Lilah said. "In Taichung."

Emery nodded vigorously. "That's amazing. What's it like? I've never been."

"It's not like one of those penthouse luxury apartments," Lilah said. "But I like it there. We go every summer for a few weeks so I can practice my Taiwanese."

"Maybe you could come to Nantucket and I could go to Taiwan. Wouldn't that be fun?"

Lilah's mouth went dry at the prospect of traveling with Emery and she only managed a nod.

"How are your friends?" Emery asked, unwrapping another ong lai so. "This is my last one. Don't let me eat any more."

Lilah hadn't spoken to Annie since the dining hall argument, and because Annie was so possessive of Cassie and

Jenny, Lilah spoke to none of them. But she waved when she saw them on campus and pretended everything was fine. This seemed to irk Annie.

"Friends suck," Emery said. "That's just the truth."

"Fake friends suck," Lilah corrected.

"Potato, potahto."

Emery unwrapped two pieces of Orbit and shoved them in her mouth.

"There's something I'm not sure if I should tell you," Lilah said. "About Scott."

"What?"

Lilah stumbled, "I wanted to tell you before, but they're your friends and I didn't know if you would want to hear it—especially from me. But then I realized you'd be better off—"

"Get to the point, Lilah."

"I'm only mentioning it because you said you're over him, right?"

"I barely cared in the first place."

"At the match against Mercersburg, Scott and Candace were talking about rich families—like families who've sent generations to Derrymore—and they were talking about your family, and Scott said you don't count because your dad isn't your real dad."

Lilah touched the back of her hand to her forehead because she could feel it starting to sweat.

Emery shrugged. She blew an enormous bubble and let it pop in slow motion.

"They've said stuff like that to my face before," Emery said, using her teeth to scrape gum from the perimeter of her mouth. "When they're talking about how they have the same ears as their parents—'Is it weird that you don't look like your mom?'—I honestly don't care. Am I supposed to be jealous of not being blood-related to my parents?"

"But Candace agreed when Scott said that's not your real dad."

"We already knew she's a total"—Emery stopped herself and put on a syrupy voice—"sweet angel."

"You're not mad?"

"I love my dad, but I have no desire to look like him."

"And you're not mad at me?"

"Don't shoot the messenger, right?"

Lilah mentally noted this phrase. Emery always had little sayings locked and loaded. They were pre-packaged quips that meant she was never at a loss for words. Lilah envied Emery's compendium of phrases. They sounded like movie dialogue, recognizable and easily understood—but Lilah could never conjure them when she needed to.

Lilah stalled by taking a piece of gum for herself. "I thought *you* wouldn't have fake friends. So when I heard your friends talking behind your back, I felt like …"

"Like there's no such thing as real friends?"

"Yeah."

"I guess I've just accepted that already." Emery stared off for a moment. "Don't I sound like such a nihilist?"

She laughed and snapped her gum loudly.

● ● ●

Emery's parents were not happy with her abrupt change of plans. They offered to cut their trip short and fly home immediately, but Emery swore that the Changs wanted to host her. The Hoopers didn't love the idea of their daughter staying with a family they had never met.

"But I stayed with Candace's cousins when I went to San Diego for surf camp," Emery said. "And they were strangers."

"They weren't strangers," her mom insisted. "They're Perkinses."

Mrs. Hooper had been introduced to Mrs. Chang at many tennis matches, but never remembered meeting her. She was bemused that Emery wanted to stay at the Changs' and asked several times when Emery had become such good friends with Lilah. Emery ignored the question.

A piece of Emery wished that her mother's offer hadn't been couched in "ifs" (*if you really want us to return, if you're intruding on the Changs, if you'd be more comfortable at home*), but she was happy to stay with Lilah until Christmas Eve.

• • •

Lilah (and Mr. Chang) had met Emery at baggage claim with flowers from the terminal vending machine and a bag of truffles from Lindt. Emery squealed when she saw Lilah and ran to hug her. The embrace made Emery unexpectedly emotional.

"I missed you so much," she said.

Lilah mumbled something inaudible.

"Thank you so much for letting me stay with you," Emery said to Mr. Chang from the backseat of the cranberry minivan. "Sorry I don't have a gift. I know you're not supposed to come empty-handed, but I was about to die in Vail."

Mr. Chang chuckled. "We are happy to have you."

Like his wife, he had an accent, but it was less pronounced. Mr. Chang worked for a software company and his English was more formal and correct than his wife's.

"I'm so excited to see your house!" Emery said.

Lilah gingerly pressed a zit in her hairline. "It's not like your house."

"What do you mean? You've never seen my house."

"But I know it's a mansion and ... our house isn't like that."

Mr. Chang said something quietly to Lilah. She retorted in a bratty way. Emery shifted uncomfortably and fiddled with her seatbelt.

"I'm sure it's great," she said. "It's so nice of your parents to let me stay with you."

When they pulled up to the house, Emery didn't understand why Lilah had been so self-deprecatory. It was a nice brick house with one big oak near the curb, but no landscaping otherwise. There wasn't a paved path to the front door or shrubs to hide the central AC unit. The dead yellow lawn ran right up to the naked house without a single flower bed to camouflage or beautify. Emery identified the oversight right away—it was an easy fix—but Lilah could never put her finger on what made her family's house appear off to the eye.

• • •

Emery couldn't conceal her fascination when she entered Lilah's room. Above the desk was a collection of roosters: bobblehead roosters, small plush roosters, tiny sueded roosters with realistic feathers.

"Why do you have so many?" Emery leaned in to examine them, her hands clasped respectfully behind her back.

"I was born in the year of the rooster." Lilah shifted her weight from one foot to the other. "It's weird, I know. My parents give them to me every birthday."

"Are these real gold?"

Emery pointed to a taller shelf on which there were fifteen golden roosters, each in its own individual case.

Lilah nodded.

"What do you do with them?"

"I guess they're valuable."

"But do you melt them down or what?"

"I give them to my kids or my grandkids I guess."

"So your entire family is roosters? Wait—do you get those red envelopes, too?"

"On Chinese New Year. Yep."

"Can I see one?"

"I might have one"—Lilah dug through her desk drawer and passed a crumpled Charles Schwab envelope to Emery. "Here's one. It's empty, though."

"Whoa." Emery accepted it reverently. "Can I keep this?"

"It's trash. There's nothing in it."

Emery ran her fingertip over the gold foil characters and gently flattened the bent corners. "So I can have it?"

Emery pulled a yard sale dictionary down from Lilah's bookshelf and slipped the envelope between the pages.

"To get rid of the creases," she explained. "Don't let me forget that."

Lilah nodded, slightly confused. Emery started digging through her large suitcase.

"Let's take some pictures."

She pulled out a Polaroid camera and emptied out her luggage: glove liners, tie-dye polar fleece, camo gaiters, sweat-wicking under layers, hand warmers, and mirrored goggles.

Lilah sat on the edge of her bed and combed through the unfamiliar plenty.

"All I have is ski stuff," Emery said, "but we can make it work. Do you have any terry cloth sweatbands or, like, Mardi Gras beads? Or war paint? I forgot to pack my knockabout jewelry."

Lilah found a blue bandana, which Emery folded into a triangle and told Lilah to knot behind her back and wear as a backless shirt.

"I can't," Lilah said. "My mom would kill me."

"Then wear it on top of a T-shirt."

Lilah did as she was told and Emery loaded her down with accessories. When they were finally ready to get the shot, Emery set the timer and placed the camera on the bookshelf. They scrambled onto Lilah's bed and jumped when Emery gave the signal.

Twenty photos later, Lilah's room was destroyed and they were exhausted.

"Thanks for letting me stay here," Emery said. "I know we haven't been close for a while, but you were the only person I wanted to see."

"Don't worry about it."

"But, like, it's not cool that we haven't hung out in ages and then I'm, like, suddenly here. You know?"

Lilah shrugged. "I don't really think of friendship like that. With real friends you can pick up where you left off and it doesn't have to be on a schedule. That's more of a …"

"A white people thing?"

Lilah looked startled.

"I heard your mom say it," Emery said.

In reference to a barbecue, a celebrity estranged from their family, and liposuction, Mrs. Chang had said, "So white."

"It's not an insult," Lilah said, hedging. "It's just that certain things that are common for white people don't make sense to a lot of Asian people. And the other way around. Like, for us, it's not considered rude to call someone fat. It's just … I don't know. Honest?"

"But didn't you say that you couldn't be honest with your parents about having a homecoming date?"

"I guess it's not honesty really. It's hard to explain—like, you can call someone fat to their face, but I'm not going to talk about a crush or my feelings or being unhappy or something. That's white people stuff."

"What is else white people stuff?"

Lilah untied the bandana tube top and smoothed it out while she thought. "This is not the case in my family but lots of my friends' families never say 'I love you.'"

"What?"

"Saying 'I love you' is a white people thing." Lilah folded Emery's turtlenecks into neat rectangles. After a thoughtful pause she asked, "When you got your period, what did your mom do?"

"I think she showed me how to use a tampon and gave me Advil for cramps," Emery said. "Something like that."

"My mom left a box of tampons on my desk and we never talked about it. She saw the blood on my underwear and never said anything."

"So you just figured it out by yourself?"

"There was health class at school so I got the gist. But that's not the type of thing I talk about with my mom. I can't even imagine that conversation."

Lilah arranged Emery's wool socks in a neat stack and continued, "But mine was better than Annie's experience. Her mom won't even let her use tampons."

"What do you mean?"

"Her mom thinks if you use a tampon you're not a virgin, so she only uses pads."

"That's so gross. You can smell when someone is using a pad—it's foul."

"I should have said that to her." Lilah looked at Emery with admiration. "She was, like, borderline calling me and Jenny sluts for using tampons. Even though Annie knows her mom is completely uneducated."

Lilah segued to Annie's dad. He had a secret family. He had gotten his mistress pregnant ten years ago and his illegitimate son wanted to go to private school. The mistress had called Annie's home phone and it all came to the fore one week ago.

"Holy shit," Emery said. "Who's Annie going to live with?"

"Huh?"

"Obviously her mom. Right?"

"They're not separating. Divorce is frowned upon in Asian culture."

"That's fucked-up."

Lilah nodded in agreement.

● ● ●

Emery liked staying with the Changs. It was very different
than her own household, but not in a bad way. Instead of
topiaries and seashell-shaped soaps, the Changs had a grand-
father clock and decorative knotwork with red tassels.

When Emery made the bed in the guest room, it only took
her one minute because there were two pillows and no duvet,
just a plush poly blanket with huge pink roses. Every window
had yellowing Venetian blinds—not a curtain or Roman
shade in sight.

The whole house was carpeted. When Emery arrived, Mrs.
Chang had given her a pair of slippers. They were orange
slide sandals, cut entirely from one piece of rubber. They
weighed almost nothing. Lilah was embarrassed when Mrs.
Chang handed them to Emery and looked down at her own
pink slippers, which she wore with socks. Emery slipped
them on immediately—though she wasn't sure if they were
protecting her from the carpet or the carpet from her feet.

Emery did her best not to make Lilah feel self-conscious
or apologetic, but a few awkward moments were unavoid-
able. Emery asked for a second towel to dry her hair and
followed Lilah to the linen closet, where several towels were
quickly unfolded and refolded before one was handed over.

"It's not dirty, I promise," Lilah said. "It's just bleach stains.
Sorry."

Lilah's house had a TV room. When Emery looked through
the doorway she was amazed: "Ohmygod! You have one of
these? Can I sit in it?"

"Um, sure," Lilah said. "It's my dad's."

Emery climbed into the La-Z-Boy recliner.

"I saw these on *Friends*. Joey and Chandler have them."

There were other peculiar things in Lilah's house: artificial flower arrangements, cut-glass bowls on top of doilies, a sculpture of Shamu. Mrs. Chang had a collection of Swarovski crystal animals showcased in a display cabinet. The centerpiece was a huge crystal swan. Emery had never seen anything like it.

• • •

"When are you getting your tree?" Emery asked on her third night at the Changs' house.

"Like a Christmas tree?" Lilah asked. "I think we have a fake tree in the basement somewhere but we haven't used it since I was little. We never do Christmas stuff because I'm an only child."

"Being an only child sucks," Emery replied supportively.

One of Emery's biggest long-term fears was a sibling. Now that she was almost sixteen, the fear had diminished, but she still asked her parents a few times a year if they would consider adopting another child (she'd act disappointed when they said they were too old).

"We should get a tree tomorrow," Emery said. "A real one. I'll text my mom for the name of the farm we always go to. Can your dad drive us?"

"I'll ask," Lilah said, grinning. "It would actually be really nice to have a tree."

Emery typed out a text and pressed send.

"It doesn't feel like Christmas without a tree, right? Hold on, she's calling … Hi, Mom! I need the address for—"

Lilah placed a notepad and pen beside Emery. Emery clicked the pen open.

"She wants to," Emery said. "Yes, she does. No ... nuh-uh. I promise I'm not."

Emery's mother urged her to be a good guest. Stop bullying Lilah into doing what she wanted. Stop pressuring the Changs into hosting an Emery Christmas Extravaganza.

"Can you just give me the name of the farm?" Emery said.

There were lights and a stand and a tree skirt that needed to be considered. Did the Changs have any of those things? Did they have ornaments?

"We can go to Bloomingdale's or something," Emery said. "I'll MapQuest it. But why not? ... Whatever ... Okay ... *Okay*. Bye."

"What'd she say?" Lilah asked.

"She said to stop 'pestering' you and to be a good guest. She's so annoying."

"It's not pestering at all. I really want one," Lilah said. "They have trees at Home Depot—let's just go there tomorrow. And we can pick up lights, too."

"Really?"

Emery clapped like an excited child.

• • •

Both of Lilah's parents worked, so she got her own breakfast and lunch, but the family had dinner together every night. All dishes were served family style: scallion pancake, bok choy, fish with lots of bones, rice. The Changs had a machine solely dedicated to cooking rice (and keeping it warm), which was never put away. It was always on the countertop. Emery ate heartily and said it was delicious. She never wrinkled her nose at the new smells.

Mr. Chang spoke little. Mrs. Chang didn't shut up. She was funny to Emery, who had never known a mom quite like her. But Lilah assured Emery that, unfortunately, her mother was a highly unoriginal figure. Even the mismatched patterns Mrs. Chang wore around the house (plaid with microfloral, Swiss dot with animal print) were standard Asian-mom fashion. When she left the house, she wore cotton-blend sweaters and slacks in solid colors.

The dinner conversation several nights in a row had consisted of Mrs. Chang nagging Lilah to attend a weekly SAT prep class. She voiced her agony in English for Emery's benefit.

"I cannot understand," Mrs. Chang said, "why Lilah is doing this to me."

She shook her head, woebegone.

"Mom," Lilah said, "I already explained it to you: It's too early. The class is for juniors. I'll go next year. If I went now, then I would be taking the exact same class two years in a row. Why would you pay twice for the same thing?"

"But then you get better and better! Two years is more study. More study is higher score. You're lucky I am *let* you do class two times."

Mr. Chang continued to eat calmly as the volume rose around him. His silence perturbed Emery. Her own father was never quiet unless he was gearing up to give a long, Final Word lecture. But three nights running, Mr. Chang had kept his opinion to himself.

His wife continued, "You need perfect eight hundred because all Ivy League expect Asian to have number one score—"

"Hold on," Lilah said. "Emery, will you please tell my mom you're not doing SAT prep until later."

Emery smiled sheepishly, a spoon of rice halfway to her mouth. "Lilah's right, it's very early to begin test prep."

"You have private tutor. Right?"

Mrs. Chang had put down her chopsticks. She waited, with fingers laced together, for Emery to answer.

"Um, not yet. But—"

"Private tutor, different story"—Mrs. Chang had learned this phrase recently and was using it with impunity—"Lilah story, group tutor. Not as good as private tutor. Different story."

Mrs. Chang smiled smugly and resumed eating.

Lilah rolled her eyes. "Fine, I'll think about it. Can we get a Christmas tree tomorrow?"

Mr. and Mrs. Chang were stunned but agreed to it.

• • •

Mr. Chang carried the tree into the living room by himself. He was surprisingly strong. The girls held the tree in place while he knelt to twist the screws into the trunk, and Mrs. Chang stood at a distance and told them which way to lean the tree until it was straight.

Emery advised them to wait twenty-four hours for the branches to drop. This was disappointing news to Mrs. Chang, who had already started putting hooks on the frosted Christmas balls she'd bought at Target. Mr. Chang, covered in pine needles, sat in the lounger and began shelling peanuts while watching a *Harry Potter* marathon.

"What other Christmas traditions does your family do?" Lilah asked.

"Let's go skating!" Emery said.

"I don't have ice skates."

"I have extra pairs. Marina could drop them off."

"I don't know how to skate, though."

"Oh. We could watch Christmas movies. I always watch *It's a Wonderful Life* with my parents."

"Is that black-and-white?"

"Yes, but it's good. I mean, it's really cheesy and overacted, but it's a tradition."

"Do you ever drive to see the lights? I did that with Annie's family once. It was pretty."

"What lights?"

"The nice houses put up lots of lights and decorations."

"And you just drive ...?"

"It sounds dumb, but I promise it's fun."

"Where is it?"

"Near the battlefield where all the good trick-or-treating is."

"In my neighborhood?"

Lilah flushed. "Oh. Yeah, I guess."

"I dunno. It feels weird to go on a drive to look at my neighbors' houses."

"Why don't you study for SAT?" Mrs. Chang interrupted. "Don't waste time."

"It's Christmas, Mom," Lilah said. "Stop talking about college."

Mrs. Chang smiled and Emery realized it was her attempt at a joke.

"We could decorate cookies," Emery said. "Do you have

sprinkles? And food coloring? I can make dough and you can make icing."

Lilah wilted slightly. "We probably don't have the ingredients."

"I'll get," Mrs. Chang said. "Tell me the list you need."

"Can we make sugar cookies?" Emery asked. "And gingerbread?"

"Everything," Mrs. Chang said.

Wordlessly, Mr. Chang went out to the driveway to start the car and blast the heat.

"Oh, look"—Lilah changed the channel—"isn't this the movie you were talking about?"

Mr. Hooper's best impression was Jimmy Stewart and Emery recognized the voice at once.

"Yes, this is it! But don't you think we should go to the grocery store with your parents?"

Lilah had slumped onto the sofa and was making no move to get her coat.

"You stay," Mrs. Chang said. "Mom and Dad do everything."

The comment sounded passive-aggressive at first, but Emery noticed Mrs. Chang was almost skipping out to the car.

• • •

When the cookies were in the oven, Mrs. Chang started in on the SAT class again.

"It's too early, Mom," Lilah said.

"Then why Annie is doing it?" Mrs. Chang asked, wiping down the counter. "I hear Diana Du do it, too. You want lowest score?"

"Call us when the cookies are done," Lilah huffed.

Emery gave Mrs. Chang an apologetic look before she followed Lilah upstairs.

"Diana's a senior," Lilah grumbled. "My mom's just making shit up. I hate when she tries to shame me by saying, 'Everyone is going to outscore you.'"

"What does your dad say?"

"Nothing."

"But he agrees with your mom?"

"Who knows."

"Why don't you ask him? Maybe he'll be on your side."

"As my mom would say, 'You are act so white.'" Lilah's impression was spot on. "I've never had a real conversation with my dad. He doesn't know how to. The way it goes is: My mom nags me, my dad is silent, so I figure things out on my own. Sometimes I'm right. Sometimes I'm wrong."

Suddenly Lilah seemed to possess the very trait Emery maligned her for lacking: worldliness. Lilah was out there, untethered, making mistakes and learning from them, while Emery was sheltered from every jagged edge.

"Do you usually do what she says?" Emery asked.

Lilah snorted. "I'm a first-gen kid. I can't trust my mom's advice because she just repeats what the other clueless Chinese moms say."

Emery's parents were good listeners. Small disagreements were talked through: Emery didn't want to go to tennis camp in Florida but that's where the most competitive players were. She wanted to paint her bedroom lilac and her bathroom fuchsia (her dad called it bordello pink). These arguments were about logistics and a compromise was always reached.

For the Changs, the rift was ideological. In Mrs. Chang's mind, the entire point of Derrymore was that Lilah would go to an Ivy. For Lilah, it was to discover her passions, to exercise her intellectual curiosity, to learn who she was. Lilah believed that to make college admissions the focal point of her education was to waste everything Derrymore had to offer.

Lilah was ready to die on the hill of learning for the sake of learning. Emery never had to consider the "purpose" of Derrymore because a spot at Penn was her birthright. She had no intention of claiming it, but it was one of the many safety nets at her disposal. Self-actualization and discovery were luxuries Emery could take for granted because she did not have to sacrifice anything—not her athletic career, not her interests, not her social life—to attain the status that Mrs. Chang wanted so badly for her daughter. Two people, apparently similar, could attend Derrymore, be in the same class, and have wildly different underlying reasons for being there: Lilah was there to begin a cycle. Emery, to uphold one.

Mrs. Chang knocked on the door and entered without permission. She placed a plate of sliced honeydew and two forks on Lilah's desk.

"Cookies are almost cooling," she said. "Come to decorate with me."

When they finished decorating cookies, *It's a Wonderful Life* was playing on TV again. Lilah cajoled her parents into watching and they reluctantly agreed. Mrs. Chang kept talking in the beginning and Lilah shushed her. By the end, Lilah and Mrs. Chang were crying openly. Mr. Chang's eyes were wet. Emery saw Mrs. Chang put her hand on top of Lilah's and squeeze.

• • •

On Emery's last night, Mrs. Chang asked, "You want me to make American food? I can make spaghetti; I am learning enchilada—"

"Please no, Mom," Lilah said. "Your spaghetti was inedible."

Mrs. Chang made a motion as if to slap Lilah. "It was first try. Don't be so mean."

"First try? You almost had a breakdown when I scored low on my first SAT mock."

"*Shhh*. Emery, you want spaghetti?"

"That's not American, Mom. It's Italian."

"White people food," Mrs. Chang said. "You know I'm talking about."

"No, no thank you," Emery said. "That's so kind of you, but I love your cooking. I don't miss American food at all."

"I knew it," Mrs. Chang said proudly. "I knew you don't like no-flavor food. I knew you are Asian inside." She thumped her chest with her fist.

Emery laughed good-naturedly and took the compliment. "I guess so."

"You invite her to Taiwan," Mrs. Chang scolded Lilah. "She love it so much."

"We were talking about it," Emery said. "I'd love to come if it's not too much trouble."

"We love having you. I tell your mom we want *adopt* you!"

"Mom!" Lilah exclaimed. "That's so offensive. I'm sorry, Emery. She doesn't know what she's saying."

Emery cracked up.

• • •

Emery left the Changs' house at noon on Christmas Eve. Her parents pulled up in their SUV and Mr. Hooper, a little rumpled from a turbulent flight, rang the doorbell.

"Thank you so much for having Emmy," he said. "We'd be more than happy to repay the favor next time you're out of town."

"We are not going so many places," Mrs. Chang said, giggling. "We love Emery. She is so good—such a good one."

Mr. Chang shook Mr. Hooper's hand with both of his and kept thanking him. Emery hugged Mr. Chang awkwardly and Mrs. Chang tightly and Lilah finally.

Climbing into the backseat, Emery greeted her mom. "How was the flight? Are you having a migraine?"

Emery's dad put the car in reverse and when he glanced out the back windshield, he looked exhausted.

"No, sweetie," her mom answered. "I'm fine. Did you send a thank you note to Candace's parents?"

"You didn't want to say hi to the Changs?"

"Of course I did," she said, waving through the window at them, "but I had to call the restaurant and make sure they could seat us last-minute. There's nothing to eat at home."

"I didn't bring a hostess gift." Emery had been certain her mom would have something for Lilah's family. A bottle of olive oil or a Molton Brown set or, at the very least, a duty-free box of Godiva. When Emery stayed over for one night with Candace's cousins, they'd received an enormous bouquet.

"I should have sent something, huh?" Mrs. Hooper said

wearily. "I'll send them—what are those pears called? The ones that the Parks gave us way back when."

"Asian pears," Mr. Hooper said.

Emery scowled. "They don't want that."

Mrs. Hooper craned her neck to face the backseat. "Why not?"

"It just feels like—that's so awkward. Why wouldn't you send them something normal?"

"You loved those pears."

"Because they were new to me. Lilah probably has those all the time."

"It's traditional to give fruit as a gift in Asian culture," Mr. Hooper said.

"But we're not Asian," Emery said.

The car was silent for a few moments before she spoke again. "Did you see their tree? It turned out really nice."

Mrs. Hooper shook her head. "I told you not to push them into getting one. How many times do I have to tell you they don't do things like that? You don't realize how expensive it is. And it's not just the cost, they don't know how to dispose—"

"They're grown-ups, Mom. They moved from a third world country and started their lives over again. I think they can handle dragging a tree to the curb."

Her mom made an "I surrender" gesture.

"You always get your way. I don't know why I waste my breath."

Mr. Hooper shot Emery a warning glance in the rearview mirror.

"It wasn't my way," Emery insisted. "You should have seen

how much they liked it—all of them. Lilah said she had never seen her dad in such a good mood."

"They don't do those things," Mrs. Hooper repeated.

"Where are we going?" Emery asked.

It took Mrs. Hooper a second to answer, "I thought you might want to get Korean food."

"But I've had Chinese food all week. I'm really craving linguine vongole."

Mrs. Hooper sighed loudly and threw her hands up. "I can never get it right."

Emery put her headphones in and texted Lilah:

My mom is so annoying

CHAPTER 22

Emery's father brought her back to Derrymore after New Year's.
Her mother had a migraine and stayed at home. They parked
behind Emery's dorm and Mr. Hooper opened the trunk.

"You know, Emery, your mother is trying."

"Trying what?"

Emery dragged a LeSportsac duffel full of new shoes and
clothes out of the trunk.

"She's trying to be supportive of your identity journey
and ... discovering your roots."

He hefted a new carpet onto his shoulders.

"Huh?"

The duffel made a muted thud when Emery dropped it on
the ground.

He lowered his voice: "Isn't that what all this Lilah Chang
business is about?"

"What are you even talking about?"

"You're getting older and you're embracing your Asian
side, which we always expected. It's good—"

"Lilah is just the only person who's not completely stupid
here. You know she's taking calc already? Candace won't
even get to calc by senior year."

"I don't know what you're referring to with Candace, but
try to understand that Mom is doing her best. She wanted to

take you—to take all of us—to a Korean restaurant so we could start to learn more about your ..."

"My what?"

He gestured vaguely—exasperatedly—and picked up the duffel.

"Just be nice. Please."

"I wasn't being mean."

Mr. Hooper centered the new carpet then hugged his daughter goodbye. She promised to check in on her mom soon.

"You know this dorm burned down when I was a fifth-former?" Mr. Hooper said, gazing up toward the intricate dentils. "They did a remarkable job rebuilding—it looks exactly the same. You could never tell the difference."

· · ·

Lilah had heard Mr. Hooper's voice in the hallway. He was always friendly, but his successful-man-who-has-more-important-things-to-do-elsewhere aura was intimidating and she waited until goodbyes were over to greet Emery. The door was propped open and she entered while Emery was sticking photos on her wall.

"Can I help with something?" Lilah asked.

Emery passed her a tangle of jewelry to unknot then turned the volume on the speakers up. Lilah peered at the Polaroids tacked on the wall and observed that she was in almost all of them. She bit her lip so Emery wouldn't see her grinning stupidly.

Noticing that Emery was dancing to the blaring music,

Lilah tried to head-bob along. When Emery emerged from the closet, Lilah pointed to the photos and made an *aw* face, pouting her lower lip to show that she was touched to feature so prominently. Emery nodded enthusiastically.

"Cute, right?" she yelled above The Fray.

Lilah had almost finished untangling all of the jewelry, but she didn't see the little bowl for rings that was usually on Emery's nightstand. She looked around the room, but before she could ask, Emery was holding it out in front of her. They laughed and Emery said "Simpatico!" with an accent.

"Shit—" Emery turned down the volume. "I need to call my mom. Do you mind?"

"Go ahead. Give me something else to do."

Emery dialed, then dumped a bunch of rugby shirts and corduroys into Lilah's lap. *Refold please*, she mouthed.

"Hi, Mom." Emery wedged the phone between her shoulder and ear. "How's your headache? I mean migraine."

Emery held up a black dress: *Cute?*

Lilah gave a thumbs-up.

It was one of the dresses she had lusted over (but been unable to fit into) for her disastrous Chapel performance last year.

Emery tossed it to Lilah. *Take it.*

Lilah couldn't say no because Emery was on the phone. She examined the label. It was Alice + Olivia, a designer Lilah recognized from window-shopping with her mom when they were feeling good about themselves. In certain moments they could browse rich-people things and not pine after them. They could generously call them exquisite (but wasteful) and admire them from afar.

Mrs. Chang had been exceedingly clear that if Emery ever offered her something, Lilah was to refuse. *Never take anything from Emery. Not an old sweatshirt, not a vacation, not a ride from her mom. Nothing from Emery. We cannot reciprocate and you must not put yourself in her debt.*

"But we've already reciprocated," Lilah had argued. "She stayed at our house for almost a week and—"

Mrs. Chang had cut her off with an impatient noise. *Different story.*

But Lilah had already accepted numerous hand-me-downs from Emery. They were never in bad condition or visibly used. Emery bequeathed all things buyer's-remorse: jewel-tone skinny jeans, a barely used bottle of Viva La Juicy, a lime green Longchamp Le Pliage, and a flannel shirt. From Emery's Christmas bounty, Lilah inherited a Kate Spade wallet, a pebbled leather jewelry box, and a trio of DiorKiss lip glosses. What Mrs. Chang didn't know wouldn't kill her.

Lilah slipped out to put the dress in her closet. It was so much nicer than her other shabby belongings that she could practically hear it whining. The hand-sequined dress looked as out of place in Lilah's closet as Emery had in the Changs' home. The Hoopers had a powder room. The Changs had a half bath.

But what good was being a size zero if she couldn't wear beautiful things?

When Lilah returned, the call was on speaker.

"… what you don't realize is that these relationships don't grow on trees, Emery. As much as your father has helped Mr. Perkins, Mr. Perkins *will* help you one day. I've told you a million times, who you know is *everything.* You're still bent out of shape by Candace's behavior on island, but you have to see it from her perspective. She wanted to socialize with the boys and you wanted to read. That doesn't sound like a very good hostess, in my opinion. You need to learn to let things roll off your back and not take them so personally—stop expecting so much."

Mrs. Hooper was monologuing. It was Emery's duty to associate with Candace and her milieu. Emery had to maintain shallow friendships because she was part of an ecosystem. She had a responsibility to more than just herself, and becoming a social pariah was selfish.

"Do you know how many parties I attend that I would much rather not? And luncheons and auxiliary meetings and retirement celebrations—they're endless. Do you think I want to host that Derrymore alumni party every five years? They trample my Japanese anemones without fail, but you wanted to go to Derrymore so I was happy to do it. What about Penn"—at the mention of the school Emery made a gun with her fingers and mimed discharging a bullet into her brain. "Your dad has been bending over backwards to give you every opportunity. It's not ideal, but this is how the world works and I've come to accept that. You'll only be hurting yourself if *you* don't.

"You'll see. One day being friends with Candace will benefit you. You can't be shortsighted about these things. You'll make it awkward between your father and Mr. Perkins if you give Candace the cold shoulder."

Lilah started to back out of the room.

"It's fine, you can stay," Emery said.

Her mom stopped abruptly. "Am I on speaker?"

"Uh-huh."

"Please take me off."

CHAPTER 23

Emery had lunch with Noah and Riley occasionally. Errol sometimes. But she always had dinner with Lilah.

Things that used to be irritating bothered her less. The way Lilah pronounced "water" as *hua-terr*. The way her eyes always darted back and forth when she was addressed. How she had never heard "Brown Eyed Girl" and never seen *Zoolander*. The self-conscious way Lilah tucked her hair behind her ears and how she covered her mouth with both hands when she laughed. Emery stopped tallying up these offenses.

But the stir-fry line was a test. At the dining hall, one of the dinner options was a DIY noodle bar with two burners. The wok and the grease smell and the sprouts and the thick noodles that turned brown with soy sauce made Emery feel deeply uncomfortable, but she pretended to be enthusiastic when Lilah suggested they cook. Lilah made a great stir-fry and Emery had been vocal in her praise at the Changs' house—but at school it felt foolish to stand squarely in front of a target.

Errol and his teammates regularly made stir-fry and Emery knew if he were cooking beside her, he wouldn't be able to resist a smartass comment. Emery had avoided the stir-fry bar for her entire first year of Derrymore, even though it was the most popular option. She had complained with Noah about how it made hair and clothes stink and how there was nothing worse than being seated in class next to someone with day-old stir-fry stench wafting from their person.

Lilah put a small spoonful of minced garlic into sizzling oil.

"I don't mind cooking if you want to save us a table," she said.

Emery hesitated—an easy out was exactly what she wanted, but she felt guilty that her discomfort was so evident. Why did she make such an effort to avoid situations that *might* precipitate snide remarks? Why did the image of a heaping plate of greasy noodles make her apprehensive? Why did she give a shit what other people said?

Because they were always talking. Because being adopted meant that people were constantly discussing her. Because she could always sense when people had been prepped: Stan Hooper's *adopted* daughter. They were over-friendly and hell-bent on making the introduction especially normal. They held eye contact too long and always mentioned how much her dad talked about her and how proud he was.

People always felt sorry for her. They imagined she had been rescued from a life of probable prostitution. Emery was, at best, three-quarters of a person, and the pieces she lacked were the vital ones. She was a scarecrow, stuffed and propped up by the scraps that her parents were generous enough to spare. Everyone seemed to agree that being rich didn't make up for a lack of biological-parent love.

Emery had more than a few good reasons to take pre-cautions and look over her shoulder. She chose a table on the quiet side of the dining hall and let her thoughts fester until Lilah arrived with their dinner.

"I accidentally heard what your mom said about me," Emery admitted.

Lilah's head snapped up from the bamboo shoots she was spearing.

"I'm so sorry. Whatever she said—"

"I'm not mad. I promise."

Emery had narrowly avoided an uncomfortable situation on her last night at the Changs'. Emery had heard Lilah shushing her mom in the kitchen and stopped before the threshold. In broken English, Mrs. Chang was saying she felt sorry for Emery. She didn't know her real mom and her parents were so old, and so white. When Lilah said that Emery had a great life and her parents were really nice, Mrs. Chang said there was no replacement for the love of your true parents and no cure for the pain of being abandoned. Adopted parents weren't the real thing.

"I feel self-conscious about cooking Chinese food," Emery explained, "because I always feel like people are watching and judging me."

"I can't imagine how hard that must be," Lilah said.

Emery perused blogs of couples going through the adoption process. She read them greedily and wondered if those babies, in nurseries that had been designed before paperwork was finalized, felt like she did. Were they resentful about the fact that they were supposed to feel exceptionally grateful to their parents? Did they believe that total obedience was the price of being rescued? The feeling of debt—Emery described it to Lilah as her plate of noodles got cold.

Lilah said all the right things: That she could never fully understand Emery's plight, that Emery's situation was so unique, that she appreciated Emery's trust, and admired her honesty. Then she said it sounded similar to being Asian.

"How so?" Emery asked.

"The debt part. My mom guilts me about everything. She says if I don't do that stupid SAT class then I'm wasting her 'immigrant sacrifice' and goes on and on about how she left her family behind in Taiwan and married my dad even though she barely knew him and she shouldn't have bothered trying to make a better life for me because I don't even listen."

"At least your mom is honest, though. She tells you that you owe her—unlike my mom who tries to make it sound like it's for my own good."

"It sort of is, though. Right? I'm not siding with your mom, but, like … if you want to go to Penn and—"

"I don't." Emery's eyes flashed. "They've been shoving that down my throat since I can remember. I'd rather go to a state school."

CHAPTER 24

Shawn had been in Emery's freshman history class. He was there for the Racist Whore Outburst and Mrs. Peiffer's mid-term replacement. After their brief interaction in Vail, Emery had spent the holiday break formulating a plan to make him her boyfriend.

First, she told Errol that she liked Shawn. Shawn was cute. He was funny. He hadn't been attached to anyone at Derrymore. She told Errol to give him her number. That afternoon, Shawn texted her. They made plans to have dinner on Saturday.

"What do you think?" Emery asked Lilah.

Lilah's mouth opened in surprise. She shut it. She wasn't surprised. Emery was always a step ahead.

"I think he's perfect for you because he's a good athlete, but he's more than that. Which is just like you. You're popular and pretty but you're also smart and—"

"Ew, stop," Emery said. "Just say if you think he's cute."

"He is," Lilah said. "Definitely."

• • •

While waiting in the dormitory foyer, Emery started to second-guess the entire course she'd set in motion. But—she reasoned to calm herself—she didn't even like Shawn (yet) and there was nothing to be nervous about. *Don't pace. Don't fidget.* She glanced out the window. When his slim figure appeared on the Isle she went to meet him.

Shawn rocked forward to hug her and they laughed awkwardly when her hair got caught in his necklace. He tucked the thin gold chain back under his shirt.

"How was your Christmas?" Shawn asked stiffly.

"It was good," Emery said. "How about yours?"

"Good. Colorado was … a lot."

"Was it fun? After I left?"

"The skiing was good. But Jake broke his wrist on the first—"

"I hate Jake." Her voice suddenly became surer (it happened any time she began to rant). "Sorry. I just do, though. He was at my beach house this summer."

"I didn't know you were friends."

"We're not," Emery said. "Are you friends with Candace?"

"I barely knew her before she invited me to Vail."

"Exactly." Emery shrugged to say that seasonal home visits didn't mean anything. "It's cold. Do you want to get dinner?"

They started off through the Isle, both thankful that they had the trip to gossip about.

"Jake and Riley are going out now," Shawn said.

"Did they hook up at that gross house?"

"You mean 'chalet'?" Shawn quipped.

She laughed and some of the nerves dissipated, and he told her she had made the right move fleeing when she did.

"I was sad you left, though."

"I'm an excellent decision-maker," she said, using sarcasm to fend off his earnestness. "It's my greatest strength."

• • •

They finished dinner but lingered until the dining hall staff started putting up chairs around them.

"Is it true JJ hooked up with Portia?" Emery asked.

JJ was Shawn's best friend. "It's true. It happened during pre-season." Shawn's shoulders slumped. "I tried to stop it, but Portia was throwing herself at him. You can't blame a guy when—"

Shawn cupped his hands in front of his chest, indicating Portia's ample bosom.

"No kidding," Emery said, extra aware of her own A-cups.

She hugged her arms to her chest and questioned whether it had been a good decision to wear her tightest, sheerest T-shirt that showed off her non-figure.

"I'm not into that," Shawn said quickly. "Portia's not my type. I like your ... mind."

Emery snorted.

"I'm serious," Shawn said. "When we were in history class last year and—sorry, I don't want to bring it up if you're uncomfortable—but I thought you handled it well and it was good Peiffer got fired. People like that shouldn't be teaching."

"Thanks," Emery mumbled. "I don't really feel like talking about it."

"I get it. Whenever I have shitty moments it takes me some time before I'm ready to analyze them. One time, I was minding my own business, waiting to get picked up from practice, and this white mom—" He noticed that Emery was shrinking into herself. "It's okay. You don't have to talk about it right now. Anyway, with the Portia and JJ thing, I know that girl has jungle fever."

"What's that?"

"When white girls are into Black guys. Last year she dated that football postgrad—he was almost twenty."

There was a rumor that Portia's dad had promised to buy her a quilted Stam bag if she broke up with the football player, who got recruited by Ohio State.

"Did JJ ... see her again?"

"Three more times." Shawn shook his head. "Probably more. But he's my best friend. So I don't judge. Noah's your best friend, right?"

"No. Lilah Chang is."

Shawn looked at her thoughtfully.

"She seems like a really good influence on you."

Emery missed his comment. It was the first time she had called Lilah her best friend.

• • •

Feed was a weekly Derrymore gustatory tradition that combined indulgent eating and scuttlebutt. *Feed?* New students and parents always questioned the word choice. It sounded impolite—feral, even. But it was appropriate.

On Saturday nights, every dorm gathered an hour before midnight to guzzle chocolate chip pancakes/penne vodka/pizza and cotton candy/fondue/cupcakes. The point of Feed was to corral and sedate.

Emery piled pasta primavera and Rice Krispie treats onto

a paper plate and beckoned Lilah over, but not before
Candace took the seat Emery had saved.

"Since when are you and Shawn a thing?" Candace asked,
mouth full of garlic knot. "Did it start in Vail?"

"We've been hanging out," Emery said unhelpfully.

"I texted Noah and he had no idea either." When this failed
to prompt a response, Candace continued, "Are you and
Shawn official?"

"I guess."

"He's really good-looking. Noah's gonna be so jealous."

Candace was right. Shawn had sharp cheekbones and a
very defined jaw. Emery envied his long eyelashes. His skin—

"He's pale for an African American," Candace said. "He
looks almost Italian or Spanish with that olive skin."

"He's half," Emery said. "His mom is white."

Candace processed the information, then put her plate
down suddenly and asked, "Is he on scholarship?"

"*What?*" Emery's forehead creased, insulted. "No. I don't
think so."

Candace tapped her chin with her index finger. "I wouldn't
ask him."

"Obviously."

"So you're not gonna ask?"

"Who cares if he is?" Emery shot back.

Candace raised her eyebrows and blinked rapidly—*it's
your life*. She reached toward a disc on Emery's other side.
"What's that?"

Emery covered the plastic case with her thigh and widened
her eyes at Lilah: *Save me*.

"A CD. Shawn burned it for me."

Lilah approached awkwardly right as Candace shouted past her at Riley, who had returned late: "Why are your knees so dirty? You slut!"

Feed was a cacophony of gossip, lies, and self-pity, where sixteen-year-olds could be unapologetically sixteen with thoughts only of the slights of the evening. By design, there was no room for perspective or self-awareness.

"How was your night?" Lilah asked, taking Candace's vacated seat.

"Do you think Shawn's on scholarship?" Emery asked quietly. "Candace just asked me."

"Because he's Black?"

"He's *half.*"

Lilah hesitated. "I know if I qualified for scholarship my parents would take it in a heartbeat. They're just barely above the income you need to get a tuition break. Derrymore is really expensive for most people."

"I know," Emery snapped. "I'm not stupid. Sorry. It's just ..."

Lilah apologized back, sorry for Emery and the stress she was under to be the person she believed she should be. Getting close to Emery was the best thing that had ever happened to Lilah, and she felt as giddy about Shawn as if it were happening to her. Candace had taken the wind out of both of their sails by implying that Shawn was a B-list boyfriend who didn't really belong at Derrymore.

At Feed there were only two recaps: it was either the best night of your life or the worst.

CHAPTER 25

"I love your necklace," Candace said.

"Oh, this?" Lilah said, touching the gourd-shaped pendant. "Thanks, it's—yeah, thanks."

She had spent ages planning her outfit for Emery's birthday party and she almost hadn't worn the gift from her grandma, which was her nicest piece of jewelry.

"Is it an Elsa Peretti?" Candace asked. "I have the bean. I'm really into abstract shapes lately."

The Wu Lou was known as the gourd of long life, Ama had explained the last time Lilah was in Taiwan. It was a symbol of prosperity and good health.

Lilah allowed herself a huge bite of focaccia to avoid lying outright. She half shrugged, half nodded in response to Candace. Emery caught the exchange and gave her an amused sidelong look. Lilah whispered, "Let her believe," out of the side of her mouth.

"Would you mind if I got the same one?" Candace asked, stirring her Shirley Temple with the straw. "My mom is taking me shopping tomorrow. Our hotel is right by Tiffany's."

Lilah shook her head and reached for the burrata.

"Good luck finding it," Emery mumbled, and Lilah pinched her thigh gently.

The party was in Manhattan at a restaurant Mrs. Hooper

had read about in *New York*. No one had kid parties like laser tag or manicures anymore. The menus said *In Celebration of Miss Emery Hooper* at the top.

Errol was seated across from Lilah, describing the famous actor who was his namesake. He was appalled no one had heard of the Golden Age thespian.

"Didn't his son go to Derrymore?" Lilah said. "And die in Vietnam?"

"Sean Flynn—thank you!" Errol said. "Someone who isn't illiterate."

"Everyone knows Lilah's the smartest in our year," Emery said.

Errol rolled his eyes but Ginny and Riley chirped in affirmation. They were the Cassie and Jenny of this group, Lilah thought. They didn't add anything, but they were necessary to make up the numbers and serve as an audience.

Lilah wasn't scared of getting talked over. She misled Candace effortlessly. She was no longer ignored or tittered at. Somehow, she had crossed to safety. Noah said hello to her in the hallways and Riley stopped to engage her in small talk. Lilah existed outside of the Emery connection—a person in her own right. She felt at ease among Emery's friends. Was the signature mocktail spiked? She sniffed the hibiscus concoction and took another sip—didn't seem so. The party was almost fun—*almost* because Emery had done her best to thwart it.

She didn't want to take an hour-long drive into the city with fake friends, she'd told her mom. But Mrs. Hooper had said to let a birthday pass without marking the occasion was uncivilized. So Emery spent the dinner sighing and counting down the minutes. She barely spoke to Shawn, who had been invited last-minute, but at least Lilah was enjoying herself.

• • •

Mr. Hooper dropped everyone back at campus except Lilah. It was her first time sleeping over, but as excited as she was to see the Hoopers' house, she wished Emery had taken up her parents' offer to stay the night at a hotel on Fifth Avenue. The only time Lilah had ever been to New York City was to see Jenny's cousin perform at Carnegie Hall.

Marina helped unload the car and had prepped the den to unwrap gifts.

"Tea?" she asked. "It's not caffeinated."

Lilah figured it must be a tradition—part of Emery's birthday ceremony. She accepted a wafer-thin ceramic cup and saucer.

Mr. Hooper poured himself a glass of scotch. Mrs. Hooper futzed with her camera.

"Why did you lie about the necklace?" Emery asked in a low voice.

"I didn't want to embarrass you. It's a Chinese thing that my grandma gave me."

Emery looked hurt. "I wouldn't be embarrassed by that."

"Just in case. And I didn't lie per se. I just agreed with whatever she said about abstract shapes."

"Is my bad influence rubbing off on you?"

Lilah smiled and shook her head.

"But are you sure you're okay?" Emery asked.

"Yeah—why? Candace doesn't bother me. She is who she is. It was a great party."

Lilah seemed fine. She must have missed Errol's comment on the drive home, even though he had been characteristically loud. Emery began unwrapping gifts, confident that her friend had not heard him say that "Lilah isn't as fobby as she looks."

CHAPTER 26

For one week, Shawn walked Emery back to her dorm every evening without trying to kiss her. Their conversation consisted mainly of making fun of Derrymore's constant use of the word "multicultural", which was ham-fistedly used in place of "minority." They mocked the multicultural committee and multicultural murals and multicultural affairs. They gossiped about the negative press Derrymore was trying to evade after someone leaked that Confederate flags were not *not* allowed in the dormitories. The Derrymore administration was waiting for the national press to report on it any day, but the prep school news cycle was in a frenzy of exposing pedophilic teachers. A particularly odious ethics teacher at Horace Mann had finally died (peacefully, in his sleep) and his victims were coming forward with their stories, one by one. The Derrymore administration sighed with relief. The only thing the *Times* loved reporting on more than predatory teachers was boarding school suicides.

As they were saying goodnight before check-in, Emery held Shawn's arm, stood on her tiptoes, and kissed him squarely.

Embarrassed, Shawn mumbled that he had wanted to but didn't know if it would be alright. Then he said something about being very surprised by her forwardness. As they made plans to meet the next day, Emery wondered if it was normal that the kiss had stirred nothing inside of her.

• • •

After they had kissed, Emery still felt awkward around Shawn, so she instated Lilah as a third wheel. Lilah liked Shawn but found him to be preachy. He was overly encouraging whenever she said anything, responding with "hell yeah" or "beast mode" to her most innocuous comments.

When Emery and Lilah were making fun of Mr. Gladstone, and how the science teacher always found an excuse to massage girls' shoulders, Shawn shared some unsettling news.

"It's pretty messed up he's still here," he said.

"Huh?" Lilah asked.

"He's the reason that Gracie girl left," Shawn said. "Didn't he, like, assault her?"

"Tennis Gracie?" Emery said. "Her dad is my ex-chef. What happened?"

"I heard from someone that didn't have the full story, but it sounded like Gladstone did something to her, but she wouldn't say what happened. So there's no proof."

Emery grabbed Lilah's wrist. "You need to switch out of his class."

Lilah nodded grimly. She had to leave for violin practice and told Emery she'd see her back at the dorms. Emery hadn't realized she'd be alone with Shawn.

Was there a way she could ask if he was on scholarship without being rude? Was the chain around his neck real gold or was it that fake stuff her mom warned her about? Were people laughing at her? Had she chosen someone who was also just-barely-but-not-really accepted?

Emery resolved to get Candace's voice out of her head. Shawn was great. She liked him. He asked her about *real* things—topics that her friends never broached. Sometimes he made her feel self-conscious: questions about her parents, comments about jungle fever, his patronizing manner toward Lilah—but it was conversation composed of real opinions and introspection. It was a thousand times better than hearing Candace talk about *Texts From Last Night* or Errol explain synesthesia. Emery chalked up her discomfort to growing pains: she wasn't used to anything thought-provoking or substantial. Shawn would be a cure for the stultifying conversation she despised.

"Do you wanna stay here or …?" he asked.

"Or" was a leading question. "Or" held the suggestion of finding a spot on the golf course, or just past the tennis courts, somewhere unlit, where they could roll around on the frozen ground.

"It's pretty cold out."

"Yeah, it's really cold," he agreed quickly.

"I'll dress warmer tomorrow," she offered. "But maybe we can just stay here and talk for tonight?"

He suddenly took her hands in both of his and smiled at her with a sincerity that made her want to look away.

"I want to get to know you," he said.

He asked her about the Hug-An-Asian fallout. He asked how she *felt*. He wasn't satisfied when she said it was stupid, that the whole thing was ignorant. He kept probing: "But what did *you* feel?"

"I wasn't even on the list, Shawn. You should ask Lilah."

"You know what riles me up about this?" he said. "They would never do Hug-A-Black. Because they know it's racist. But they also know that Asians never stand up for themselves." Shawn looked at her hard. "If I were you, I'd be mad that I *wasn't* on the list."

They sat in silence for a moment before she said, "Jake and Ian called me a bitch. I wouldn't let her sign and they called me a bitch."

Emery's voice caught on the last word.

"Let who sign?"

"Lilah. They did the eye thing"—Emery took a deep breath to keep her voice from shaking—"the slit thing."

"Huh?"

Emery pulled the corner of her eye back with an index finger.

"But Jake's family hosted an Obama fundraiser—" Shawn pursed his lips and looked grim. "I need you to do something for me. Look at me, Em."

Emery flinched imperceptibly at the use of her nickname.

"You have to tell me when these things happen," Shawn said. "Okay?"

"I hate talking about it. It took me a long time to stop thinking about it."

"You can't do that." Shawn's voice became stern. "That's the worst thing you can do. You were protecting Lilah. She needs you. For her—and for me—don't bury your head in the sand. Okay?"

• • •

On February fourteenth, a pile of half-dead daisies was delivered to the common room of every dorm. There was a loud *aww* as Candace extracted the twenty bundled pinks that had already been checked repeatedly—only to dash each girl's hopes as she flipped over the tag and pretended that she hadn't expected to see her own name. They were from Candace's mom.

Emery sorted through the ragged flowers and found the ones addressed to her. Shawn had sent daisies to both her and Lilah. Emery gently banged the bottoms of the stems against the table to align them.

Lilah's were white and hers were red.

• • •

Lilah was carrying a bowl of grapes when Annie called her name.

"Do you want to sit with us?" Annie asked.

Jenny and Cassie scooted unnecessarily to show there was plenty of room. It was as close to an apology as Lilah would ever get. But it was vindicating to know that they were worse off without her. Lilah sat down primly.

"How were your breaks?" she asked.

"Good," Annie said.

"We heard Emery was at your house," Cassie said. "Your mom told my mom."

"She stayed for a little," Lilah said.

She bit into a grape and waited to see if her invitation was contingent on sharing gossip.

"Was it fun?" Jenny asked.

"Are you friends again?" Annie asked.

They already knew the answer to the latter. Emery hooked her arm through Lilah's when they walked anywhere. She screamed Lilah's name across the Isle. She had assigned Lilah a distinct ringtone and occasionally borrowed her deodorant. Their friendship had evolved drastically from the discretion of the previous year.

"We are," Lilah said. "Did you get anything good for Christmas?"

Cassie and Jenny waited to see how Annie would respond to the forceful change of subject.

"I got a perm," Annie said. "At a nice salon. They gave my mom champagne."

It looked as if Annie had stuck a fork in an electrical socket. Lilah knew what look Annie was going for, but the botched perm had overshot Gisele-style beachy waves. In middle school, Lilah had pressed Cassie's crimper onto a section of hair for a full minute—it appeared Annie's whole head had been abused in this same way.

"It looks nice," Lilah said.

Annie's hair was so fried that it was shiny. It looked brittle and coarse at once.

"Really?" Annie touched her hair self-consciously. "My mom said it looks worse than my regular hair. I like it, though."

"It looks good," Lilah repeated.

Cassie said she received some graphic novels she had asked for. Jenny said her family didn't exchange gifts. Lilah had a sudden urge to tell them that she had baked gingerbread and trimmed a tree and watched a Jimmy Stewart movie—but she kept it in. Maybe she'd try to flash her phone wallpaper, which was a picture of the Christmas tree lit up in her living room.

"We saw Shawn walking Emery back the last few nights," Cassie said. "Are they going out?"

Lilah smiled coyly, as if it were her own love interest. "Yeah, but … it's still new."

"Is it a secret or can you tell us about it?" Jenny asked.

During freshman year, Lilah had doled out shreds of Emery's life for Annie's approval. When Lilah reported back with a description of the boar bristle brush Emery used, they'd googled its cost and gaped. Annie had been too caught up in her Emery obsession to criticize Lilah's reconnaissance missions, and those moments of captivation were confused with closeness. But Lilah no longer craved Annie's validation and had no reason to trot out details of Emery's life.

"It's not a secret," Lilah said. "They're going to spring formal together. But it's weird to list facts—like, what do you want to know?"

The other three girls quickly agreed that there wasn't much more to say now that the coupling was confirmed. They switched to discussing a boy, Chuhao, who was obsessed with Annie and would arrive to class ten minutes early to save a seat for her.

Fascination with Emery's life used to be a shared experience, but Lilah had graduated from outside-looking-in status. The same thing happens when the first girl in a clique has sex—up to that point, everyone's opinion counts equally, but after the first one advances from theory to practice, all the virgins suddenly seem unsophisticated and childish.

Lilah spent the rest of the conversation carefully attuned

to Annie's attitude and demeanor. When she floated a few comments that would have drawn cutting remarks in the past, they rolled by without aggression. She felt quiet satisfaction in the shift.

CHAPTER 27

By mid-March, Candace was clamoring for Emery's attention. When Candace wanted to watch a lacrosse game or show her a Lonely Island video, Emery was busy with Shawn. When she needed Emery's opinion on the plunging neckline of her formal dress, Emery was teaching Lilah how to shape her brows. When she finally got Emery's attention at Chapel, Candace proposed that they recommit to *Class Dress* by posting every day and getting a real photographer (one of the artsy upperformers with an expensive camera) for the blog—but Emery wasn't interested. Candace threatened to continue *Class Dress* with Riley. Emery said it was a great idea.

"Riley's clothes suck, though," Candace said. "She always wears mine."

"She can borrow my stuff. I don't care."

"But we got so many page views."

"It was just our moms. And their friends."

"My mom said she knows someone who can help us grow it."

"I'm too busy now."

"Because of your *boyfriend*?"

Candace's tone was somewhere between teasing and nasty. Emery knit her eyebrows together in mock confusion.

"Sara?" She brought her face inches from Candace's. "Is that you?"

The jab resonated. To be a Sara was their greatest fear—her combination of totally transparent envy coupled with a failure to understand that she was the butt of the joke was abhorrent.

Candace backtracked: "I was obviously kidding."

"Sara? Sara, please calm down, Sara. You're a strong, independent, *single*"—Emery weighted the word—"woman."

Candace laughed insincerely. "Shut up."

It was a rush to watch her toggle between rage and embarrassment.

Emery's phone buzzed and she checked the message. "Lilah's waiting for me. I'll see you later."

Candace looked like she had been slapped.

• • •

At Shawn's request, Emery taught him how to make stir-fry. She used Lilah's recipe.

"Don't be so heavy-handed with the soy sauce." She pulled his arm back from the wok. "That's how white people make it."

Shawn chuckled. "Show me how to do it the authentic way."

Since the Hug-An-Asian conversation, Emery had shared more with Shawn than she had ever told any boy. Noah included. She even told Shawn the story her dad had shared over break.

"There was an employee your mother wanted me to fire," Mr. Hooper had said, tapping his cigar against a ceramic ashtray Emery had made in third grade. "Did I ever tell you about this? This guy—let's call him Jacob—Jacob was up for a promotion. He was a known ass-kisser, and he was so-so at his job. He was married to this absolute piece of work—I don't remember her name. The two of them would tag-team me at the holiday party, thinking they were ingratiating themselves when really, the more they talked, the more damage they did.

"Then we adopted you. We were so proud and couldn't help but show you off every chance we got. At the same time, the board was starting to talk about launching a new branch in Korea, and it was a tremendously exciting time in my career.

"But Jacob saw this as an opportunity. He and his wife had told me multiple times they weren't interested in having children (they thought this would get him promoted faster). Then one day, Jacob comes into work with a Chinese baby. He's bringing his kid to the office every day, not getting any work done. Or if he doesn't bring him, Mrs. Jacob swings by at lunch and creates a huge to-do.

"He doesn't get the promotion. (He doesn't deserve it.) He's irate. He tells me he's gone above and beyond for the company. He tries to talk around it but eventually he spits it out: he adopted Jacob Junior to prove his commitment to me and the company. I ask him, 'Where is your baby from?' He says, 'China.' We stare at each other for a minute. I say, 'The new branch is in Korea.' The color drains from his face."

Shawn didn't think it was as funny as Emery thought he would, but he liked when she talked about her parents.

"Did your dad fire Jacob?"

Emery shrugged. "Probably. I mean, he doesn't do the firing himself, but yeah. Probably."

She offered another family moment so Shawn wouldn't think she was avoiding the topic.

There was a family photo on the wall above the breakfast nook in the Hoopers' home. The photo had been taken when Emery was nine. It included three generations of her mom's side. Her father was in the back row, barely visible, and Emery was in the front row, second from the right, surrounded by cousins.

Last Thanksgiving, Aunt Sylvie had been standing in front of the photo and said, "Your eye just goes right to Emery, doesn't it?"

She made a beeline motion with her finger.

Her husband said, "I was just thinking the same thing."

"It's that hair," Aunt Sylvie said. "Like a black hole—absorbs all the light around it."

They hadn't noticed that Emery was sitting at the kitchen island, eating toaster waffles.

Shawn had an expectant way of listening that made Emery want to elicit a strong reaction: shock, heartbreak, indignation. He was always waiting for a punchline and she wanted to deliver.

In the month and a half they'd been together, Emery didn't feel much closer to him, but she assumed the more they confessed to each other, the sooner they'd move into the next realm of intimacy. Everything he fished for—what it was like to have white parents, to be adopted, to go to expensive private schools—she surrendered.

"Don't act like you don't know about private school," she said.

"Not like you. My dad didn't start making money until I was in middle school. I remember what it's like to be poor."

"Middle-class," Emery corrected.

"Same thing."

Shawn's father was a surgeon. When Shawn was born, his dad was still in medical school. He made partner when Shawn was in sixth grade.

"I went to public school."

"So did Lilah."

"That's Lilah. Not you."

Emery rolled her eyes and he kissed her. It was a game they played. He poked at her privilege and she halfheartedly defended herself. He was never satisfied until she confessed something painful.

Did you think you were white growing up? Do you think your parents love you as much as they would biological children? Would you have gotten into Derrymore without your dad's connections? Do you actually like The Beatles? Be honest. I want to challenge you. No one has ever challenged you about these things.

He was right.

"I admire you so much," he said, after a particularly heartrending self-reflection. "A month ago, you wouldn't even acknowledge that you were adopted."

"Don't exaggerate."

"Pretty much."

"I barely knew you. I thought you were nosy."

"I needed to know if you were *real*. Everyone here is so fake. I knew you were real in Peiffer's class, but you try to suppress it. I just want to help you be the best version of yourself. My dad always says, for people like us, getting out of our own way is the hardest part."

CHAPTER 28

Lilah and Emery were putting on makeup in front of the mirror when Mrs. Hooper called.

"You're on speaker, Mom," Emery warned. Just in time, she smacked a mascara wand out of Lilah's hand: "Primer first. Never put mascara on bare lashes. Hi—sorry. Lilah and I are getting ready for spring formal."

"Do you two have dates tonight?" Mrs. Hooper asked.

"No, and I can't really talk now. I have to focus."

Emery fluffed her kabuki brush and blew into it.

"Okay, sweetie. I just wanted to make sure the alterations came out okay. Did Paolo do a good job?"

"Yes, the dress fits perfectly. Thank you for dropping it off. Sorry I was out when you came by."

"I know you're busy studying. Lilah was a dear."

"Uh-huh"—Emery patted blush into the apples of her cheeks—"I have to go. Love you."

"Love you. Send me a picture of you girls. Say hi to Candace for me!"

Emery hung up.

"See how much better the mascara sticks when you use primer?" she asked. "What did you tell my mom?"

"I said you were at the library," Lilah said.

"Alone?"

"She didn't ask."

"Okay good. Thanks for covering for me."

"There was a close call, though. Candace came in right when I was getting your dress and—"

"Ohmygod, I'll kill her. What'd she say?"

"She was trying to talk to your mom so I told her that Ian came by looking for her."

"He did?"

"No."

"Ha! You're the best. I swear to god if Candace keeps pissing me off I'll accidently send *that* picture to her mom. No—her *dad*."

"The one in Ian's lap? You wouldn't."

Lilah knew the picture. Candace was straddling Ian in Vail, surrounded by empty beer cans. Emery had sent it to herself from Riley's phone.

"In a heartbeat." Emery applied Clinique lip gloss and smacked her lips together. "I haven't told my mom about Shawn yet."

"How come?"

"It's not the right timing."

They finished getting ready in silence.

"Do you mind if I wear the dress you gave me?" Lilah asked.

"Which one?"

"The black one with the sequins."

"Go ahead—you really don't need to ask. I completely forgot about it."

• • •

Shawn acted like he was struck when he saw Emery. He clutched his heart and staggered a few steps on the lawn outside of the girls' dorm. She wore a grey one-shoulder mini dress with ruching from armpit to hip. Emery had known at first sight that it was the only dress for her.

"Stunning," Shawn said.

Errol chimed in, "Hooper cleans up nice."

Emery elbowed him. "Shut up—don't be mean."

"I meant it!" Errol insisted.

Lilah took pictures of Shawn and Emery. Shawn took pictures of Lilah and Emery. Feeling benevolent, Emery posed for a few with Candace and Errol. She avoided Jake and Riley.

The dance hit a rough patch when Ian and Scott arrived drunk and the entire soccer team was enlisted to smuggle them back to their dorms before they were caught. When an older player beckoned him over, Shawn kissed Emery goodbye. The DJ hadn't played the slow song yet and Shawn would never be back in time to dance with her.

"Get them expelled," Emery whispered in his ear.

He smiled knowingly and raised three fingers: scout's honor. But Emery knew he would play his role well and help disguise his teammates so the dutymaster wouldn't see that at the center of the group were two sloppy, drunk assholes.

Codes proliferated at Derrymore. They were much more serious for boys than girls. Shawn was expected to jump into action for his teammates, for his dorm mates, for his roommates. For any boy who had done something stupid and needed assistance.

Derrymore operated under a two-strike rule, so if your friend already had one strike and you had a clean record, you would be called upon to take the fall and absorb the second. Emery had never heard of girls sacrificing themselves like this for each other.

The code culture only burdened Shawn since he never did anything that would require others to martyr themselves for him. Emery had a feeling that if he had shown up drunk to the dance, the soccer team would have been much slower to mobilize.

She looked around for Lilah and spotted her with the quadruplets. It was a surprise—and slightly amusing—to feel a twinge of jealousy.

CHAPTER 29

Emery said it was ridiculous to date someone for more than three months and only kiss. Middle schoolers did more. Lilah said that wasn't necessarily true—shouldn't you be guided by your ... hormones? They giggled.

"I'm not talking about sex," Emery said. "Just the next thing. I feel like I'm the only one who hasn't seen *one*."

Candace had. Riley had. Emery expected that Noah had, too.

"You feel ready?" Lilah said.

"I'm curious," Emery said diplomatically.

She had stopped Shawn the first time he felt up her shirt because she didn't want him to. The second time, a week later, she stopped him because she felt she should. The third time, it was habit, and she wished she hadn't because he stopped trying.

Candace said she wanted to go all the way with Ian, but he hadn't asked her to be his girlfriend—so it had to wait. Emery had asked if that label would make a difference. "Definitely," Candace said. "We're sixteen. It's the ideal time to lose your virginity."

Lilah wasn't a prude. She didn't balk when Emery told her about Candace and Ian.

"If she feels ready, then sure," Lilah said. "But if you feel like you need to check sex off a to-do list, that's a different story."

Emery smirked. "Different story."

"Ohmygod—I sound like my mom."

They dissolved into laughter and Emery asked if Lilah had ever touched a penis. Lilah shocked Emery when she said, "Kind of."

At homecoming freshman year Lilah said she had made out with her date and felt it pressing against her hip.

"I didn't touch it with my hand or anything," she said. "I'm not even positive that I felt it. But I'm pretty sure."

Emery imagined chubby freshman Lilah in the velvet dress kissing the boy with the bad haircut.

"I just don't believe Candace," Emery said. "I don't think you really *want* to do any of that stuff until you're older. She's just trying to fit in."

Lilah considered disputing this but decided against it. She half nodded.

That evening, Emery was prepared when Shawn rolled on top of her. His hand fished tentatively for the hem of her quarter-zip and he placed his hand on her bare waist. When she nodded, his hand continued slowly up to her bra. She waited for something momentous to happen. He squeezed. He groped. It felt like he was checking avocado firmness. She considered making some noise of pleasure but when she tested it in her head it sounded ludicrous.

His mouth was still on hers when he shoved his hand beneath the underwire and pinched her nipple. Emery opened her eyes in surprise but shut them when she saw Shawn's eyes closed, brow furrowed in concentration. It didn't hurt, but it didn't feel *good*. It was the same sensation as when her pediatrician pressed around her pubic bone—she held still and overcame the desire to squirm away.

The underwire cut into the top of her boobs and she imagined how unappealing and small they must look, mashed down. The image was so far from sexy that she pulled away from him.

"Are you okay?" he asked.

Emery fixed her bra forcefully, wiggling and twisting until it sat comfortably.

"I'm fine," she said and pressed her hand to the back of his head to continue kissing.

She snaked her hand down his side, to his hip (like she had seen in movies), and felt around to the front of his pants very deliberately. His hips lifted and she found what she was looking for. Once she could feel his erection through his jeans, she didn't know what to do.

It was much firmer than she'd imagined. Lilah had said she thought it felt like a saturated sponge, but that was off by a mile. Emery grasped it the same way she checked her bike tires after pumping them up at the beginning of the summer. She squeezed, checking for resistance.

He groaned. The sound was too much. It felt adult and lustful. Emery stifled a laugh.

She squeezed one more time and pushed him away. He was breathing heavily and his eye contact was burning.

"Was that okay?" he asked. "It wasn't too much?"

"No, it was fine. It was good."

She snuck a glance at his pants to see if the thing was still there, and imagined how she would describe it to Lilah. An unripe banana? She had already forgotten how it felt. She'd meant to spend more time with it, but the rigidity had startled and repulsed her. When she realized in order to gather more intel she'd have to endure this again, she was distressed.

Shawn sat up and pulled her close.

"I really care about you," he said.

"I care about you, too."

"And I would never do anything to hurt you."

"I know that."

"And I would never pressure—"

"I know, Shawn," she said. "I wanted to."

"How was it?"

"Um—"

"Does it scare you?"

"No! It's just weird. It just sits there and then … you know."

"We can go at your pace. I don't have any expectations for how fast this moves."

"Okay, okay. Don't make me feel awkward."

He kissed the side of her head.

CHAPTER 30

Ivy Day is around the same time every year. All in all, accept-
ances abound. Parents show up with congratulatory gifts that
were purchased months ago. But there is a healthy swath of
delayed gratification: while every senior expected to get into
a top school does, it is often by way of waitlist.

Getting waitlisted is the cruelest purgatory because it
shatters the sweet pleasure of public approbation. Colleges
use the waitlist as an exercise in humbling the entitled.
Schools know that they cannot deny Scott his rightful place
nor Candace hers—but the waitlist will make them miserable
for a few months. While friends visit future alma maters, the
waitlisters imagine what it would be like to attend Vanderbilt
or Carnegie Mellon. They make secret plans to transfer and
mentally commit to spending freshman year buckling down
and getting straight As. But then the lackadaisical "if you
wanna come, you can come" message arrives in June from
UChicago or Duke or Cornell (never from Harvard). There's
relief mingled with joy but bitterness is the prevailing note.
After a life of line-cutting, they finally get a taste of how it
feels to be an afterthought.

Which brings us to the exceptions at Derrymore: the few,
the unlucky, the rejected. For them, the humiliation lasts
forever. Not only must parents dispose of premature Brown

caps and MIT sweatshirts, there is also the sickening joy of undeserving peers. They have to see mediocrity rewarded and calculated donations pay off. They have to see a 650 math SAT get into Princeton and a serial plagiarizer admitted to Columbia.

Entire careers, marriages, and Weltanschauungen are ignited by a no from Stanford.

• • •

Lilah's neighbor, Diana Du, got Swine Flu. She also got into Brown.

"But she got rejected by Penn and Yale."

Lilah said "Penn" softly, not knowing if the word would irk Emery.

"Brown is good," Emery said, annoyed by the whisper. "It's a real Ivy."

"Asians don't know Brown. Diana's parents won't pay that much money for a school that no one has heard of."

"*What?* Who hasn't heard of Brown?"

Emery's outrage was invigorating because the quadruplets unquestioningly accepted their parents' attitudes, and Emery's reaction made Lilah feel justified in her conviction that her parents' way of thinking could (and should) be ignored.

"So, where are you gonna apply?" Emery asked.

It was one of those fourth-wall-breaking transitions that is obvious but still unexpected.

"I'll probably apply to a couple Ivies," Lilah said. "But those are reach schools. I've started researching financial aid at the types of schools my parents wouldn't pay for—top forties. It's way easier to get a scholarship at a non-Ivy."

"Like, a full ride?"

Emery had heard this phrase and wanted to sound like she was more knowledgeable than she was.

"Those are hard to get, but, if possible, yeah. If I don't have to depend on my parents to pay for college then I can actually make my own decision."

By way of support Emery said, "My dad always says, 'The only real freedom is financial freedom.'"

"How about you?"

"I honestly don't know. And I swear I'm not being secretive."

"I didn't think—"

"I hate when people lie and pretend their dream school is, like, Pepperdine, just because they know they'll get in. But then—miraculously—they're at an Ivy." Emery tested a lip stain on the back of her hand. "You know I don't want to go to Penn, but Shawn keeps saying I'll end up there because it's a 'family tradition.'"

Emery spat the phrase like he had—as if describing the despicable actions of war-profiteers or robber barons.

"It's not that I *want* to do the easy thing"—Emery's fists were balled up with the effort of articulating herself—"but how do I know if the hard thing is necessarily the 'right' thing? I mean, isn't there a possibility that the easy thing *is* the right thing?"

• • •

The Hoopers celebrated Easter at Rosewall every year. The country club had always been a haven for Emery. But for the first time ever, she felt uncomfortable walking into the main clubhouse.

"Good morning, Ms. Hooper," the receptionist said through a wide smile.

"Morning," Emery replied curtly.

It was unfair to be rude to the unwitting middle-aged receptionist tasked with greeting members at Easter Brunch (and subject to Colbie Caillat on repeat), but something about her smile and the way she said good morning rang false to Emery. Her unwavering eye contact felt like scrutiny, and the cheerfulness of her voice sounded like it had to cut through a layer of resentment.

Emery smoothed her pastel dress down. Did it look like a costume? She looked around at the headbands, seersucker, and gingham. Everyone had gotten the memo.

Mr. Hooper was in his element—shaking hands, pounding friends on the back. *Good to see you. How's the family?* Mrs. Hooper, too: The wonderful gazpacho recipe in *Bon Appétit*, the something or other was in bloom. Her friends asked, *Was that really Emery? It couldn't be—how grown-up! How beautiful.*

Emery smiled mechanically and texted Shawn. She wouldn't be drawn into the circle of women describing farmhouse sinks and plantar fasciitis.

Outside, on the East Lawn, the egg hunt was underway. Emery watched a little girl in a purple pinafore hip-check a suspender-wearing toddler to claim a plastic egg.

When she was seven, Emery had won the prize for most eggs collected. She received a chocolate bunny that was as tall as she was. Emery told her second-grade teacher it had been the best day of her life and the message was conveyed at parent-teacher conferences. The Hoopers still loved to share the anecdote almost ten years later.

She got a reply from Shawn:

How's country club easter?

She sent a picture of herself looking bored.
He replied:

You're above that

CHAPTER 31

"I'm going to Taiwan with Lilah this summer," Emery told Shawn as they crossed campus after dinner. "My dad bought our flights over spring break."

Shawn was always telling her that she needed to be more in touch with her Asian heritage.

"That'll be good for you," he said. "How long are you going for?"

"One month, so I can still go to Nantucket for a few weeks before preseason."

"Wouldn't want to cut into those critical Nantucket weeks."

Emery shoved him gently.

"Is Lilah going to Nantucket with you?" he asked.

"Next summer. Not this year because, with Taiwan, that's a *lot* of time for us to be together. She agreed that it might not be good for our friendship since there's a chance we'll be roommates next year."

"She said that?"

"I said it. She agreed."

It was common knowledge that best friends were not supposed to room together, but this advice was routinely ignored. Emery had seen many falling-outs amongst her female peers, but she had never seen the wisdom come to pass for their male counterparts.

"What're you going to do in Taiwan?" Shawn asked.

"Lilah's my tour guide. She goes every summer. They have a house there—an apartment."

"You should look up some museums and history stuff that you want to do while you're there."

Emery didn't want to ruin the mood so she just said, "Good idea."

Then she told Shawn she had been thinking a lot lately and she felt ready to take their relationship to the next level.

"Really?" he asked, understanding immediately.

She knew where they could go to be alone: the shed by the tennis courts where the hoppers were kept. She had a key.

The experience was messier than she expected and it took too long. Thankfully, they found a bottle of sunscreen. The lubricant made it easier, but her wrist ached.

"Are you okay?" he asked when it was over.

"Did I do it right?"

"You did it perfectly."

Emery didn't voice her skepticism. It had been—more than anything else—tedious, but she was relieved to have it over with.

It was the first warm evening of the season, and campus was swarming with couples tucked away in semi-secluded spots. Good weather was something Derrymorians did not take for granted. In the bitter winter, they went to the woods with fleece blankets purchased expressly to keep bare asses off frozen ground. But springtime was Derrymore at its most hopeful: daffodils in bloom and crepuscular hand jobs.

CHAPTER 32

At Derrymore, activism was a slightly provocative car wash, a barbecue in bikini tops and cutoffs, endurance hula-hooping during Chapel. It was selling cupcakes to benefit the hungry or delivering milkshakes to support battered women. Most of the time, the sums were generous (but not preposterous) because these charity-a-thons always ended with someone's dad writing a check.

But the year prior, the Humanitarian Aid Society chapter at Derrymore had been embroiled in a scandal that resulted in two senior girls getting their admission offers rescinded. The six figures "raised" by the two co-presidents had nothing to do with fundraising and everything to do with fatly padding résumés. Before the implosion, the two seniors (field hockey co-captains) had received awards from HAS headquarters and did the daytime talk show circuit, holding forth on what it meant to be a Young Philanthropist.

Two weeks after their *Good Morning America* appearance, it came to light that the funds raised did not square with the impressive sum they had touted. It wasn't confirmed, but everyone assumed their jilted third friend (always the odd one out of the pair's successes) turned them in. An amateur investigation revealed that the girls had raised slightly under one thousand dollars (their parents furnishing the rest) and their stirring website was not, as claimed, something they'd built, but the work of an experienced web designer.

Such deception fell under Derrymore's catch-all rule: students could be disciplined for anything "unbecoming of a Derrymorian," which was used to punish offenses ranging from shooting squirrels with BB guns to offering oral sex in exchange for a seat on student council. The two students' transgressions were reported to Princeton and Georgetown, where they had, respectively, accepted admission. The Princeton-bound girl's offer was withdrawn, but fear not, she ended up at Georgetown with her co-captain/conspirator. (Everyone knows a larger endowment correlates with a higher moral standard.) The Jesuit school asked each for a self-flagellating letter and the incident was forgotten.

• • •

Lilah didn't think of her brainchild as "activism," because the word was synonymous with perfunctoriness and fraud. In her mind, *Interrogate* was a reaction to the nauseating feeling Hug-An-Asian had prompted. It was a way to manage discomfort that she would otherwise bury—a way to take something disturbing and allow herself to be fascinated by it.

Lilah was talking so much that she hadn't touched her dinner—meanwhile, Shawn and Emery were almost done with their pierogis.

"I like the name *Interrogate* for the magazine because that's what I want it to be," Lilah said. "Like, asking hard questions and really putting Derrymore under a microscope. I was thinking there could be an interview with a maid or a cook on one side of the page"—she hinged her hands open and closed like a book—"and then an interview with Headmaster Runciter on the other side."

"Verso recto," Emery offered. "If you can pull it off, it would be really good for college apps."

"That's not why I'm doing it, though," Lilah said. "Derrymore is so caught up in itself and we never talk about the real world beyond our bubble. I want to make people aware we're in one—that's the very first step."

"What questions are you going to ask?" Emery said.

"Things like how many kids do they give scholarships to? Is there a quota for different races? What percent of legacy kids are admitted? Are punishments and expulsions different based on how much money your parents give to the school?"

Emery was about to say never in a million years would Lilah get permission—

"So, answers we already know," Shawn said.

"But backed up with data," Lilah said.

"Lilah coming in hot with the numbers," Shawn said. "Quantify the bubble. I love it."

"Do you think it feels too controversial?" Lilah said to Emery.

"You shouldn't be scared by controversy," Shawn said. "If you're interested in asking hard questions then you'll need to get over that."

Lilah's jaw clenched slightly before she said, "Em? What do you think?"

Emery had checked out when Shawn started talking. She was preoccupied with thoughts of returning to the tennis shed to revise what could only be described as a letdown. She wanted the urgency and heat that Candace had described. Something had clearly gone wrong the first time and she was determined to right it.

"Um, yeah," Emery said. "It sounds really productive. Better than a stupid fashion blog for sure."

Lilah wasn't sure if Emery was distracted or disapproving. If Shawn weren't there, Lilah would have made the explanation more pointed and less general: *Interrogate* meant to question who got to belong, and who didn't.

• • •

Annie gave Lilah an iTunes gift card for her birthday. Their friendship had resumed cautiously from Lilah's side and remorsefully from Annie's.

Emery gave Lilah an iPod Touch and took her to see *Hair* on Broadway. Both girls shed tears when Claude's hair was cut short, but long after curtain, Emery was still inconsolable.

CHAPTER 33

Shawn badgered Emery about *Interrogate* all through spring semester. Lilah had generously offered her a co-president title, but Emery had already put in serious legwork for the Alumni Reunion Committee. She had just been voted ARC vice president, which all but guaranteed the president title for her senior year.

"Even if *Interrogate* crashes and burns"—Shawn took no notice of Lilah's affronted reaction—"it'll be a better use of time than doing the seating chart for the class of nineteen-forty whatever."

"Our endowment is so close to eclipsing Choate's," Emery said. "Every detail matters."

She didn't mention that a fluff title at a pretend magazine wouldn't do her résumé any favors.

"Is that how they're motivating you?" he asked. "When I'm an alum, I'm not giving a single dollar to Derrymore. Charity should go to poor people, not trust fund kids."

"What about scholarships?" Emery asked.

Lilah nodded vehemently.

"You think it's fun for JJ to see Errol's dad driving a Maserati when his family can barely afford textbooks?" Shawn asked.

"A larger endowment means bigger scholarships," Emery said.

"So more poor kids can feel inferior to their rich class-mates? No thanks."

"ARC is important to me," Emery said. "Just because you hate Derrymore doesn't mean I have to. Plus, what would I even contribute to *Interrogate*?"

"You can interview people," Lilah said. "You'd be great at that."

"Has anyone signed up yet?" Emery asked.

"Not yet," Lilah said. "I asked Dean Andrews to make an announcement at Chapel but he never got back to me. That was a week ago."

"You should write a column," Shawn said to Emery. "You have so many personal stories that are relevant."

"Maybe I'm not that self-centered and I don't need to be *in* the magazine."

"Em," Shawn said, "you're the one who said your dad adopted you as a career move."

"I did not."

"You said he adopted you *just* as his company was expanding into Korea. I can't be the only one who thinks that timing is suspicious."

"You're putting words in my mouth."

Shawn bungled a quotation about cowardice and bravery and got up to leave. He cleared Emery's plate for her, as he always did.

"He lectures you a lot," Lilah said.

"That's just how he is," Emery replied. "It doesn't bother me."

"Even what he said about your dad?"

"Shawn challenges me. He makes me think about things I don't want to think about." Emery picked at the nail polish chipping on her thumb. "Can I ask you something? Do you feel uncomfortable at Derrymore because of the Maserati stuff and all of that?"

Lilah took her time answering. "At first, I was sort of amazed—especially freshman year. But then I got desensitized to it. You guys don't think about money and it's … very different than what I was used to."

"Like shopping?"

"Not just that. Even though Annie did ask me if it was true that you had every color of the Tory Bunch ballerina shoes. What're they called?"

"Burch. Ballet flats. Oh god—I was so tacky last year."

"But it's not only about clothes. It's the way you order takeout all the time and get lots of packages in the mail. And Shawn has, like, two iPods and two laptops and a Rolex watch. No offense, but he can be a hypocrite."

"Yeah, but"—Emery tried to conjure some kind of defense but came up short—"yeah."

"My dad is obsessed with Rolexes. I don't think he'll ever get one. But like I said, that's how I felt before. Now it doesn't faze me."

"And that's a bad thing?"

"Getting used to inequality?" Lilah smiled wryly. "Probably."

• • •

During the last weeks of school, Emery and Lilah planned their upcoming Taiwan trip. Every detail from the footwear Emery would pack to the street foods Lilah would introduce her to was covered ("You should get Imodium"). Junior year was supposed to be grueling: their schedules would be crammed full with AP courses and there wouldn't be a moment to take their foot off the pedal come fall, so maximizing summer was a must.

In what remained of the school year, Lilah recruited writers and editors and graphic designers for *Interrogate*, which was how she met Hector.

Hector (a junior) was a Photoshop whiz with a known Asian fetish. Emery told Lilah not to grant him an interview, but Lilah said Hector's work was significantly better than the other applicants'. Emery said she didn't trust him and accompanied Lilah.

Hector was in the library watching *Neon Genesis Evangelion* on his laptop when they arrived. As soon as Emery introduced herself she wished her skirt were six inches longer. His eyes traveled over her, hyperactive in their attention to detail. She was relieved when Hector turned his attention to Lilah.

Lilah seemed impervious to his staring and a tic he appeared to have where his tongue would touch the corner of his lip then disappear back inside his mouth. Emery shuddered each time he did it.

"I've been working on something for you," Hector said, eyes flicking between them.

Emery crossed her arms in front of her chest. He turned his laptop screen toward them and Lilah leaned in, but Emery remained planted against the back of her chair.

"Ew," Emery said. "Is that—"

It was a graphic image of an octopus and a woman engaged in bestiality. The octopus' eyes gave a sense of its face and that face was suctioned to the woman's crotch. Emery glared at Hector.

"It's a famous painting," Lilah said.

Emery refused to look at the screen; her hand shielded it from view.

"It's a Japanese woodblock print that I edited to look like a photograph," Hector said. "It took me weeks."

"Was this for fun or for an assignment?" Lilah asked.

"Fun."

Emery turned the laptop back toward Hector using one finger, as if the machine itself were dirty.

"You know showing this to us could be taken as offensive?" Lilah said. Her voice was matter-of-fact. "The hyper-sexualization of Asian women is something I want to write about in *Interrogate*."

Hector shrugged. "I didn't mean to offend you. I was just showing my most impressive work."

"Octopus porn?" Emery said.

"Degas painted little girls. Lewis Carroll was a pervert. Woody Allen ..." Hector trailed off suggestively. "People say that I have yellow fever, but I just like Asian culture. How is that perverse? It's not like I'm into kids or something sick."

"*Sailor Moon* is schoolgirl fetish," Emery said, indicating a sticker on his laptop.

"I watch it for the animation," Hector said.

Emery sneered in disbelief. "Sure."

"What if I were an anglophile?" Hector asked. His tone was non-contentious. "There's so much Union Jack stuff at Derrymore—flags and T-shirts and crap. That's not stigmatized, right? Obsession with Europe is never frowned upon even though it's the same fetishization. But the difference is I'm not a dilettante. I actually study and appreciate Asian culture. Everyone else just likes Wayne Rooney and Arctic Monkeys and fancy hotels and they don't know anything about it. I'm in AP Japanese."

"Show us more of your work," Lilah said.

Hector's portfolio outshined all the other candidates' by a long shot.

"Why do you want to be on *Interrogate?*" Emery asked, hoping to trip him up.

"I've never done any clubs at Derrymore because they're all bullshit 'leadership positions' for college. But Lilah's doing something that I actually believe in, and if I can make some cool stuff while I'm at it, why not?"

Lilah mumbled something in response and Emery was dismayed to see she was blushing.

CHAPTER 34

Lilah and Emery landed in Taiwan in the late afternoon. The food on the flight had been overwhelmingly abundant and good. Lilah ate until she felt sick and continued on anyway. Emery slept ninety percent of the flight and told Lilah to wake her up for desserts only. Lilah had thought they would gossip all flight, but she hadn't anticipated the separate pods in first class. To speak to Emery, she had to unbuckle her seatbelt and walk across the aisle.

Lilah had stayed with Cassie's family for the weekend before the flight, because the Hoopers were at a family friend's wedding and Mr. and Mrs. Chang were already in Taichung. They had arrived a couple days earlier to settle in and prepare the apartment for the girls. It was a clean, minimalist two-bedroom on the twenty-fifth floor of a high rise. Lilah's room had two twin beds and a vertiginous view that elicited a genuine *whoa* from Emery.

Upon entering, Emery asked for slippers, which caused Mrs. Chang to clap and hug her.

"I'm so smelly," Emery warned. "You don't want to hug me."

"You are my second daughter!" Mrs. Chang said. She took a deep breath and drew Emery close to her. "I only smell flower and butterfly."

Lilah fended her mom off and accused her of hugging

performatively. Emery forced Lilah to take the first shower to spare everyone a salutational mother-daughter argument. She thought she caught an appreciative smile from Mr. Chang as she launched into a summary of her journey.

"It's a beautiful country," Emery concluded. "I can't wait to see all of it."

"I have surprise for you," Mrs. Chang said. "You will love. At dinner, I tell you and Lilah."

"Tell me now," Emery said gamely. "I'll pretend to be surprised at dinner."

Mrs. Chang smacked Emery's arm playfully and refused.

"How can I help with dinner?" Emery asked.

Mrs. Chang asked her to make rice—a symbolic task, too simple to really constitute help. But Emery had never made rice and Mrs. Chang clapped her hand to her mouth, aghast. Mr. Chang couldn't stop chuckling.

Mrs. Chang showed Emery how to rinse the rice, drain it, rinse it again until the water ran clear. Mr. Chang was still laughing to himself.

"A Korean girl who doesn't know how to make rice," he said in wonder.

● ● ●

When the surprise was revealed at dinner, Lilah was livid. Mrs. Chang had signed Emery up for Taiwanese language lessons. Class began the following day.

"Mom," Lilah said. "That's not okay. You could have at least warned Emery before she came."

"You too!" Mrs. Chang said.

"Me too what?" Lilah asked.

"I sign you up for advanced reading and writing. Your speaking is so bad, too. I can barely understand."

"*What?*" Lilah said. "Everyone speaks Mandarin here. No one even speaks Taiwanese anymore."

"Metro announcements are in Taiwanese," Mr. Chang said.

"You are here one month," Mrs. Chang said, ignoring her husband. "What you doing for such long time?"

"We planned to go to the beach," Lilah said. "And I packed so many books."

Mrs. Chang made an unconvinced noise and said, "Too much reading. Eat! You have to sleep soon or you will be tired for class."

• • •

"I can't believe that my mom did that," Lilah said. "I'm so sorry."

"Honestly, I'm not mad," Emery said. "We were probably gonna get bored going to the beach every day anyway. Maybe we can meet some people and go clubbing."

Lilah laughed nervously as she climbed into bed.

"I'm not excited for college stuff to start when we're back at school," Emery said, fluffing her pillow. "It's just going to be even more competitive than usual."

It surprised Lilah to hear such a statement from Emery, since she came fully equipped to dominate the competition with the right name and every privilege one could hope for.

Emery continued: "My mom and dad are trying to not piss me off, and every time they bring up college they try to be fake-casual about it. They're like, 'Oh, I just happened to run into so-and-so whose son is applying to Georgetown. What do you think of that?' And I'm like, 'Wow, I couldn't care less.'"

"At least your parents are trying to not bug you," Lilah said. "My mom talks about it non-stop. I bet the only reason she signed us up for the class is because she's terrified that I won't have something on my résumé for this summer."

"It's summer! Colleges don't care if you do nothing. Just say you played tennis the whole time."

"I wasn't planning on doing nothing. I have so many ideas for *Interrogate* that I want to organize because I know there's going to be so much work when we get back."

"What kind of ideas?"

"I guess I'm working backwards from things that happened, but I don't want it to just be 'Hug-An-Asian is Bad'—I want to say something about the bigger picture at Derrymore. Like, about the culture overall. Annie told me something that a teacher said to her, and I thought it could be a good article—if she lets me write about it."

"Was it Peiffer?" The room was tense for a moment, then both girls giggled manically. "You can say her name! She's not Voldemort."

"No," Lilah said. "It was the science teacher with the lesbian haircut."

"Oh, Mrs. Morten. She flirts with Scott in class. It's so shameless and gross."

"Annie stayed after class to brownnose—which she does a lot—and Morten was like, 'There's more to life than grades.'"

"Hm." The lights were off but the window shades were thin and their eyes were adjusting to the semi-darkness.

Emery turned on her side and propped her head on her hand, facing Lilah. "What do you think she meant by that?"

"I think she was saying Annie is a grade-obsessed, nerdy, typical Asian kid. Why? You don't think so?"

"No, I definitely do. It's also just a retarded thing to say because everyone at Derrymore is obsessed with grades. That's the whole point."

"Yeah, does she want Annie to not care? And fail the class?"

"She probably said it because Annie is annoying and always asks how much assignments will count toward final grades and stuff." Emery's hand shot into the air in an imitation of Annie. "*Will this be on the test? Will that be on the test?* She's such a stereotype, no offense."

"I heard that if you're Asian it's a bad thing to get a perfect SAT score. My mom saw one of those super-expensive New York City consultants talking about it on the news, and they said it makes you seem like a machine who has no personality. Not that I'm going to get an 800."

"I guess it's lucky that I can just check the box for 'white' since my last name is white."

"Is it okay if I mention that in *Interrogate?*"

Emery turned onto her other side.

"I guess? I don't think it's that interesting, though. I'm so tired I can feel my head pounding. Let's go to sleep."

• • •

Emery loved the Taiwanese class. It was only three hours in the morning and she lorded over her classmates. They were all versions of freshman Lilah—uncool, Taiwanese American teenagers whose meekness was exceeded only by their self-consciousness. Boys and girls alike were enamored, and she turned the class into a cult of Emery.

When they asked pointed questions—*Are you rich? You're popular, right? Do you only have white friends?*—she smiled and answered patiently. When they stumbled over their words and failed to make eye contact, she made them comfortable. When they stared, she didn't glare back. She volunteered the information they wanted: how she was adopted, what her father did, details about her relationship with Shawn. Their fascination was palpable and she rewarded it.

She even asked about their lives. When they were self-deprecating she scolded them kindly. She was quick to express sympathy and admiration. She was affectionate and gave out compliments recklessly. Emery was a celebrity at a meet-and-greet intent on making all of her fans fall even more deeply in love.

Emery's progress was average. But even when her mangled pronunciation became a class joke, it didn't reflect poorly on her. It was proof that she was untouchably American, and this quality was held in highest regard. Emery lambasted her inability to grasp the grammar and bullied the teacher into filling out a chart with makeshift verb conjugations (she knew Taiwanese was not a Romance language but, please, if she could at least see something resembling the I/you/it and we/y'all/they versions she was accustomed to—maybe it would help). The teacher penciled in the chart with anglicized spellings of what Emery asked for. It didn't help.

At Derrymore, Emery didn't have the freedom to bestow kindness upon the Jennys and Cassies. She had no use for followers of their ilk. But in Taiwan, she could afford to be benevolent. She basked in her own generosity and smiled into their pimpled faces and overlooked their faux pas.

Emery befriended a boy named Thomas who reminded her of middle school Noah. They ate lunch and spent the afternoon together while Lilah endured her (much longer and more demanding) advanced class.

After being dismissed from class each day, Emery and Thomas sat at a picnic table outside the academic building and saved a snack for Lilah. For the first week, Thomas tried to flee whenever Lilah arrived, but Emery finally convinced him that he was not intruding. The trio talked for another hour until it was time to return home for dinner. They parted ways at the metro station after Thomas asked Emery what kind of snack she wanted him to bring the next day.

"Isn't Thomas so nice?" Emery asked. "I feel like he's gonna invite us to meet his family. But I don't really want to go."

"He's so in love with you," Lilah said. "And he's cute. For an Asian guy."

"I thought so, too. Hey—maybe we can set him up with someone. There's this super-shy girl in my class and they'd be adorable together."

Lilah almost walked into a parked scooter because she was staring down at her phone.

"Are those all from Hector?" Emery asked.

Abashed, Lilah tilted her screen to show a full inbox. The Changs' phone plan didn't include international texting but Lilah convinced her mom that she needed to text her friends in order to stay in the college application loop. They negotiated that Lilah could send ten (and receive ten) messages each day. Lilah was re-reading Hector's messages from the day before.

Emery had been attributing her lack of communication with Shawn to the twelve-hour time difference. She'd have to come up with a different reason.

● ● ●

The bedroom closet was packed with the contents of Emery's two suitcases. Emery drew the blinds while Lilah fingered a denim minidress with a bustier top hanging on the rod. It took some convincing, but Lilah agreed to try it on.

"Turn around," Lilah said, preparing to undress.

Emery grumbled but did as she was told.

"Can you zip me?" Lilah asked.

They stood in front of the full-length mirror and gawked.

"Wow," Emery said. She made an hourglass motion with her hand. "That looks so much better on you than me."

"I'm so full from dinner," Lilah said.

"Shut up. You look so skinny."

"I could never wear it."

"Why not? You look twenty-five—in a good way. Like, New York City–bitch twenty-five."

Lilah gestured to her breasts, threatening to spill out of the dress.

"That's how it's supposed to fit," Emery said. "I wish mine looked like that."

Lilah pushed her boobs together in obscene cleavage and they screech-giggled.

Mrs. Chang's voice came through the door, "Everything okay?"

"Yes!" the girls answered hastily.

"Unzip me," Lilah whispered. "I don't want my mom to see."

"That you're a *woman*?"

"It looks weird on me."

"It looks good! What if you're fooling around with Hector"—Emery lowered her voice at Lilah's censoring look—"and he goes to unhook your bra? The ones you have are totally fine for just wearing but they're not, like— you cannot let a guy see those, Lilah. I'm not even being mean."

Lilah shimmied out of the dress and pulled on an over- sized Pochacco T-shirt. She shut the lights off.

"I don't think he'll care—"

"Because he's not interested in sex?" Emery asked, not meaning for her tone to betray hopefulness.

"No. He definitely is."

"Definitely? Why? What did he say?"

"Just … He makes kind of cheesy innuendos."

Emery was glad Lilah couldn't make out her appalled face in the darkness. "Like what?"

"Nothing that goes *too* far. I said something like, 'I can't wait to not be long-distance anymore,' and he said, 'When we get back, there will be no distance between us.'"

Emery beat her heels against the mattress and they laughed as quietly as they could.

"Don't be mean, Em!"

"I have"—Emery drew a deep breath—"a cramp."

Lilah threw a small pillow and it bounced off Emery's chest.

"My boob!" Emery whisper-screamed, setting off a new round of giggles.

When they caught their breath, Lilah made another admission: "He calls me 'cutiepie' in our texts."

She twisted the sheet around her fists, waiting for Emery's judgment.

"That's cute," Emery said, sitting up and pulling her knees to her chest. "Shawn only calls me Emery. We don't have any nicknames for each other. I'm even listed as Emery Kit Hooper in his phone."

"As opposed to?"

"Like an inside joke or something. Candace is in Ian's phone as 'Caddie my favorite girl in the world Perkins.'"

"But she put that in, didn't she?"

"Even so."

"This is just hypothetical, but would you ever go out with someone like Thomas?"

"Like, someone Taiwanese?"

"Or Asian in general."

"Probably not. Would you?"

"I did," Lilah said. "At camp. He was extremely nerdy with those glasses that change into sunglasses. And he asked me to the dance and then we were boyfriend/girlfriend for the last three days even though we barely spoke. When we danced, his hands were on my shoulders and my hands were on his shoulders."

Emery put her arms out stiffly like Frankenstein's monster and swayed back and forth until Lilah crumpled with laughter.

"I can't wait for you to come to Nantucket next summer," Emery whispered.

They talked late into the night, and both girls fell asleep smiling.

• • •

Emery awoke to a message from Candace, who was visiting her cousins in La Jolla. In the grainy photo, she was wearing a wetsuit and posing in front of an enormous soft-top. Emery replied with a photo of stinky tofu from the night market.

> I wish you could smell it
> It puts Ian's cleats to shame

Candace said the tofu looked disgusting and told Emery that she had cut Ian off completely.

Emery praised her friend and said she deserved better than noncommittal Ian, but didn't believe it was really over. They'd be hooking up as soon as fall semester arrived.

> What else is going on in civilization?

As she waited for Candace's reply, Emery remembered that she forgot to ask her mom if their phone plan covered international texts. But it had already been weeks of uninhibited texting and neither parent had said anything.

Candace's reply was so long it came in three separate texts: Riley was traveling in South America with her family, so *Class Dress* was on hiatus. Noah was fishing for an invite to anywhere with anyone. Errol was at IMG for the summer. When Candace got to peripheral people, Emery had already confirmed she was having the best summer. She said she'd be home in a couple weeks.

• • •

Emery earned the enmity of a girl in her Taiwanese class. Blossom gave Emery an intense once-over each morning, and even though this was the only time she'd deign to look directly at Emery, Blossom's neck was often craned at odd angles to catch Emery's voice talking about her tennis team or her PSAT score or the American Girl doll she had growing up.

Emery had made an effort to include Blossom in the circle of admirers, but Blossom resisted. When Emery was showered with compliments and questions (How did she do her fishtail braid? Where was her charm bracelet from? What was the name of her nail polish?) Blossom was the only one who never participated, despite dissecting each of Emery's carefully assembled looks with laser focus (and ordering a bottle of Vamp).

Blossom began dressing more elaborately, trying to compete with Emery while never acknowledging her. Emery wore a silk scarf as a headband and the next day Blossom had a cheap polyester one wrapped around her ponytail. Emery mentioned her trip to Positano—Blossom wouldn't shut up about her family's timeshare at Rehoboth Beach. Emery took great pleasure in Blossom's quiet, seething hatred. She made a point of complimenting the most absurd part of Blossom's getup: *I love your knee-high gladiator sandals. That clip-in hair feather is adorable. Where did you get those acid-wash shorts?*

Blossom brushed each remark off with a cold "thanks" and pretended to be engrossed in her Taiwanese exercise.

• • •

Thomas told Emery to not provoke Blossom.

"Me?" Emery said. "She's rude, Thomas. You know she is."

Emery tilted a bag of rice crackers down her gullet.

"I know she is," Thomas said, "but just ignore her."

He opened a can of apple soda and passed it across the table.

"I'm trying," Emery said, taking a sip. "If she'd just be normal to me, I wouldn't even notice her."

Thomas rarely engaged in gossip about their classmates, and though he was non-judgmental, he never gave her the satisfaction of a laugh when she came up with a clever putdown. After Emery unleashed her analysis of the day's class, they segued into topics that Thomas had more to say about. He talked about his favorite sci-fi books and explained *kanchō* and debated Emery about the differences between Taiwanese and Korean faces.

They stared at each other and Emery pointed out differences while Thomas kept pointing out similarities.

"I need a mirror," Emery said. "I don't think I see my face the way you're describing it."

"Here"—Thomas took a picture on his phone and held it up beside his face—"you can compare now."

Emery squinted. "Maybe I don't look like the average Korean. And maybe you don't look like the average Taiwanese person."

"I'm not even completely sure I'm Taiwanese. That's just what my parents were told."

"Huh?"

"I'm adopted, too."

"What?"

"I told you when we met."

"You did?"

Thomas smiled and nodded.

"Have you been here before?" Emery asked. "Like, this country?"

"It's my first time."

"I thought you were staying with family."

"I'm staying with a host family."

"Do you like them?"

"I do."

"Would you live here?"

"I plan to."

Emery's eyebrows shot up. "For study abroad?"

"Sure, but also for real." Thomas started to laugh at the scandalized expression on Emery's face.

"What?" She wiped her mouth. "Crumbs?"

He shook his head.

"But why?" she asked.

"I feel normal here. I like feeling like that."

That evening, when Lilah and Emery reached the heart-to-heart portion of the night, Emery described the conversation with Thomas.

"I felt so sad for him," Emery said, "and how he's felt so out of place his whole life."

Lilah was spared from answering by a sudden glow outside their window.

Emery sat up. "Weird. It's not Fourth of July."

"No," Lilah said, "but I don't think that's celebrated here anyway."

"Oh yeah. I guess not."

●　●　●

When they returned from class on a Friday, it was surprisingly quiet in the apartment. Usually Mrs. Chang was waiting in the kitchen to grill them on what they had learned. The previous week, Emery had stumbled through *Hello, my name is Emery. I am an American*—and Mrs. Chang's eyes had welled up. Lilah had written a one-page biography of Mrs. Chang's life in Taiwanese, which Mrs. Chang read and then said, "Dad and Mom did not 'fall in love'—we matched together. No one gave me the choice."

Emery peered into the master bedroom. "She's not here."

"She must be at the market," Lilah said.

"Should we call?"

"I'm sure she's fine."

"It's strange, though," Emery said, "because she usually leaves the rice out for me. Are you sure she's okay?"

"I think she had an errand to run," Lilah said, opening the fridge. "Yeah, I just remembered. She'll be back soon."

Emery looked at Lilah suspiciously, but Lilah was rearranging items in the fridge with intense focus.

"You're acting weird. I'm gonna make rice."

"Oh, you don't need to. I can do that in a bit."

"It's the only thing I've helped with at all. I can't do nothing."

"You brought all those gifts that made my mom almost pass out."

They laughed at the memory of Mrs. Chang's face when she saw the robin's-egg blue gift bags arranged on the dining room table. Mrs. Chang had put the silver carafe on the coffee table and the silver frame in the entryway (with no photo). The empty gift bags had been placed in a position of honor on the media console.

Emery had been very clear with her mother that she wanted to bring *nice gifts* for the Changs.

As she started to scoop rice into the rice maker's metal bowl, the front door opened violently. Mrs. Chang was standing in the doorway loaded down with bags and balloons.

"No rice!" Mrs. Chang said.

"Ohmygod, Mom," Lilah said. "You scared us."

"Help me!" Mrs. Chang said. "I have so many things."

Emery took a large package from Lilah's mother.

"Is this … a cake?"

Mrs. Chang was struggling with grocery bags that were weighing down her arms.

"You got the strawberry shortcake, right?" Lilah asked.

Mrs. Chang said something in sharp Taiwanese and Lilah apologized.

"What's all this for?" Emery asked.

"Anniversary!" Mrs. Chang said. "Emery's adoption anniversary!"

Emery brought a hand to her heart. She almost dropped the cake.

"How'd you know?" she asked, steadying it. "I completely forgot."

"Long time ago, your mom tell me so. She said you always have big celebrations with Mom and Dad."

"I invited Thomas," Lilah said.

Emery's lip trembled as she watched Lilah untangling balloons and Mrs. Chang re-rearranging the fridge.

• • •

As soon as Thomas went home, Emery asked Lilah for paper and pen. Lilah tore out pages from her journal and handed over a pencil topped with a tiny nigiri. Emery was writing so quickly that her hand cramped but she powered through. She tried to record everything from the evening: the spongy cake with whipped cream frosting, the potted laceleaf Thomas brought as a present, the toast Mrs. Chang made in her honor, Mr. Chang's impression of Lilah that had them howling. The details were slipping quickly and Emery wrote down half sentences to keep things from floating away. *Norah Jones* was to remind herself of the album Mr. Chang put on (only to be overridden by Lilah, who switched it with an old Jennifer Lopez CD). *Red envelope* was to remember the shiny sleeve that Lilah filled with small bills ("Next time we get zongzi, you have to talk to the vendor"). *Pineapple cake* was for the fancy box of ong lai so Mr. Chang bashfully presented. *9:42* was the time Emery looked at the clock and wished the night would never end.

Emery tucked the pages into the zippered compartment of her suitcase. Lilah was lying on her side, texting.

"Who are you talking to?" Emery whispered.

"Hector."

"About what?"

When there was no response, Emery got into her bed and opened her laptop. She knew she should be happy for Lilah, but something chafed when she saw Lilah smiling into her phone screen.

"Have you seen this email from school?" Emery asked and then read: *"Derrymore will not tolerate any sort of behavior, from students or parents, that intends to sabotage another student's college admission results. This includes reporting student infractions or misdemeanors to admissions offices, college coaches*—holy shit. Do parents do that?"

"Hector was telling me about this," Lilah said. "Basically, parents were calling colleges and tattling. Like saying so-and-so smokes weed and drinks or cheated on a test."

"And they say, 'Accept my kid instead?'"

"I think the calls are anonymous."

"Does it work? Do they reject anyone based on these calls?"

Lilah shrugged. "I'm not sure."

"What the fuck," Emery said. "What losers. My parents don't have time to sabotage someone else's life."

"I could see my mom doing that," Lilah said. "Annie's mom definitely would."

"Are you serious?"

"Remember when I told you about the first chair violin thing? And how Annie saw my application? I was so scared that Annie's mom would call the Derrymore office to report me."

"Maybe she did," Emery said.

• • •

A packet came for Lilah at the end of their trip. Emery knew what it was because her mom had asked if she could unseal the hefty Derrymore folder a week prior:

Can I open without you?

Sure

The manila envelope was resting in the center of the Changs' dining room table as if it were news from the Queen. Lilah's eyes bulged when she pulled out a stack of fifty pages. There were suggested reading lists, university rankings, and previous years' matriculation.

Emery explained that they would be assigned a Derrymore college counselor at the beginning of junior year. Then she added that most families hired private consultants to supplement their school-affiliated one. She considered omitting this fact out of financial sensitivity, but it would be patronizing—and possibly deceitful—to not mention it. Plus, the Changs weren't *poor*-poor as far as Emery could tell (though she'd be the first to admit that her sense of poorness was not fine-tuned and—just as Lilah couldn't quite perceive shades of wealth—Emery's ability to differentiate needs-financial-aid-desperately from would-be-greatly-helped-out-by-financial-aid was inferior).

Lilah's forehead was creasing with anxiety, made worse when she asked about the seminar schedule, which was printed above a list of the Common Application essay prompts. The seminars included Early Decision Strategy and the Personal Essay—basic stuff, according to Emery.

"Basic to whom?" Lilah asked. "How do you know all this?"

Emery shrugged. "You just pick it up from other people."

"You are knowing everything," Mrs. Chang said.

Emery nodded sagaciously.

• • •

Emery's teacher improvised yearbooks out of construction paper and distributed them on the last day of class. She handed out markers so they could sign and leave HAGS (Have a Great Summer) messages for each other. Blossom signed each yearbook with just her name and left early without thanking the teacher. Emery caught Blossom's eye as she was fleeing, but Blossom looked away hastily. Emery discovered why a moment later. There were hushed noises of displeasure and sounds of wounded sympathy from the girls hovering over Emery's yearbook.

"She's so jealous."

"Who does that?" asked one girl, whom Emery had given the bracelet off her wrist.

"I should cross it out. Can I cross it out?"

Emery pushed them out of the way gently and saw the single sentence Blossom had written: *They only like you because you pretend to be rich and white.*

"You *are* rich," one of her defenders said.

"That's not why we like you."

"None of us like Blossom."

"You're so much prettier than her."

"She was jealous of your clothes. She told me so."

"It doesn't bother me," Emery said, smiling. "I always make enemies. I feel bad for her."

"Can I sign?" Thomas asked.

Thomas struck a neat line through Blossom's words so they were still legible, but to be ignored.

CHAPTER 35

Boarding school is an engine powered by the apocryphal. Its allure is a blend of legends and half-truths punctuated with just enough fact to keep skeptics from prevailing. There are notorious alumni fables and institutional lore. Something that happened ten years ago (a drowning in the pond, a teacher-student affair) lives eerily in the present. But where appetite for myth lives, so too does speculation. The students of Derrymore probe incessantly into one another's lives. No frontier is off-limits.

• • •

The school year opened with a bang. The story of Noah's humiliation spread through Derrymore faster than mono.

Devin, Noah's roommate, couldn't get his Wi-Fi to connect, so he opened Noah's laptop to check if it was down school-wide. Devin screamed, "Gay porn!" and that cry brought the entire floor to attention.

When Noah returned from the bathroom, twelve guys were crowded around his computer and the sound of grunting filled the room.

• • •

Emery's door almost smashed Lilah's left hand but she drew it back just in time. They had lucked out—instead of being roommates, they had been assigned singles right across the hall from each other. Lilah had been lying on the floor with her legs propped up to drain the lactic acid (Coach Norton's recommendation) when Candace barged in wearing an orange faux-fur coat and aviators with purple lenses. Riley was close behind in a pink mohair sweater on top of a red corduroy dress.

"I feel so bad for Noah," Candace said. "Is he okay?"

Emery didn't look up from the racquet she was re-gripping. "Huh?"

"Check your phone," Candace said.

Emery dug it out of her tennis bag. "My dad says: 'How was practice?'"

"No one told you?" Candace said. "Scott and Errol texted me—"

"Saying what?"

"It's so awful." Candace could barely conceal her delight. "Devin caught Noah watching gay porn and told everyone."

"And then 'everyone' told everyone else?" Lilah interjected.

Emery's eyes darted toward Candace's face, but the disdain she expected to see was nowhere to be found.

"It's so messed-up," Candace said. "You should call him, Em. He didn't pick up my call, but he'll answer yours."

Emery took a long sip from her water bottle. "Why are you dressed like that?"

"We're taking photos for *Class Dress*," Riley said.

"You're still doing that?"

"You said I could," Candace said. "We have over ten thousand views every day."

"Are you serious?"

"We're being interviewed by *Teen Vogue* at the end of January"—Riley squealed and Candace elbowed her in the ribs—"and we're gonna work with a professional photographer who—"

"This is too much to process," Emery said.

Candace continued: "He shot Leighton Mees—"

"Not that—Noah's thing. How can people be so mean? Don't they have anything better to do?"

"Oh yeah. It's reprehensible."

Candace smiled a distracted smile that Emery had seen on a thousand different occasions. *Who was diagnosed with ADHD? They finally found out about whose nose job? The husband is having an affair with which au pair? How awful.* It was fleeting sympathy accompanied by disinterest and a desire to get back to their own news.

When Candace realized Emery was not going to make a speakerphone call for their entertainment, she left. Emery's first order of business was to check *Class Dress*. It looked completely different. Candace's mom had called in favors galore and the website looked like a fashion magazine. Lilah said that Candace and Riley looked like real models and Emery begrudgingly agreed. After checking to see if she had been scrubbed from the earlier posts (she had been), Emery called Noah.

At first, he tried to argue that it was a misunderstanding. He had been watching "regular porn" and his computer must have skipped to the next video. Emery was willing to go with it, but Noah stopped himself mid-sentence.

"Did you know?" he asked.

Emery considered lying but decided against it.

"How long have you known?" he asked.

"I don't remember not knowing."

"I knew you knew," he said. "I wanted to tell you. I never wanted to tell Candace."

He confided that he didn't feel safe telling Rich People anything. Emery *mm*'d understandingly and wondered how she had managed to evade the title.

• • •

Lilah stopped by Emery's room to drop off mail.

"It's me," she said, knocking lightly. "You had a J.Crew catalog that's been there since May and a letter from Thomas."

"That's so sweet of him," Emery said. "I can't believe he wrote me from Taiwan."

"He lives in Virginia, Em."

"Shit. I always forget. You can leave it on my desk, thanks." Emery was cleaning the lenses of her sunglasses. "How is my laceleaf plant?"

"I think the caretaker is watering it."

"I found our photos from last year winter break. Do you want them?"

A Steve Madden shoebox was filled with the Polaroid pictures that had adorned her walls the previous year. The photo-plastered look was passé, Emery explained.

"Help yourself."

There was a picture of Lilah in ski goggles, one of Lilah's dad asleep in the La-Z-Boy, another of the lone fork Mrs. Chang had set out for Emery at dinnertime. "I forgot you couldn't use chopsticks before Taiwan," Lilah said. "You got so good. I love these pictures—are you sure you don't want to keep any?"

Emery didn't answer. She was searching under the bed for the back of an earring that had escaped.

"We should have a reunion with all of our Taiwanese class people," she said, straightening up. "Don't you think that would be fun?"

"I didn't really make any friends in my class," Lilah mumbled. She picked up Andre Agassi's memoir, which was sitting on a light grey tray on top of a dark grey pouf. "I like this monochromatic look. It's so different from last year."

"Thanks." Emery dustbusted a corner that was dotted with silver glitter. "I wanted it to feel grown-up and I liked how your room in Taiwan was all one color."

Lilah pictured the apartment. True, the room was uniformly bland shades of oatmeal—but that was lack of design, not a design choice. Emery's comment betrayed a childish self-absorption that rejected inputs failing to square with how she believed the world worked. A room conceived without a decorator was not something Emery considered. This convenient worldview also allowed Emery to ignore the fact that Shawn's friendship with Ian and Jake was uninterrupted despite their horrible treatment of her and Lilah.

He was on his way to see Emery's new room. Lilah declined an offer to join them for dinner—she had plans with Hector.

"Is it finally ready?" Shawn's voice was muffled but unmistakable through the window.

Lilah replaced the book and slipped out as Emery struggled to lift the frame from its sticky casing.

"Am I colorblind?" Shawn asked, head peeking in.

It was all grey everything: duvet, throw pillows, area rug, framed prints.

"My godmother told me that grey is the most calming color," Emery said, "and since everyone says junior year is going to be the hardest year of our lives, I want to create the most Zen atmosphere possible."

"Or what? You won't get into Penn?"

Emery flicked the screen and it rattled.

"I'm not going there," Emery said. "Do you like it?"

"It's beautiful," Shawn said overzealously. "You know I don't have any opinion on interior decorations. Come outside. I don't like talking with a barrier."

Shawn was buzzing because all the seniors on his team were committing to colleges. He couldn't wait to follow them out of Derrymore and dreamt of the schools he and Emery might attend together. They talked about the future. Neither acknowledged the fact that they had barely spoken over the summer.

"Anything but a car sticker school," Shawn said.

Emery had come up with the term last Ivy Day. A car sticker school was a name brand. It was the type of school that Derrymore parents were dying to plaster on their back windshields.

"I'll never get why people are so obsessed with Ivies," he added.

Emery felt under attack but was wary of stoking another argument. On the first night of preseason, they had spoken about applications, and when Emery mentioned her dilemma in checking white or Asian for the demographic box, Shawn had become furious that she'd even consider being "so deceptive," and accused her of self-loathing. To avoid a follow-up lecture she bit her tongue while he bemoaned elitist culture.

"It's just so predictable: Derrymore, then Penn, then a job at your dad's company. Is that all you want in life?"

All he wanted to talk about was college, but Emery had something entirely different on her mind.

• • •

Emery had a certain image of herself, and being sexually behind the curve did not jibe with it. She was petrified of being grouped with the asexual Asian and Indian Derrymore crowd—or worse, falling into the category of those who became sexually hyperactive in college to make up for a late start. Recently, everyone had been talking about an alumna who'd graduated two years earlier, Yichen Wen. Yichen (who was so anonymous that *The Derry* ran a mock Missing Person ad for her) had undergone a sexual awakening at UCLA, changed her name to Gretchen, and gotten a boob job.

Classmates who had never said hello to Yichen/Gretchen were now perusing her Facebook, riveted. Candace brought her laptop to Emery's room to show her Gretchen's risqué albums. Gretchen, apparently, was fond of the obscene tongue-through-peace-sign pose and fishnet stockings. She cut her own bangs and had learned to do a smoky eye.

"I didn't care about her when she was here," Emery said. "I care even less now."

"But look—she's dressing like a stripper. It's so weird. How can someone change that much?"

"Didn't Sara get fat? Go to her photos."

After Candace left, Emery stalked Gretchen's photos for twenty minutes. They were preposterous—and ignited a new fear that anyone would gawk at her as she was gawking at Gretchen.

CHAPTER 36

There was a respectable turnout of twenty for *Interrogate*'s first official meeting. Emery couldn't make it because of an ARC commitment, though she'd halfheartedly offered to skip if Lilah needed the moral support (*Not necessary! But thanks for the offer!*). Lilah described the magazine's mission and found it surprisingly exhilarating to speak in front of the small crowd, many of whom were taking notes. She assigned articles and remembered Emery's advice to sound like she knew what she was talking about even when she didn't.

After the Q&A finished, Lilah felt giddy while going over the art for issue one with Hector. She had loved being asked how she came up with the idea for the magazine. It made her feel interesting—which she imagined was adjacent to popular—but she'd kept her answers short for fear of boring her audience.

Hector showed her a folder full of sketches.

"I don't want you to spend too much time on this," Lilah said. "I know how much you were looking forward to a whole year of senior spring."

"I didn't really mean that," Hector said. "I only pretend to be lazy. It's a sham."

Hector pulled her into his lap by the waist. They

whispered with their noses barely an inch apart until a librar-
ian cleared her throat loudly and gave them a stern look.

Lilah had never been shamed for inappropriate closeness
before. The reprimand made her feel almost as good as having
Interrogate officially underway.

• • •

Junior fall lived up to its reputation. It refused to ease them in
and instead behaved like a Candace shaggy dog story: relentless
and unaware of the harm it was causing. Between SAT prep
sessions and tennis matches, Emery almost forgot to send her
godmother a thank you note for the sweater from Gorsuch.

Emery couldn't fathom how Lilah was also working on
Interrogate. Even though she had quit violin, Lilah was taking
an extra math course and the most advanced Chinese class
that Derrymore offered.

It was so difficult that fluent Mandarin speakers could
barely scrape an A. Lilah explained that it was common practice for students to have their parents write their papers.

"All the Chinese parents do it," Lilah said. "Tsai laoshi is
such a hard grader that she literally gave Annie's mom a B."

"Are you serious?" Emery asked.

"My dad got an A minus, so my mom took over and I got
an A. Her Mandarin is better than his, but his Taiwanese is
better than hers."

"All the parents do this?"

"They have to. We'd get Cs if they didn't."

"That's so immoral." Emery laughed. "I thought you were
such a goody two-shoes."

"No—it's not like that. Everyone does it."

"It's still cheating"—Emery shrugged and cocked her head—"I won't tell anyone, don't worry."

Emery didn't notice Lilah's flustered expression because she was wondering if her mom could get an A in her English class.

• • •

While Emery was largely indifferent to the magazine, Annie was bursting with curiosity. When Annie asked what the point of *Interrogate* was for the tenth time, Lilah suggested Annie come to a meeting (they were weekly now) so she could see firsthand. Annie declined in a tone that was barely polite and just one shade removed from contemptuous.

"It's just about being Asian, right?" Annie said.

Lilah kept her scowl in check—she was past letting Annie insult her. She said no firmly (but dispassionately) and explained that she wanted to dissect the makeup of the "Most Typical Derrymorian" and understand what prevented someone like herself from achieving such status. Lilah wanted to pin down so-called intangibles and get to the core of why some Derrymorians succeeded in their sleep and others sank despite best efforts.

Annie asked a few questions about direction and philosophy—and she got it. Annie grasped Lilah's vision better than anyone (even Hector), which reminded Lilah why she had tolerated Annie's abuse for so long. When Annie managed to silence her competitive voice, they made each other think.

In middle school they'd had a book club—just the two of them. Annie had eliminated all other would-be members because the trial meeting had been lousy with "dumb opinions and literal interpretations." From that point on, Lilah and Annie alone read *Kira-Kira* and Janet Wong's poetry, and then a book neither of them fully grasped about a man who, one morning, wakes up in the body of a woman and simply accepts it.

Annie was opinionated but respectful during those discussions. She didn't lash out or put Lilah down. Their book club was one of Lilah's favorite adolescent memories: she'd had a sparring partner, and it was that much more miraculous that the person who challenged her in the best way was one who usually made her want to hide.

"Is Emery doing *Interrogate?*" Annie asked, breaking the spell.

"Not this first issue," Lilah said, "but maybe in the future. She's really busy with alumni and reunion stuff."

Annie went on a rant about ARC being a bullshit committee for slackers who couldn't commit to a real club like Model UN or Mock Trial. Lilah secretly agreed.

"What about Hector?" Annie asked. "Are you two a couple?"

Lilah suddenly had an image of Annie, Jenny, and Cassie discussing her as they used to discuss Emery—and she didn't hate the idea of it. She nodded.

The way Annie asked her next question—with overacted spontaneity—revealed how she had been waiting for an opening to pounce: "Maybe I'm misremembering, but didn't Hector date one of those Japanese exchange students last year?"

Lilah took a beat, her sense of superiority fading fast.

"He didn't date any of them," Lilah said. "He dated Yichen—Gretchen, whatever—the year before. But you probably knew that already."

• • •

Lilah recounted the exchange student jab to Emery. She wanted to see if Emery would side with Annie and malign Hector, but Emery wouldn't take the bait.

Emery knew Lilah was probing for a reaction and cared less about Annie's amateur attempts at bullying than the fact that Lilah was testing her.

"Yichen is such a Ryan wannabe," Emery deflected.

Lilah was new to this game so she backed off rather than doubling down. She didn't recognize that Emery was discomfited more by the confidence Hector instilled in Lilah than by his dating record. That plus the newfound importance Lilah had amongst the *Interrogate* staff was beginning to erode the mentor/mentee angle of their friendship—and Emery couldn't anticipate what it was being replaced with.

Preparing *Interrogate*'s first issue had become so all-consuming that their nightly catch-up sessions were less and less frequent. On more than one occasion Emery went across the hall only to be disappointed that Lilah was busy editing articles or approving photos.

Lilah changed the subject by mentioning that she had read Hector's college essay. Emery immediately sat up. College essays were a new source of fascination: pre-packaged, horrible little confessions that forced you to cough up what made *you* different.

"I can't believe he showed it to you," Emery said.

Lilah didn't know whether the comment was meant as an insult or just felt like one, and filed it away for later inspection.

"He knows we have that seminar later today so he sent it to me," Lilah said. "I thought it was nice of him."

"Can I see?"

Asking to see someone's essay is like asking to see their diary—but more invasive. In a diary, it's permissible to be stupid and mean or sloppy and crude. You can admit to transgressions and desperate longings in a whisper. But a college essay demands far greater humiliation. You must shout, you must be declarative, you must speak from the bilious heart of earnestness.

In teenagers' defense, "What Matters and Why" in 650 words is an impossible prompt because it demands self-definition from a body of people who are changing so rapidly that they cannot pin down who they are with any accuracy. The most confident student will be cut down to size in the face of the college essay because he must betray what he believes is special about himself. No matter how special you believe yourself to be—no matter how special you *are*—when put down in plain English, it sounds awfully insignificant.

Lilah pulled up the document and Emery devoured it.

"Hm," Emery said, sounding disappointed. "It's better than I thought it'd be."

•   •   •

They showed up just in time to get seats at the back of the lecture hall where they usually yawned through presentations by Nobel laureates or congressmen or over-tanned PGA presidents. All the juniors who came afterward had to sit on the floor. A woman named Tanya began the seminar by saying that she wasn't going to sugarcoat anything and the quality that made her a good college counselor was "realness." The topic of the day was the personal essay.

"I'm not going to lie," Tanya said. "This will not come easily to most of you. Because most of you do not have a sense of self. Yet. Your counselors will help you find one—not fabricate, we never fabricate anything—because colleges can tell when your sense of self isn't fully formed.

"What is sense of self? It's knowing who you are, even if you don't know what you want to do with your life. It's fine if you don't have a step-by-step plan, but you have to know what principles you live by. Are you motivated by money? Are you motivated by recognition? Do you want to change the world? You should have consistent self-presentation throughout your essay so they know what you're selling."

Emery considered what she was selling. Nothing came to mind, but her parents would hire someone to help her find it.

CHAPTER 37

In October, Dean Andrews was waiting in the hall outside of Emery's last-period class. He asked her for a word in his office. Blood immediately rushed to her head.

Had he found out about the homecoming note she and Noah sent to Lilah freshman year? Had one of the tennis underformers reported her for bullying them about crossing the Isle?

Emery's limbs went noodly as she followed the dean to his office in the rotunda. She started forming an alibi, but when he sat across from her, he was wearing the familiar expression of someone about to ask a favor.

"How's the semester going?"

"Well, thank you."

"I heard you're doing great work with the Alumni Reunion Committee."

"Yeah, I—ARC is going great. Am I in trouble?"

"No, not at all"—Dean Andrews laughed. "Everyone sees me as the grim reaper around here. I do have responsibilities outside of expelling rule breakers."

Emery chuckled weakly.

"I've actually called you in here for selfish reasons. Every year we do a—for lack of a better word—'photoshoot' to gather images for our prospective student literature. We always pick a few students who we feel represent Derrymore: ones who embody athleticism, intellectual curiosity, and multicultural-ism. Does that sound like something you'd be interested in?"

Emery was so relieved not to be in trouble, her response was much heartier than intended: "I'd love to be part of it."

"And forgive me for being presumptuous ..." Dean Andrews made a *mea culpa* gesture. "Your other half?"

Though Emery's interactions with Dean Andrews had always been brief, it was a given he knew the ins-and-outs of her personal life. At Derrymore, information was currency for teachers and students both. It wasn't cheap gossip in the he-said-she-said sense—it was knowing when to dispense and when to withhold. It was pretending to not know something you heard a week ago (Ian's brother got a DUI) to flatter the Johnny-come-lately (Riley) who would later let something more valuable slip (Shawn's dad was a chronic philanderer) because she enjoyed the feeling of authority. No one suc-ceeded at Derrymore without a gift for circulating and proffering information when it counted.

Emery wouldn't be shocked if Dean Andrews knew that she'd had a crush on Scott way back when. And for her part, Emery knew that the dean's nephew had withdrawn before he could be expelled for stealing girls' bras from the swim team locker room.

"I'll tell Shawn at lunch," she said. "I'm sure he'll want to do it."

"We're aiming for Monday morning, when there should be good weather. You'll be excused from first and second period. If it rains, we'll move it to Wednesday."

Emery thanked Dean Andrews and set off for the dining hall.

• • •

Shawn offered Emery a bite of grilled mahi mahi. She made a face and turned her head away.

"We'll get to be the face of the school, Shawn," she said.

"A fake face, Em. They're using us to make it seem 'multi-cultural.' It's all fake."

"How is it fake? We go to Derrymore. We're real students. You're against it on moral grounds and it's not a moral issue. It's just a photoshoot. July Perkins did it."

"We're not representative," Shawn said. "You think it's an honor, but they're taking advantage of you."

"You're so paranoid about getting exploited. People *want* to be in the prospectus."

"Who cares what other people want? Who cares if Candace's brother was in it? The fact that other people want something doesn't make it valuable. You're so brainwashed."

She crunched down on a piece of garlic bread.

"I'm not doing it," he said. "You can go ahead—and I'm sure you will—but don't complain to me when you go to the 'photoshoot' and it's a Black kid, an Indian kid, and you."

She kicked the leg of Shawn's chair rhythmically. "I don't need your blessing."

"You never listened to the CDs I gave you," he said over her.

"I did," Emery answered.

"Huh?"

"I listened to them. I said I hadn't because I didn't like them."

"What?"

"I didn't like them."

"*Late Registration* is the best—"

"They're not my taste."

"Then you have no taste."

"Why do you think I care what you think?"

"I forgot you only like white music."

"What's your problem?" Emery blurted.

"You have no sense of self. That's *your* problem."

• • •

The next day, Emery told Shawn that their relationship didn't make sense anymore.

He offered an apology, but also demanded one in return. She had nothing to apologize for and she told him so. He finally walked away, defeated.

Emery had never brought up Shawn to her parents. She'd considered telling them after Taiwan, but a particular incident stopped her. When Lilah came over to the Hoopers' for dinner, they asked her to recite some Taiwanese. Lilah quickly swallowed a bite of risotto and, in the language of her ancestors, said what a beautiful home the Hoopers had and how grateful she was to join them for dinner. After an awkward pause when Lilah didn't know whether she should go on, they acted delighted and Mrs. Hooper clapped enthusiastically.

"Incredible," Mr. Hooper said with too much gusto.

They never asked Emery to perform what she had learned and she didn't offer.

• • •

Lilah was the only person who knew about the breakup, so Emery calculated a couple days before the news traveled through Derrymore's porous grapevine. But Candace passed along a message that implied Shawn had been quick to let the world know he was single.

Scott apologized. Not directly, of course, but he sent a messenger.

"He told me to tell you he feels really bad," Candace said. "And I could tell he meant it."

"For what?"

"The Hug-An-Asian thing."

"From last year?"

"We had a heart-to-heart and he talked about it for, like, an hour."

"Shouldn't he apologize to Lilah? He hugged her, not me."

Candace snorted. "I'm sure she liked the attention. Besides, they're not friends."

"And we are?"

"You and Scott? Obviously."

Emery's pulse quickened. Scott passing messages through Candace could only mean one thing: he had been biding his time all along. She could already hear herself reassuring Scott he wasn't a rebound.

"She got way prettier," Candace said.

"Who?"

"Do you think Lilah would model for *Class Dress?*"

Emery didn't answer.

CHAPTER 38

Lilah invited Emery to tour colleges with her family over winter break, but the invitation was declined. The Hoopers were feeling very neglected after she'd spent the summer in Taiwan and she couldn't deprive them of college visits.

Like many Derrymore parents, Mrs. Hooper thought of the college process as her sacred domain. Emery's academic career had been carefully assembled brick by brick, the foundation laid long before she was born. Volunteering and hosting and Christmas cards and sympathy gifts—the culmination of twenty years' soft power would pay off during senior year. Mrs. Hooper viewed college tours with her daughter as a reward for making Emery's life a series of low-hanging fruit harvestings.

If Emery were being square, it wasn't just about humoring her parents. She wanted to stay in five-star hotels and order room service. The Hanover Inn and twenty-dollar ice cream sundaes were not on the Changs' agenda. Lilah had also become selfish lately: on the night of the breakup, Lilah still went to the *Interrogate* meeting even though Hector could have run it no problem. In Emery's mind, touring colleges *alone* would prompt Lilah to remember how important their friendship was.

Emery thought her parents might resist when she asked to invite Noah (they had repeatedly said how excited they were to spend one-on-one time with her) but Mrs. Hooper was thrilled.

"I'm so glad you want Noah to come," she said. "I haven't seen him since your birthday party. I really didn't like seeing all your longstanding friendships fall by the wayside."

They visited Swarthmore first. Then they went to Penn, even though Emery repeatedly stated she had no interest in touring or applying.

"I already know what it looks like," she said. "I've been to Dad's reunions so many times."

"You have to keep your options open," Mrs. Hooper said.

Mrs. Hooper arranged a sit-down with the dean of admissions for Emery and Noah. There was an excruciating lunch with one of Mr. Hooper's ancient Wharton professors. Noah did an excellent (and disgusting) impression of the octogenarian eating a heavily dressed Caesar salad.

Emery was glad for Noah's company because she needed to discuss a burgeoning rapport with Scott. She made Noah pinky-promise not to tell anyone about the flirtatious text messages. She wanted to witness Candace's unadulterated envy when they returned to campus and Emery had inside jokes with Scott.

• • •

At Princeton, the tour guide swore up and down that she was not an Ivy League–caliber student. She proudly announced that she had average grades and below-average SAT scores. Her essay, she swore, had gotten her in. It was obvious bait and Noah fell for it. He shoved to the front of the tour group and dragged Emery with him.

"What did you write about?" he asked the tour guide.

"I am the first generation in my family to go to college. My parents are illegal immigrants from El Salvador." The girl beamed.

"So what did you write about?" Emery asked.

"That I'm first generation and—and the stuff I just said."

"But what was the essay *about*?"

The girl glared at Emery and led them brusquely into Frist. Emery pulled Noah's elbow and fell back into the middle of the group.

"What are you going to write your essay on?" she asked.

"My parents' divorce maybe. Or being an only child. I know it's supposed to be about a hardship or an obstacle."

"Then why aren't you writing about coming out?"

"It feels … I dunno. Mercenary? Like, cheap. Do you think I should?"

"It's your 'sense of self,' isn't it?"

"I still won't get into an Ivy. I wasn't even going to tour Princeton—"

"Noah, stop. This is Derrymore all over again. Just write the gay essay and don't bitch out for once."

"What are you going to write about?"

Emery gave him a scornful look, like he had just asked her net worth.

"It's personal."

In the evening, Emery resumed her thread with Scott and they bonded over a shared complaint well past midnight. Scott lamented that no matter what he achieved on his own, it would always be credited to his family. Emery confided that she had the same woe and added:

> **I'd rather die than go to Penn**

Having it easy was their crime. If they succeeded, well, who wouldn't with those advantages? And if they failed—ha! Pathetic. (Especially with all those advantages.) Everything would be framed in terms of those inescapable advantages that, it should be pointed out, they *never asked for*.

Scott reasoned that if everyone would judge them no matter what, they might as well reap the benefits and just coast. Capitalize on their privilege and be the spoiled trust fund kids that everyone accused them of being. Emery sent:

> **Haha**

Quickly followed by:

> **Do you really mean that?**

There were no more replies that night and, in the morning, he didn't clarify.

• • •

The Changs canceled college tours at the last minute. They didn't tell Lilah why and would only say it was a bad time for Mr. Chang's work schedule. When she got upset, they told her not to be spoiled. College tours were not a necessity. Only white people did them. *Use the time to study*, Mrs. Chang said. Lilah rebelled by watching *Laguna Beach* (DVDs borrowed from Emery) and reading Hector's copy of *Dispatches*.

After an agonizing winter break, the new semester finally began and *Interrogate* set the student body buzzing. First issues were scattered on every table in the dining hall, and wherever you turned, students were poring over Lilah's creation.

Underformers were begging to join. Seniors who had never given Lilah the time of day pitched ideas on the inequalities they suffered: who got to have a mini fridge or an AC unit, the pet policy (fish only), learning disability accommodation. The editor-in-chief of *The Derry* nominated *Interrogate* for the Best Publication Award even though his vote guaranteed that the student paper's twenty-year winning streak would end.

Lilah loved being known. Before *Interrogate*, she would have guessed roughly fifty percent of the Derrymore student body would be able to confirm she attended, and thirty-five percent could name her. She'd always thought that some people were destined to fly under the radar, and others—like Emery—were *known*. She hadn't imagined that one could graduate into known status.

Lilah knew that people were only approaching her because of the magazine. But the more she thought about it, the more she preferred that to being known for having a rich family or being generally popular or having a reputation with boys. Lilah had an Actual Reason for being known. She likened the distinction to reality TV stars: people disparaged them by probing into what they were famous for. Could they sing? Dance? Act? *No?* Talentless good-for-nothings. But Lilah had a real talent, which she suspected had something to do with Emery fabricating a cockamamie excuse to keep Lilah from modeling the denim bustier dress in *Class Dress*.

• • •

When Emery entered the dormitory, a row of girls was reading quietly in the usually rowdy common room. Everywhere she went, *Interrogate* was being discussed.

"It's surprisingly polished," Errol said. But when Emery mentioned the next issue, he said, "How many more complaints can she come up with? She's lucky we let her slander us the one time. It's taking free speech *ad absurdum*."

Noah inspected the masthead. "So Lilah's the founder, president, and—*ooh*—editor in chief. *That's* a good title. I bet colleges love that."

"I didn't know she was such a go-getter," Riley said. "She should win Most Changed—"

"It's just a magazine," Emery snapped. "She didn't cure cancer."

CHAPTER 39

Emery couldn't find her periwinkle sweater. It was her most beloved knit and the only garment she was never careless about. People said they recognized her across campus by the blue-purple shade even before they could make out her distinct features. Lilah wouldn't have borrowed it because it was so personal—it would be like borrowing underwear or something monogrammed.

Distance had cropped up between the two girls and it felt unnatural to barge into Lilah's room unannounced. But to knock like a stranger would be a definite statement, formally declaring that things had become weird.

"Hey, did you borrow my sweater?" Emery allowed her voice, false and high, to precede her. "Sorry, I didn't mean to startle you. But I can't find it. It's fine if you did, but I need it back."

It took only the slightest hint of confrontation to make Lilah feel like she was in trouble. She froze while arranging daisies in a Vera Bradley travel thermos she had found in the kitchen.

"Oh shit"—Emery brought her hand up to her throat—"it's Valentine's Day? I totally forgot to send daisies this year. It looks like you got a lot, though. Are those from Hector?"

"Mostly, yeah."

Lilah had been in the common room when the delivery

arrived, and had observed Riley and Ginny tallying up their own (and everyone else's) scraps of piecemeal affection. Emery had remembered to send them daisies.

"I returned your sweater," Lilah said. "I swear I was going to ask, but you weren't there. Is it not in the bottom drawer?"

She crossed the hall and Emery followed.

"It's here," Lilah said, visibly relieved.

"Oh. Weird"—Emery glared at her dresser—"I don't know how I missed it."

"I'm sorry. I should have asked."

"No. Um. It's fine. That's weird I didn't see it."

Lilah opened the drawer one more time to double-check the sweater was there.

"I wanted to look nice for the *Interrogate* meeting on Friday because a lot of new people are joining, but it didn't look good on me."

"I'm sure it looked fine on you," Emery said, quashing an urge to ask how many new people.

Lilah shook her head. "How were your college tours?"

The subject eased them into a comfortable dialogue, and in a few minutes, Lilah was helping remove pills from Emery's cardigans with a cashmere brush.

Emery asked about Lilah's first meeting with Tanya, the college counselor. It had been frustrating because Tanya wouldn't even entertain the idea of applying to an eight-year in-state program combining undergraduate and medical school.

"I didn't know you wanted to be a doctor," Emery said.

"My parents told me to ask about it. They said if I don't get into a top three college, they want me to do this eight-year thing."

Lilah said the conversation with Tanya had centered pri-
marily around scholarships. Emery responded instinctively:
"*Why?*"

Mr. Chang had lost his job. They'd sold the apartment in
Taiwan. Money was tight and the Changs were obsessed with
value. Only the very best schools had value, according to
Lilah's mom. The schools her parents had never heard of—
the Pomonas and Haverfords—were throwing money down
the drain. It was Ivy or bust.

"There's no way I'm getting into Harvard, so if I can't get
a scholarship to UNC or somewhere then I'll have to do this
eight-year thing," Lilah said.

"Do you even want to go to medical school?"

"I want"—Lilah took a thought-gathering breath—"I'd
like to not be a burden to my parents. I want them to feel
like Derrymore was a good use of their money. They're
really unhappy that I've spent so much time on *Interrogate*.
I know they're gonna say it's the reason I don't get into a top
three."

Not sure what to say, Emery offered Lilah some Baked
Cheetos from the bag she'd just opened.

"It's okay. It'll be okay," Lilah said, shaking her head.
"Tuition is our biggest expense, so as long as I get a scholarship, it'll be fine. The eight-year thing is just a backup." Lilah
noticed a copy of *Interrogate* peeking out from under Emery's
mail and pointed to it. "What did you think?"

"Oh"—Emery wiped her fingers on a hand towel, leaving
bright orange streaks behind—"I didn't get a chance to read
it yet."

Lilah apologized—a nervous laugh escaped. It had been

presumptuous to think her best friend would take the time to look into what she'd been slaving over for months. Lilah's eyes flicked to the blithely stained towel. Annie had coveted and then stolen its mate mere days ago.

When Lilah had seen the fluffy white fabric, with blue piping and a delicate tree embroidered, hanging over the end of Annie's bed, she'd asked how it got there.

Annie said it had been sitting on the windowsill in the bathroom for weeks. That didn't make it okay, Lilah replied. Annie said there was no award for the Most Moral Derrymorian. She didn't regret it.

"Why do you defend her?" Annie had asked. "She's the most self-centered person in the world. You know she wouldn't do the same for you."

Emery had stood up for Lilah when Ian and Jake tried to hug her. She supported Lilah in battles against Mrs. Chang. Emery was an excellent ally to helpless Lilah—but a capable Lilah did not evoke the same generosity.

"Are you still pen-paling with Thomas?" Lilah asked.

"Huh?"

"The letter he sent you."

"Ohmygod. I never opened it. I think I lost it. That was the same time I was trying to be a vegetarian."

• • •

Noah was late to Latin and spent the whole class shooting Emery dramatic looks. She mimed writing a note, but he wanted the satisfaction of divulging and managed to wait until the bell rang.

"What is it?" she asked. "You were so distracting and obvious."

"You'll never guess who's dating."

"You."

"Ha*ha*. No, really. Guess."

"Just tell me."

"It's Scott and Candace!"

Emery stared at him blankly.

"She told me," Noah continued. "Right after Chapel. They were hooking up over break. She wants to tell you herself, so don't tell her I told you."

Emery replayed all of her recent conversations with Scott. He'd never mentioned that he even saw Candace over Christmas.

"It's like you've always said," Noah said. "It's so predictable. They were basically bred to be together."

"She said she thinks of him as a brother," Emery protested.

"You always say she's full of it," Noah said. "But I bet they'll win Cutest Couple for yearbook—"

"What the fuck. She's such a liar. I bet he didn't apologize at all."

Emery took a sharp breath in and exhaled loudly.

"Also, you didn't tell me Shawn wrote an article," Noah said.

She squinted and shook her head. It was too much information all at once. She asked what he meant, and Noah said that Shawn's *Interrogate* article about Black athletes being exploited by colleges was "pretty smart." Emery couldn't tell if the tight feeling in her chest was from finding out that Scott had duped her or Lilah had betrayed her.

CHAPTER 40

In their first meeting, Mr. LaChance asked how Emery's dad was. The counselor had an air of slickness that she disliked right away. She replied "good" then he said "great" and those two words were enough to accomplish what Mr. LaChance wanted to accomplish—namely, establishing that he knew Emery was her father's daughter.

It was a type of exchange that was becoming more common (with both peers and adults): a non sequitur about Nantucket or a fake-casual "Do I recognize you from Rosewall?" The entire point of these bids for recognition was to signal *we are on the same page* and—usually—of the same world. But, unlike most people, Mr. LaChance wasn't trying to show that he ran in the same circles or frequented the same locales as the Hoopers. The counselor simply wanted to lay on the table that Emery was not applying to schools as Emery Hooper, but as Stan Hooper's only child.

He pulled up a map of the US on his computer. He pointed out colleges in northern California, southern California, the Midwest, and the South. After a couple minutes he confessed that the map was just a mandatory exercise in open-mindedness. No self-respecting Derrymorian had any reason to look beyond the Northeast. Mr. LaChance's laugh was rascally.

Mr. LaChance was Tanya's counterpart and co-chair of the college counseling department. He was well into his sixties and known for his impeccable track record. He was also famously blunt.

"I have your whole file here," he said, tapping a folder of documents. "Read it front to back. Everything there is to know about Emery Hooper. And you've been assigned to me—which speaks for itself." That laugh again. It was sinister. "Where are we applying early decision?"

"I'm not sure I want to commit to something binding. I'd like to keep my options open if possible. I like the idea of Williams or Swarthmore—"

Mr. LaChance made a face when she mentioned Shawn's top choices.

"Small schools? You'll be bored. It'll feel just like Derrymore. I think Penn is the obvious choice for you. We can throw Swarthmore onto your list for the hell of it, but there's no reason to mess with a winning formula."

"What about Stanford?"

Mr. LaChance did not mince expressions. He wore his skepticism plainly in the sneer of his mouth.

"Tell me"—he tapped his pen against his desk—"the Common Application has a form for awards and honors. What awards and honors have you received?"

"Next year, I'll be tennis captain and ARC—"

Emery caught herself. The ARC presidency had been such a sure thing in her mind that when the votes were tallied and Ginny won, Emery had thought she'd misheard. The underformers clapped and trilled as Ginny pressed her hand to her heart. It was obvious where Emery had lost the vote—she had done nothing to ingratiate herself to them, and Ginny was her usual pushover self. It wasn't rigged, but was definitely personal, and when Ginny suggested Emery continue on in her role as vice president, Emery had reacted impulsively. She'd quit.

"Those are leadership positions," Mr. LaChance interrupted. "There's a separate form for those. Just focus on awards and honors now."

"I don't think I have any of those," Emery confessed.

"Not on the national level?"

"No."

"What about state?"

"No."

"What about just within the school? The history department award or MVP on the tennis team?"

"No"—Emery fought to keep her voice from quivering—"I don't have any."

Mr. LaChance gazed at her unblinkingly. He waited a few seconds then cleared his throat.

"Right. I think we can both admit—"

"Actually," she said. "There is something. I've been helping my friend with a magazine she started. It won the Best Publication award. Would that count?"

"It would depend on your role. What does this publication cover?"

"Uh … a lot of different stuff," Emery said. She struggled to recall anything besides Shawn's article. "There's a piece about how Derrymore exploits—"

"Ah!" Mr. LaChance cried, sweeping his white hair back with the same motion the lacrosse players were famous for.

"The bleeding-heart rag. It's audacious—colleges like that. You're an editor?"

"Sort of."

"Not sort of," he said severely. "Make it happen. And it's got to be more than a measly editor role if you really are dedicated to 'keeping your options open.' Get a position with a fancy title. Make it up if you need to. You said it's your friend's magazine, right? Easy."

• • •

As she walked to the dining hall, Emery considered Mr. LaChance's acknowledgment of his reputation as counselor to important students—important did not correlate to top-tier. In fact, she realized almost all of his assignees were legacy kids. Their parents and grandparents had attended Ivies and (surely) donated consistently and, in recent years, especially generously.

Taken in contrast with Tanya's students (who included Annie and, surprisingly, Noah), LaChance's were noticeably whiter and richer. Tanya and LaChance were known to split the strongest applicants amongst themselves, but it seemed obvious now that LaChance got the sure-thing, homerun batch and Tanya got the hardworking, earn-your-way-in kids.

Emery wanted to despise LaChance, but he was the wrong target. His quick enthusiasm for jumping aboard the *Interrogate* train proved that it was not a question of his ego versus hers. LaChance had no horse in the race—he hadn't humbled her for his own gratification. He simply called a spade a spade.

Emery found Lilah by the salad bar.

"I was literally in the middle of texting you"—Emery

snapped her phone shut and made her request with little forethought: "I know it's out of the blue, but I just wanted to ask"—she smiled endearingly—"are you still interested in a co-president?"

Lilah frowned, grasping artichoke hearts in a pair of tongs. "For *Interrogate*?"

"Uh-huh."

"But it's already out."

"But there's a second issue."

"The second one is almost done."

"Oh. Wow."

Lilah drizzled balsamic and carefully phrased her next statement: "I really appreciate the offer, but I think that would just confuse people now since it's, like, kind of set that I'm the president and Hector is VP. But it would be awesome if you wanted to write an opinion—"

Emery's sweaty hands dropped her phone and the battery skittered out. She cursed as Lilah crouched down to retrieve it.

"Thanks," Emery said. "Sorry—I just, I remembered I have a meeting with Mr. LaChance."

"Oh! Go. Don't be late. I heard he's strict."

Emery went straight to the dorms. She'd never considered that Lilah might refuse.

The Derrymore crowd didn't refuse favors. You "saw what you could do" and never said "no" outright. In the case of a dead end, they did each other the courtesy of couching it in "we can work something out" language. Lilah's rebuff had been flat-out and immediate. Even if she knew, without a doubt, that Emery's sudden interest in *Interrogate* was college-driven, a real friend would have given her the title.

• • •

As the week progressed, Emery cooled down by reminding herself of two things: Lilah's dad had lost his job, and it would look extremely tacky to shun Lilah after being denied a favor.

She swung in the opposite direction and lifted the embargoes on Hector and *Interrogate*. Suddenly, Emery was chock-full of insightful questions and demonstrative curiosity. The magazine was absolutely going to Lilah's head, but it wasn't Emery's responsibility to keep the EIC's ego in check. Why not humor her?

It was what Lilah had craved all along—a sign that Emery cared and saw her as more than a Noah-esque lackey. It also proved that Annie's assault on Emery's character had nothing to do with actual concern for Lilah and everything to do with jealousy.

Lilah was elated to (belatedly) discuss Shawn's article and talk about the new one Raymon was writing on Derrymore's opium trade origins. In her enthusiasm, Lilah offered up the third issue's theme: money. The biggest feature concerned "The Hidden Costs of Derrymore," and Lilah planned to write it herself—unless Emery wanted the assignment.

"I want to quantify all the things you need that aren't 'mandatory,' but they basically are. Like formal dresses and private college counselors, and you know way more than I do about—"

Emery declined, and asked if Shawn was writing another article. Lilah said probably, but quickly added that she would eliminate him from the issue if Emery wanted. She apologized and explained that publishing Shawn's athlete exploitation article had never struck her as an act of disloyalty, but she could see how Emery might take it that way—and she was incredibly sorry.

"He pitched it to me. I didn't ask him to contribute. But I should have asked you."

Emery shrugged. "It's whatever."

Lilah mentioned that Noah was writing an article about LGBT rights.

"Good luck with that," Emery jeered, her polite facade dropping. "Writing is not his forte."

When Emery asked absentmindedly about the cover for the next issue, Lilah blanched.

"I don't know," she said. "Hector's painting something, I think. I gave him free rein. It hasn't been finalized yet."

"Do you guys say 'I love you' to each other? Have you ... done stuff?"

Lilah wasn't used to so many questions about herself. Was it possible Emery had overheard Annie's "self-centered" critique?

"He told me he loved me for the first time over winter break. I said it back. And, well ..."

It hadn't happened yet, but Lilah *really* loved Hector. She felt ready. She wanted her first time to be with him.

"Don't rush it," Emery said. "I don't think you're ready. It's not that great and it hurts a lot."

Lilah was crestfallen, but Emery ended the conversation without further comment—as if her opinion was the final word.

• • •

Emery maintained that she was looking out for Lilah. She was merely preventing a decision that, in all likelihood, would lead to the same mild regret and serious disgust she'd experienced after her first time. There was nothing worse than pushing yourself because of expectations and timing and boyfriends who may or may not be getting fed up with waiting.

But Shawn hadn't pressured Emery. She'd pushed herself (as she always did) to hit all her marks on cue, no matter what her gut was telling her. She'd had her first kiss and beer and boyfriend right on time. She'd never doubted that she would have sex in that short window deemed correct—not too early to be considered fast, and not prudishly late—because the idea of arriving at college a virgin was abhorrent. Emery checked the box punctually and with little consideration for her own readiness or desire.

Emery tried to argue that she was protecting Lilah, but her counsel was not impartial. Truth be told, Emery was terrified that Lilah was eclipsing her in yet another category.

It wasn't fair that Lilah got to run a magazine (with Shawn taking orders from her no less) *and* experience sex while madly in love. Lilah was supposed to be Lilah, and she hadn't played her role properly in some time.

Emery felt deceived. Lilah had always seemed to admire the things Emery excelled at—Halloween costumes, social maneuvering, French dessert names—but she had been planning something bigger all along. Lilah's journey was supposed to conclude with being an ersatz Emery, but she had become someone entirely apart from her.

CHAPTER 41

The campus teemed with former tenants: five-year alumni with first-job glows, ten-year alumni with young children, fifty-year alumni stooped and nostalgic. Alumni weekend brought about an unexpected victory for Lilah. The deputy editor for *Time* was a member of the class of '80 and found himself flipping through *Interrogate* during the headmaster's welcome remarks. He told Dean Andrews that he needed to make some splashy donations in support of young journalists and he wanted to fund the magazine.

"My boss' kid didn't get into Derrymore," the deputy editor said, laughing gruffly. "This will really get my twist of the knife in. Who's the editor? I'd like to talk to him."

Dean Andrews didn't know, but promised someone would be in touch shortly.

• • •

When Lilah received an email from Dean Andrews praising *Interrogate*, her first reaction was fear. Had he gotten wind of the upcoming critical op-ed on Hug-An-Asian Day? He asked her to come by his office during her free period to discuss some "exciting news."

Lilah had never been in Dean Andrews' office before

because 1) she had never been in trouble and 2) she had never capitalized on the dean's open-door policy. Dean Andrews encouraged students to stop by and shoot the breeze, even supplying snacks to lure them in. The idea of waltzing into his office and helping herself to Mint Milanos was absurd, even though the Errols and Scotts of the world confidently and unhesitatingly did so. Some people can belong Anywhere. They walk into a room and fit. They're good at starting new schools and moving to new cities. Lilah was not such a person.

Dean Andrews did not recognize her right away and Lilah introduced herself awkwardly from the doorway, pointing to the copy of *Interrogate* that was being used as a coaster for a Roosevelt coffee cup.

After commending her intrepid spirit and willingness to ask hard questions, he told her about the outside funding. It wouldn't change the operation of the magazine in any way, but it was an incredible honor. And compliment.

"It's not charity," he clarified.

Then he rattled off a list of suggestions for future stories: the first Black student to attend Derrymore, the first class to accept women ('87), generous need-blind scholarships, the solar panel installation Derrymore was preparing to unveil.

"You can have these"—he handed over his notes—"for reference."

Lilah wondered if this was an order, threat, or something else.

"It would also be great if you could mention—"

He listed a bevy of multicultural initiatives from the past

year that had been photographed professionally and posted on the Derrymore website.

"And another thing I've been meaning to do," Dean Andrews continued, "I'll give you a nod at Chapel and tell everyone to get involved. I'm sure there are plenty of students who would love to join."

Lilah had asked months ago for this specific favor. Was he acknowledging that he'd ignored her email? Was he pretending he never saw it?

"Actually, would you mind making that announcement at the beginning of next semester? We just finalized the second issue and it's a lame duck period. It would be pretty … useless to make the announcement now."

Dean Andrews' eyes narrowed the slightest bit. Lilah kept a neutral smile on her face, her heart pounding from the last-minute decision to get her tiny jab in.

"Of course." He cleared his throat. "Of course. We wouldn't want enthusiasm to flag by the time you start back up in the fall."

• • •

Shawn had his position on the athletic foundation. Scott had somehow been voted the Honor Representative of their year. Errol was elected to the only student position on the Derrymore board. Even Candace had *Class Dress* to distinguish herself. How had Emery come up empty-handed?

Every time she saw Candace wearing Scott's sweatshirt it reminded her that she had nothing—not a boyfriend, not a sinecure. If you had asked Emery over Christmas break whether she considered herself a successful Derrymorian, she wouldn't have hesitated to answer yes. Little had changed since then, but her inferiority had been exposed.

Potential was all she had, but she had treated it as if it were a sure thing. She was in the midst of a flirtation, the ARC vote hadn't been cast, *Interrogate* was just a silly project—each of those things had panned out very differently than Emery had anticipated. She promised herself that she wouldn't be so stupid in the future and wished she had internalized Coach Norton's catchphrase: *It's not a break until you hold.*

CHAPTER 42

Shortly after Hector graduated, Lilah broke up with him. She found out that, despite his claiming otherwise, he had dated one of the Japanese exchange students. A girl named Natsu tagged him in an album called **~*pHoToS fRoM mY oLd CaMeRa**~* the last week of May. The caption read *American boyfriend XD*.

Hector said it didn't count as a relationship because they never even kissed. He said "boyfriend" was a clumsy translation for a Japanese word that meant someone who was more than a friend but not something serious, more like a mutual crush. He had asked Natsu out on her last day at Derrymore and they'd emailed for several months. That was all. Lilah believed him, and she might have forgiven him if the quasi-girlfriend had been from Berlin or Cape Town—but she knew the rumors about his dating record, and she knew what Emery thought of him.

• • •

Emery was indignant but unsurprised when Ian was admitted off the waitlist to Berkeley. She knew what his secret weapon was: the essay-for-hire.

Ian used the same essay tutor his older brother had:

George, a Stanford graduate and Groton alumnus. Mr. Hooper arranged for George to spend the summer in their guest house and tutor Emery exclusively.

"He's going to help with your Penn application, right?" Mr. Hooper asked.

"Dad," Emery whined. "Don't start this again."

"Tell him you want to apply early decision. Let's get this college business over and done with."

"Pressuring me is not gonna change my mind."

"Do you remember my promise? I'm a man of my word."

"I know, Dad. I know."

"And I'll even sweeten the deal—you can bring Lilah."

Mr. Hooper promised Emery a trip to anywhere in the world if she applied early decision—full commitment, no reneging, no entertaining other options—to his alma mater. She didn't even have to get accepted. As long as she took a leap of faith, he was ready to go to Mykonos or the Seychelles—even Las Vegas.

• • •

Emery's mother was on the phone nearly every day with the consultant she had hired. Emery thought Hedley was a hack and told her mother so. After he advised her to close her eyes and visualize herself at her dream school for ten minutes every day ("You're trotting down Locust Walk—there's a crisp breeze coming off the Schuylkill"), Emery refused to join the calls. At a later date, Mrs. Hooper passed on Hedley's advice to buy and wear college merchandise as a way to increase her chances of admission. Emery's eyes met her dad's and they tacitly agreed to let Mom *believe*. Hedley billed the Hoopers by the hour.

Mrs. Hooper relied heavily on Hedley to calm her nerves and was excited to add George to her support contingent.

• • •

George had dinner with the Hoopers on his first night and, after their initial shock at his being Black, won them over with alacrity. He complimented Mrs. Hooper's wallpaper and her chicken paillard. He agreed heartily with Mr. Hooper's take on David Brooks ("the only columnist worth a damn") and expressed admiration for the Lego model of Fallingwater in the mud room ("a Father's Day gift from my Emmy").

"Glad to have you, George," Mr. Hooper said, finishing his after-dinner decaf.

"Please let us know if you need anything," Mrs. Hooper said. "We're so appreciative that you're working with Emery. We've heard such great things about the results you've produced."

Emery hoped George didn't see her father's eyebrow go up.

George said goodnight and crossed the backyard to the guest house.

"The Shepards have made hefty donations for the past decade," Mr. Hooper said. "George seems like a good fellow, but I wouldn't give him all the credit."

Mrs. Hooper made a thoughtful noise. Emery bit her tongue.

"Good fellow," Mr. Hooper repeated. "Couldn't even tell."

"Tell what, Dad?" Emery asked sarcastically.

"I keep forgetting Noah's light in the loafers too. I never would have guessed. Your mother said it was obvious, but—"

"George seems like such a gentleman," Mrs. Hooper said. "That bone structure is so *regal*."

Mr. Hooper had offered an exorbitant rate (more than triple what the Shepards had paid for Ian and Jon combined) to ensure Emery would be his one and only client. George had accepted.

• • •

Emery watched George pump up the tires on a beach cruiser. They were biking to Millie's as a bonding exercise. He needed to get to know her in order to make her essay really sing. Over ceviche and lobster quesadillas, George explained that the strength of a Common App essay came from its un-replicability. Emery told him she wanted to write about being adopted, and how she felt comfortable in her parents' world for the most part but, at times, terribly outside of it. She was taken aback at his unenthused response.

Emery wanted praise for her profound honesty and self-awareness. Three years ago, she wouldn't have considered herself an outsider of any sort, but Shawn and Lilah had demonstrated how the sharp edges of outsiderdom could be weaponized.

"It could work," George said tepidly. "But say there are ten thousand applicants and fifty of those essays are about being adopted. How is yours different from the other forty-nine?"

Emery didn't have an answer. When she showed him her first draft, George said a few lukewarm things then told her that it covered too much ground.

"What if we focused on your adoption party in Taiwan?" he said. "I love that visual and it feels very full circle-y. But I need you to dig deeper and find something with more substance. Maybe something vulnerable that can be spun into 'growth'—ideally something *seemingly* unflattering."

Emery continued writing and George continued pooh-poohing. Her ideas were contrived and her voice was clichéd. Making it about her birth mom's tragic sacrifice was melodramatic (and speculative). She relied too much on adoption tropes and tugging on heartstrings.

"Don't write a 'my dog got put down' essay," George explained. "It reveals that the *worst* thing you've ever gone through is imagining someone else's pain. If that's true, you don't want to admit that."

It went on like this for weeks.

• • •

Near the end of June, Emery called Lilah. They had been texting sporadically for weeks (mostly about where their classmates were applying) but hadn't spoken for almost a month.

"Hi!" Lilah answered. "Are you busy? Is it an okay time to talk? How's Nantucket?"

Even when Emery called her, Lilah always worried that she was encroaching. Emery said her essay was turning out to be much trickier than she'd anticipated. June wasn't going to happen, but maybe Lilah could visit in July. Lilah said no pressure, no rush—she was busy helping her dad look for jobs.

"I didn't get ARC president," Emery said. "I don't know if I mentioned that before."

She managed to sound casual but the loss was stirring panic beneath the surface. Lilah expressed outrage and said Ginny was undeserving and underformers were stupid. Emery listened while silently accusing Lilah of hoarding *Interrogate* titles.

"Hector and I broke up," Lilah said, reciprocating with a bit of her own misery. For girls, it's always easiest to share bad news in a call-and-response format.

Lilah explained the circumstances with the Japanese exchange student and Emery didn't rub it in. She didn't say *I told you so* or anything else about Hector's proclivities.

Emery asked if Lilah was writing her college essay on *Interrogate*. Lilah said she was not.

CHAPTER 43

When her parents said it was time to go, Emery always asked which car they were taking. Lilah thought about that question each time she asked to borrow The Car.

Lilah's family had one vehicle. She had one winter coat. At least she had three nice dresses.

She was surprised that her mom said yes and granted her permission to pick up Annie. Medical school had become such an inflammatory subject that college became an off-limits topic during dinner. Lilah had taken to spending her summer break on the sweltering back deck to avoid her mother's hurt glances and, when these failed to elicit a reaction, withering glares.

The comment that wreaked havoc was: *I'll go to med school if all else fails.* Lilah's mom couldn't wrap her head around Lilah's logic—who would turn down dirt-cheap tuition and guaranteed medical school admission to be the poorest person at an overpriced, non–Ivy League?

"I'm already that at Derrymore," Lilah had said.

The silent treatment lasted for four days.

Lilah was astonished the car wasn't used as a bargaining chip until she remembered that her mom lived to put Annie's mom in her place. A passive-aggressive comment years ago about Lilah "probably not get into Derrymore" had kept the flame of pettiness burning.

While a six-year-old Volvo might not sound impressive, cars were a constant competition between families. Mrs. Chang loved referring to Annie's mom's Kia as "a great value." No one knew that Mr. Chang had lost his job.

As soon as she climbed into the passenger seat, Annie asked what colleges Lilah was applying to. Lilah named a few but said she was trying to keep her list short because application fees could be up to $75 each.

Annie didn't react to the fee comment and Lilah wished she hadn't said it.

"How about you?" Lilah asked.

"With all due respect," Annie said, "I'm not telling anyone. For me, it's a private matter and I'm not comfortable sharing."

Lilah managed to keep her eyes on the road despite the insult. *For me*—as if Lilah had displayed indiscretion by answering the question asked of her.

"When are you going to Nantucket?" Annie asked, reaching down to bring her seat forward.

"Soon. George is—Emery's essay guy is living in their guest house and she said I can come after he leaves."

Annie shifted her weight to drag the chair forward and it clicked into place loudly. On the one occasion Emery had sat in the passenger seat, she'd reached to the right side of the chair looking for an electric switch. When Lilah instructed her to feel for the metal bar beneath the seat, Emery lifted the lever with too much force and the chair shot back dramatically. Her screech had made Mrs. Chang and Lilah laugh.

"That's rude to keep you waiting," Annie said.

"She never promised anything."

"And that makes it okay?"

Lilah didn't answer.

For the second time in the brief conversation, Lilah wished she hadn't divulged because Annie played her cards close to her chest while nosing into Lilah's business. She was thinking about how caginess came so naturally to her friends when Annie suddenly said, "I was really mad when you abandoned us. You really hurt Jenny and Cassie."

"I didn't abandon you," Lilah protested.

"You chose Emery over us. Twice." Annie's voice was small and she was looking straight ahead as she spoke. "We felt like shit when you made it so obvious we were your second choice. But it's okay."

• • •

The bulk of Emery's summer reading consisted of message boards where students (and sometimes parents) posted the essays and scores that had gotten them into college. Emery studied the essays and compared their stats to hers.

"I don't get why anyone would share this voluntarily," Emery said.

"Who knows," George said. "To help other people— unfathomable as it sounds."

"It's to brag."

George was pestering Emery about where she was applying.

"Penn State," she said.

George's eyes lit up for a nanosecond before darkening.

"Did my dad tell you to push Penn?"

"Yes," George said. "He offered me a huge bonus if I can get you to apply early."

"I knew it. You're just—"

"What's wrong with Penn?"

Emery twisted her mouth. "I don't want to be predictable."

"So college is about throwing people off? You want to nonplus them?"

"It's not about that. My sense of self is not Penn. Everyone thinks my life is gonna go in a straight line"—her flattened palm zipped through the air—"and it is. It has been."

"You don't want to be a passenger in your own life."

George said it not with sympathy, or even much under-standing, but with such accuracy that Emery needed to pause so her voice didn't break when she spoke next.

"You'll get the bonus no matter what," she said. "Dad always pretends like he's not going to give you what you want, but he does in the end."

• • •

The last Penn reunion Emery had attended was Mr. Hooper's 30th. She was ten, hated wearing a name tag, and was excruci-atingly bored. Nothing bad happened. There were no incidents or gaffes. No one mistook her for a Chinese family's kid. None of Mr. Hooper's old friends talked to her like she couldn't speak English. In fact, they accepted her into their little club with startling alacrity. They took for granted that she would seek higher education at the Philadelphia institution.

"We have photos of Emery in a Penn onesie the week we brought her home," Mr. Hooper said to his college buddies. "And every subsequent year of her life, come to think of it.

This is the first time she's insisted that it stifled her 'self-expression.'"

Mr. Hooper's air quotes made his friends laugh as he gestured to the MTV T-shirt Emery believed was the height of fashion. He ruffled her hair and she pulled away from him, surly and cute at the same time.

"Dad," she whined, leaning her forehead into his lower back.

"Girls go through a rebellious phase," one of Mr. Hooper's friends advised. "Better earlier than later, I say. My Katie— twenty-two now—wouldn't come to a reunion after she turned twelve."

"Heartbreakers," another chimed in.

"Is that so?" Mr. Hooper asked, struck.

"Ah," Katie's dad said, "just be patient. When it's time to apply, mark my words, she'll come running: 'Do you know anyone who can write me a letter?' Katie wanted nothing to do with Penn for the longest time, but she ended up applying early."

"She'll come around," someone added. "They always do."

"And when Katie got in—happiest day of her life. Of all our lives! Now she's at McKinsey."

The men chortled and Emery gave them the stink eye from behind her dad.

"Okay fine," Mr. Hooper said sportingly. He picked Emery up and hugged her to him. She was almost too tall for him to do this anymore. "You've suffered enough. Are you ready for sundaes?"

Emery's demeanor changed instantly. While she gorged on butterscotch at Franklin Fountain, she momentarily forgot the comments about the typicality of her rebellion and her fated change of heart. Her ten-year-old mind was distracted by Reese's pieces and maraschino cherries, but the rankling conversation lodged in her subconscious. Her entire life was not only predictable, but inevitable.

CHAPTER 44

Emery rewrote. George critiqued. They'd start to get some-where, but then he'd repeat requests for more vulnerability, more rawness.

George advised: Don't say "the tennis coach," use Coach Norton's name to make it feel more personal. Don't say "I felt like an outsider," write that your journal was overflowing with feelings of unworthiness.

He kept asking her to be more introspective, but what else was there to mine? Every childhood trauma had been consid-ered: the mean boy who said the Hoopers would exchange her for an African baby, the dreams she had about waking up white and resembling her parents, the time a classmate's mom accused her of carrying a counterfeit Coach wristlet.

"So what, though?" George said. "You suffered. We all have. What is this essay *about*?"

Emery's question to the Princeton tour guide had come back to haunt her. But it was a necessary reality check. Of course she had more to offer than a dime-a-dozen sob story.

Upon reading her fourth draft, George said, "*Ooh*. This is different. How come you never mentioned this before?"

• • •

In August, a toast. George raised his Arnold Palmer and declared the essay finished. Emery yelped and hugged him.

"Are you sure?" she asked.

George placed his hand on top of the essay. "Don't tinker with it anymore. This could only have been written by you. It's brimming with voice and it makes the reader feel like he knows you. It's perfect."

"It's not too braggy?"

"Hey—you went through a lot to get there. You deserve to tell it the way it happened. *Don't mess with it.*"

"I can't believe it's done." Emery exhaled. "You're sure it doesn't sound like … someone else?"

"Not at all. This captures you to a T. Don't overthink it."

"I'm so ready to submit it."

"That's because you have a better sense of what you want now. And a better sense of who you are."

Emery choked on an ice cube.

CHAPTER 45

When Emery returned to campus for her final preseason, it was a nasty shock to encounter a co-captain. True, Lilah consistently beat her in straight sets, but the idea that their leadership abilities were equal was unthinkable. Lilah still couldn't undress in front of other girls without using the sports-bra-over-regular-bra method. How would she ever haze freshmen and captain effectively? Coach Norton announced they would split the honor and Emery employed a hug to hide the bafflement on her face. There was no appeals system.

As the co-captains walked back to the senior dorm, Lilah babbled about how unexpected it was, how flattered she was.

"You deserve it," Emery said flatly.

"We should celebrate!" Lilah said.

They ordered pizza and Lilah insisted on paying for half with her summer job money. (She had tutored middle schoolers for the SSAT.)

"Are you still working with George?" Lilah asked, blotting her slice.

"No," Emery said. "It's weird because we spent the whole summer together, but we'll probably never talk again. We were so close, then, poof, nothing."

"Oh, so your essay is done?" Lilah asked carefully. "Do you mind if I ask what you wrote about?"

Emery launched into a prepared statement: "I finished it already, otherwise I'd show you. I just don't want to get confused about editing it more, you know? Too many cooks."

"I'm sure it's great."

"I wrote about that summer in Taiwan and how it was, like, really formative for me. And being adopted."

"That's awesome. I'm sure it's amazing."

"Thanks. What's yours about?"

"You can read it—if you want."

The essay opened with Lilah's dad losing his job. It was about the anger she felt at her parents for fooling her into believing their life was stable. It was about how she was torn between making practical decisions and idealistic ones. It was about how uncertainty and fear could make people play it safe. It was about how Lilah had decided not to let fear dictate her choices or cow her into ready-made solutions. It was about how she defined "worst-case scenario" as knowingly and willfully making decisions that would make her unhappy.

"It's kind of … heavy," Emery said. "I thought we were supposed to tell a story?"

"You think it's too much of a screed?"

"A what?"

"Like a tirade. That's what Annie said."

Emery blinked several times. "You showed Annie your essay?"

"We hung out a little bit. In the summer."

Emery folded her paper plate into a small triangle. "I really don't know. I just did what George told me to do. But I think yours is good? It's just different from mine."

"Yeah. Thanks. I'll keep that in mind while I'm revising."

Emery placed the essay face down on Lilah's desk and there was an unfamiliar sensation of not having anything to say to one another.

They never addressed the fact that Lilah had never made it to Nantucket. There were no mentions of future trips or promises that next summer would make up for last.

• • •

Proprium humani ingenii est odisse quem laeseris. Mr. Arthur had assigned Tacitus for fall semester.

"It's human nature to hate those whom you have harmed," Raymon translated.

"But what does it *mean*?" Mr. Arthur urged.

"When you fuck up," Errol said, "you hate the person who reminds you of your guilt."

"Language," Mr. Arthur growled. "Is it true? Do we really do this? Is Tacitus extrapolating to all of mankind unfairly? What about womankind?"

Emery avoided joining the discussion and counted down the minutes until class was over.

The entire Derrymore campus was eagerly anticipating the third issue of *Interrogate*. Students quoted Shawn's last article as if he were a famous journalist.

"There's an article about porn in this issue," Emery over-heard one of the editors say, confirming that Noah had managed to turn his article in on time.

Each time the magazine came up, which increased stead-ily as the release date approached, Emery ground her teeth.

She always wondered how it would feel to be a songwriter and hear an entire stadium sing along to lyrics you wrote in private. Lilah was getting to experience that.

When the third issue finally arrived, the cover stunned Emery. It was a Hector original riffing on *The Scream* (a painting that every Derrymorian studied in Foundations of Art). Instead of a fence behind the figure, it was a low retaining wall, like the ones all over Derrymore's campus. Instead of orange and blue, everything was brick and ivy colored. And instead of a ghostlike figure with a black cloak, there was a grotesquely rendered girl wearing a cable-knit sweater. A periwinkle, cable-knit sweater.

THE MONEY ISSUE was emblazoned in a gaudy typeface. Lilah had put her best friend on the cover. It was an accusation and a parody—the meanest kind of satire.

Riley and Candace congratulated and complimented Emery. They didn't get the joke.

• • •

Annie burst into Lilah's room at the beginning of study hall. Cassie and Jenny followed behind, both carrying issues of the magazine.

"We've been looking for you," Annie said. "I can't believe you did that."

Lilah was eating microwavable rice and pickled radishes in front of her computer. "Huh?" She wiped her mouth with a Kleenex.

"Can you sign this for me?" Annie said. "I want to frame it."

"What are you talking about?"

Annie held up her copy of *Interrogate* and thumped the cover. "There I was thinking that you worshipped her, but you were just waiting to strike."

Lilah grabbed the issue from Annie's grasp and scrutinized the cover. "No—that's not it at all. It's not *her*. It's just—"

"Who else could it be?"

"It's an archetypal Derrymore girl. Just an anonymous rich kid."

Cassie and Jenny exchanged glances.

"What?" Lilah demanded. "You guys don't think so?"

"It's her sweater," Jenny said. "Isn't it?"

"I thought you were finally taking a stand," Annie said.

"The girl's not even Asian," Lilah said, examining the figure. "Does everyone think it's ... her?"

Hector had asked if he should paint the hair blonde—to be safe—but Lilah had insisted on leaving it dark. The identity of the figure was ambiguous.

Even without knowing that Emery had registered the removal (and return) of the periwinkle sweater, the quadruplets were scared for Lilah.

• • •

Emery flipped through *Interrogate* until she found what she was looking for: *by Noah Humbird*. He hadn't found time to visit her in Nantucket, but he had found time to write a self-pitying personal essay about his unceremonious outing.

With all the "what I realize now" and "looking back on my former self" statements, it was obvious that this tacky tell-all was also Noah's college essay. After years of asking Emery to edit his papers, he'd turned to Lilah for the most important one of all.

• • •

Her application was finalized. Mr. LaChance approved a few last-minute changes to the essay and gave her the green light. Emery pushed submit.

A toneless text to her parents announced that everything was in, then the device was powered down. A quick scroll through the artist list to find Michael Bublé, volume up on "I've Got the World on a String." Celebratory pomegranate juice and a muttered curse when crimson was dribbled onto ivory sweats.

Emery's stomach was turning. She told herself it was relief.

Binding Decision.

The words were bloated.

• • •

"Emery?" Lilah knocked a second time. "Em, it's me. I'm coming in. I need my stain remover."

They hadn't spoken since the issue came out and Lilah had decided to play dumb. There was no need to apologize—she had done nothing wrong. She'd stand by the same argument she'd presented to the quadruplets: it was simply a paradigmatic Derrymore girl. If Emery believed the cover depicted her, then she *was* self-centered.

Lilah swallowed dryly, trying to imagine herself saying the words out loud.

"Em?"

Lilah spotted her stain remover on the nightstand. As she was reaching for it, something in the printer caught her eye—Emery's college essay.

As much as their friendship had evolved, Lilah could never completely shake her fascination. It overrode good sense and she took the pages out of the printer. Baffled, she re-read the first paragraph three times.

It was about being omitted from the Hug-An-Asian list and the isolation of being adopted—and how it had driven her to start a magazine.

Lilah stopped to listen for footsteps then continued, her heart pounding.

I never thought of myself as an activist until ...

Lilah read at a breakneck pace.

When I decided to put myself on the cover ...

She didn't realize she was holding her breath.

I founded *Interrogate* to explore the hurt and curious pieces of myself—

The door opened.

"What the fuck?" Emery snatched the essay out of Lilah's hands. "What are you doing?"

Lilah stuttered, "Stain remover."

"Why were you snooping?"

"I didn't mean to."

"Please get out. I'm late for class."

Emery locked her door emphatically.

• • •

Lilah couldn't sit still so she knocked on Cassie's door. When there was no answer, she tried Jenny's. All she wanted was a distraction, not to talk about it. If she spoke to Annie, everything would come tumbling out, but she was caught standing paralyzed outside of Annie's door.

"Who's there?" Annie barked and wrenched the door open. "What are you doing?"

Lilah stepped inside and closed the door behind her. She wrung her hands and remained frozen in one spot.

"What's wrong?" Annie said. "You're acting weird."

Can you keep a secret? I have to tell you something. Will you promise to—none of these intros worked, so Lilah just word-vomited it. Annie's face was taut with disbelief and indignation.

"Do you think she pretended to be you?" Annie asked. "On her whole application?"

"I can't remember everything she wrote, but she talked about being adopted so I don't think so."

"Did she say she was a co-president? Or *the* president?"

"The president. By herself."

Annie made an incredulous noise. "She's shameless."

"She also copied some, like, random things from my life."

"Like what? You should write this down before you forget."

Lilah ignored the pen and paper Annie held out to her.

"It was something about a Wu Lou necklace and my rooster collection and listening to classical music when she studies."

Annie made a few notes on the pad.

"You need to report her for plagiarism."

"But it's not plagiarism. She wrote it."

"Then for lying. It's unbecoming!"

Lilah didn't answer.

"You should at least pretend like you're going to report her—just to scare her," Annie said. "She's rich and she has a golden ticket to Penn. Why does she get to take anything she wants?"

Lilah's breath quickened at the suggestion.

"I don't think I should."

"Why are you so scared of her?"

"I'm not."

"She used your magazine and your *rooster collection*. What will it take to see that you're not actually friends?"

Lilah pulled her sleeves down over her hands.

"She told me her essay was about how our summer in Taiwan changed her life. I really believed her."

One thing Lilah didn't mention was how Emery's essay concluded by saying that she'd put herself on the cover of *Interrogate* as a self-aware acknowledgment of her complicated relationship with money.

CHAPTER 46

After classes, Emery discovered a bouquet of ranunculus waiting outside of her door. She drew up a list of who they could be from: Shawn, Noah, Lilah—each one owed her an apology, but Lilah most. The *Interrogate* cover was the biggest betrayal, and the fact that it had come after all the blathering about blacklisting Shawn from the magazine made it even more duplicitous.

She picked up the glass vase and shut the door quickly, but quietly, behind her. The ranunculus were a sickly peach color that looked as if it wanted to be pink, but had been bullied during a critical period of growth. A small envelope was tucked among the blooms. Emery plucked it delicately from the bouquet and unsealed it.

There were so many letters in her life. The letter from the adoption agency formally signing her over to her parents (framed in her dad's study). The acceptance letter from Derrymore. The open letter announcing Mrs. Peiffer's termination. The Raymon homecoming letter. Thomas' unopened letter. Letters bore news. They told you where you were in your life.

The small notecard was thick and the florist's handwriting was loopy:

Dear Emmy—Your mother and I are so proud of you. I can always count on you to make the right (and EARLY) decision. Start thinking about your dream vacation and tell Lilah to renew her passport. All our love, Dad and Mom

There was never any decision. Choice was the one luxury Emery was not accorded. Binding decision didn't just apply to her Penn application—it was the terms of her whole life.

The front door of the dormitory banged open and the halls filled with sounds of blissful teenage self-centeredness.

The thought of enduring practice was unthinkable—and facing Lilah, even worse. Emery locked the door, climbed up into her lofted bed, and pulled the duvet over her head. She had planned to spend this time strategizing and coming up with something actionable that would embody her dad's motto regarding mistakes (*Get out in front of it*), but she fell asleep.

When she awoke, the dining hall had stopped serving dinner. All of her stress exhaustion had been wasted on the nap and she wished she had sleeping pills to silence her conscience. She felt it in her stomach. It wasn't like muscle soreness, which ached. It was closer to tendonitis—unexpected twinges and sharp pains that forced her to confront that something was wrong. When Emery had gone to the trainer to get her wrist taped up, he said her tendonitis wouldn't go away unless she fundamentally changed how she struck the ball—if she continued playing the same way, the pain would only intensify.

Emery turned on a small desk lamp and sifted through her bottom desk drawer until she found what she was looking for. The stapled-together pieces of colored paper looked like something from kindergarten rather than two years ago. Emery had accumulated many yearbook-style mementos and she always left them on the kitchen counter so her mother could read the notes her peers left, see how well-liked Emery had been, and then file them away in the Hoopers' meticulously organized keepsake collection. But she had never shared the Taiwan one with her mother. Emery kept it to herself and hadn't looked at it since the day it was signed. She flipped through the entries while sipping an Odwalla smoothie.

I'd wish you good luck, but I know you are going to be successful …

Thank you for being so nice to me! I was so intimidated when I first met you …

You made this class so fun. I never thought I'd enjoy summer school!

The last note was from Thomas. Beneath Blossom's bitchy message he had written:

The only reason someone wouldn't like you is that they don't know you. You're one of the smartest funniest people I've ever met and I'm going to miss you. Thanks for being my friend even though I'm not as cool as you. I have a feeling we'll be friends for life.

She had such an urge to call him, but she had never replied to his letter.

Thomas would tell her to apologize. He would tell her to confess.

Emery tucked the makeshift yearbook inside of her unread copy of *Interrogate*, threw it in the trashcan, and dumped her Mango Tango on top of it.

• • •

Lilah tossed and turned all night. When her alarm went off, it felt like she had barely slept. Annie was on her case at breakfast:

"If you really believe in *Interrogate*'s mission, you'll turn her in. Isn't the entire point truth and justice and 'sunshine is the best disinfectant'?"

Lilah's Cap'n Crunch was becoming mush. She pushed the bowl away and hitched up her ill-fitting American Eagle jeans from the belt loop on her right hip.

"If you let her get away with it then she wins," Annie said. "As always. She gets credit for all your hard work and you *continue* to let her walk all over you."

"She'll know it was me."

Lilah bit a hangnail off her index finger.

"That didn't stop you from putting her on the cover. Put her in her place for real this time." Annie downed eight ounces of orange juice. "The way I see it, you have a once-in-a-lifetime opportunity. People like Emery always get away with murder. But you can show all these rich kids that they can't just float the rules—"

"Flout," Lilah corrected.

"Whatever. Don't be the weak Asian who lets everyone cheat off her. People like you fuck up the curve."

Annie's voice had risen significantly and Lilah *shhh*-ed her. Her finger was still to her lips when she noticed Riley wearing Emery's denim dress, which was at least one size too small. Lilah hooked her finger through the belt loop again, but when she lifted, it ripped off and she slammed her hand against the sharp edge of the table.

• • •

The note was a little crumpled, but still legible. Lilah had packed and brought it to school every year—it had moved on and off campus as many times as she had—for no specific reason. She never revisited the hateful invitation, but she always knew where it was. Noah's neat cursive stared up at Lilah as she tucked the note into a powder blue folder she'd received at a UNC information session. She'd only bring it out if Dean Andrews seemed skeptical of her claims. It wasn't blackmail. It was proof of Emery's character.

The door was open, but the dean wasn't in his mahogany-paneled office when Lilah peeked in. It was furnished just like the golf clubhouse at the Hoopers' country club: tufted leather chairs, oil paintings of hills, and an antique globe. Lilah didn't think her stomach could feel queasier than it had at breakfast, but it knotted into cramps that were worse than her most painful periods. The past twenty-four hours had been spent agonizing, and now that she finally resolved to pull the trigger, he wasn't there.

The rotunda was empty and the only sound was her own jagged breathing as she stood in the doorway. Maybe it was better the dean wasn't in. She could write him an email and attach an image of the note. *You should always leave a paper trail*—she had heard that somewhere. She could also email the admissions people at Penn and tell them that Emery was a fraud. George! That was the essay guy's name—maybe he could be coaxed into sharing how much of Emery's essay was actually *his* handiwork. There was so much to do—

Suddenly, the dark paneling parted and Dean Andrews appeared wiping his hands. Lilah jumped.

"Hi, there," he said. "Didn't mean to startle you."

Lilah's arms had shot up protectively and she was stuck in a frightened stance.

"Private bathroom. One of the perks of being dean. How can I help you?"

It was clear that he didn't recognize her, despite their previous meetings and the fact that Lilah was president of the only Derrymore publication sponsored by a media titan.

"I have to tell you something," she said shakily.

"Oh?" His expression darkened. "The door, please. Have a seat."

It was all part of the job.

• • •

Trembling made it impossible for Lilah to go through the motions of studying. Her classical music playlist was on repeat but she wouldn't have been able to tell you if she was listening to Vivaldi or 3OH!3.

Dean Andrews had taken copious notes and asked her to repeat several parts of the story. He had appeared concerned but calm, and betrayed nothing in his reaction for the entire twenty-five-minute interview. He had neither validated nor dismissed her, but his sangfroid shook Lilah's certainty that it was an open-and-shut case. She thought she deserved at least one noise of disgust or a disappointed head shake or a muttered *Unbelievable*, but the most expression he exhibited was a slight frown when she described her rooster collection— and that could've been confusion.

Even though Dean Andrews was treating the matter with the utmost seriousness (and was already making a call as she left his office), Lilah didn't feel reassured. The way he had asked, "Emery never held a role of any sort on your magazine? Not even as an unofficial advisor?" made her wonder if he thought she was lying. There was a world in which this would backfire spectacularly and end up with Lilah getting in trouble.

The thought made her sweat even though her room was cool. The best way to protect herself—and ensure Emery felt the cold sting of justice—was to make sure her story was airtight. There had been no natural opening to show Dean Andrews the homecoming note so it had stayed in her folder, but she'd present it at the next opportunity along with a time-line of *Interrogate*.

Lilah wiped sweat off her upper lip with her sleeve. Not *her* sleeve—the burgundy faux-fur-lined Marc by Marc Jacobs hoodie belonged to Emery. Lilah had "borrowed" it for weeks (Emery preferred the black one) and had never been asked to return it. But it wasn't generosity that allowed her to keep it. Emery was simply unable to keep track of her earthly possessions because the pace at which her wardrobe expanded exceeded her ability to make use of it.

Lilah unzipped the hoodie and placed it on her bed. Every piece of clothing, every bag and belt and scarf that Emery had pawned off on Lilah was extracted from closet and dresser. The pile that accumulated was staggering: Helly Hansen rain jacket, Nantucket long sleeve, abused London Sole flats, St. Ives face scrub, silky Joie blouse, low-rise Hudson jeans, a $40 T-shirt from a Coldplay concert, Hunter rainboots (with fleecy socks), BareMinerals complexion kit, Lancôme Juicy Tube gloss, chestnut-colored riding boots, tub of cellulite firming cream, and a braided hair headband that was two shades off of Lilah's hair color.

Even though Lilah's mom had told her never to accept anything, she couldn't stop Emery from abandoning things in her room. Yet for everything Emery had divested, she had taken freely and greedily from Lilah. It wasn't just Lilah's time (the hours spent color-coding Emery's closet) or her attention (the endless discussions about *everyone else's* ego problems), Emery had stayed at the Changs' home and never reciprocated. She'd dangled Nantucket in front of Lilah for years but never invited her and, through it all, managed to make Lilah feel indebted despite the fact that Emery was the Taker all along.

So what if Lilah had a few hand-me-downs? Why did it matter if Emery had given her a pair of calfskin gloves and sweatpants from Fred Segal? It mattered because Lilah had never intended to amass such a collection, and when she looked at it head on, she couldn't deny how much it resembled a bribe. It would align perfectly with rich people behavior to lay bribe groundwork with no particular goal in mind, anticipating that it would pay off one day. It cost Emery nothing to unload a pair of Nike Frees or Ray-Bans and rest easy knowing that, should the need ever arise, she could call in all these debts. It was the Back Pocket Insurance Policy that Derrymore families relied on so heavily. They had backup plans layered on top of safeguards padded with shortcuts. The key was to unobtrusively collect ammunition, give no indication that you were quietly prepping for war, and then, when everything imploded, your forces were already positioned to attack.

Emery's deposits in the friendship bank were casual and inconspicuous, but the withdrawal would be seismic and final—this was the unspoken contract between un-equals. Among equals, the terms were stated clearly and notarized. Derrymore kids didn't flinch at signing legal agreements with their parents, promising to abstain from alcohol and drugs on boarding school property. Social embarrassment could be warded off with apotropaic attorneys and formal contracts.

Once she returned everything, Lilah would free herself from obligation. No borrowed bandeau or Bean boots could obfuscate the truth that Emery was a bully and a liar. She said goodbye to her treasures.

• • •

Annie refused to do it, but Cassie and Jenny were talked into doing Lilah's dirty work before dinner. From an upstairs window, they watched Emery leave the dormitory and walk in the direction of Dean Andrews' office.

"But she could just be going toward the dining hall," Jenny said.

"No, her walk was anxious," Annie said. "I'd bet anything she was called into his office. It's happening. She'll be out of here tonight."

"Take everything now," Lilah ordered, making sure the burgundy hoodie was sitting at the top of the pile, "before she gets back."

Cassie and Jenny hauled two large Century 21 bags filled with Emery's things and placed them outside of her room.

"Mission accomplished," Cassie reported back.

"I can't believe she gave you all of that," Jenny said.

"She didn't really," Lilah said. "It was just borrowed stuff, but I never asked for it. Are you ready, Annie?"

Annie nodded and held up her laptop, which showed a blank document. It was her idea to make a list of Emery's crimes: "If you have evidence, you can't lose. Prove that the essay is just one single incident in a long history of unbecoming behavior, and they'll have no choice but to expel her."

It would be surprising if Emery was expelled outright. In most cases involving the discipline of high-profile students, Derrymore let them withdraw so their permanent records remained unmarred. Either way, it'd be announced at the end of Chapel tomorrow and Emery would be out of her life.

Lilah scrolled through text messages searching for anything incriminating Emery had ever written. (She wouldn't let Jenny or Cassie help her sift through emails because there were mean jokes at their expense.) Five minutes went by without anything to record.

"Still nothing?" Annie complained.

"How about this: I told Scott that sweet angel went to visit Ian last weekend"—Cassie and Jenny gasped—"but 'sweet angel' is Emery's code for 'ugly bitch,' which is her codename for Candace."

Annie squinched her nose. "So Emery told Scott that Candace is cheating on him? That's not bullying. That's just backstabbing. It's not illegal to be two-faced."

Lilah searched for another minute.

"Ugh. She always types 'love' when she means 'hate.' It's almost like she was preparing for an audit."

After exhausting the text messages and getting through most of the emails, there wasn't anything juicy enough to warrant recording.

"You don't need it," Annie said. "The homecoming note is just icing on the cake anyway. The essay thing is enough to get her kicked out. Can we go get dinner?"

Over chicken pot pie, the quadruplets reassured Lilah that she was doing the right thing—the brave thing. Emery was a Taker and a User masquerading as a Giver. Standing up to her would feel so gratifying when the other shoe finally dropped. Plagiarism was the most straightforward expulsion that existed: it fell under Derrymore's one-strike policy.

Before Lilah could repeat that the essay wasn't exactly plagiarism, Annie said: "I bet Dean Andrews was just pretending to be indifferent. He probably wanted to cheer. I'd never want his job."

"Because it doesn't pay well?" Jenny asked.

"Because the rich kids always get their way, but in walks Lilah—his guardian angel! She's giftwrapped and delivered the one true desire of his heart: a rich kid who can't be saved."

"I don't think he hates them," Lilah said. "Isn't he one of them?"

"Whatever. That's not the point. Emery thought she could steal your life story and you're showing her that she's not entitled to everything after all." Annie took a big slurp of chocolate milk. "That sweet angel thing is pretty funny, though."

• • •

When they returned to the dorm, the bags in front of Emery's door were no longer there. Lilah's blood ran cold. Expulsions were famously quick at Derrymore. Students were whisked away within hours of their sentencing. Not being allowed to say farewell to friends was a key part of the punishment.

They speed-walked to Lilah's room and, once the door was shut, whisper-screamed at each other.

"*Shh! Shh!*" Lilah hushed. "You need to go walk by her room and see if there are any lights on. Be discreet."

Cassie and Jenny went immediately.

"Ohmygod," Annie mouthed. "Do you think she already moved out?"

Lilah gaped back at her. This was it.

Cassie and Jenny said the lights were off. When they put their ears to the door, it was silent. Lilah sent them to Candace's room. They reported that Candace emerged to make tea then called her brother on speakerphone—but she didn't say anything about Emery. The quadruplets huddled for another hour and agreed to meet for breakfast at 7 a.m.

Lilah rehearsed what she'd say as she handed over the folder to Dean Andrews. *I don't mean to beat a dead horse—and I appreciate how efficiently you've taken care of things—but I wanted to give you this for record-keeping purposes.* To accompany the note, she typed up a document that explained its context, how Raymon was involved, and who the perpetrators were. She squirmed a little at throwing Noah under the bus (he had been a decent friend for the past year; they attended black box performances together), but Lilah couldn't help that he was collateral damage. He had written and illustrated the note after all. She couldn't recall if bullying fell under the one-strike policy.

A little after midnight, she climbed into bed exhausted but not sleepy. Her mind's eye kept returning to the heap of Emery's stuff that had been returned unceremoniously. Lilah was never in it for the spoils—meanwhile, Emery had pillaged details of Lilah's life with undeniable intention. She'd assumed parts of Lilah's identity, co-opted the alienation Lilah had described, and glued everything together with lies. Lilah had never meant to dress like Emery or pilfer a single thing from her gross, materialistic life. And to prove any resemblance was an accident, Lilah had dumped everything the moment she realized what she was turning into—thank goodness she'd caught herself before becoming infected.

The homecoming note was an indisputable smoking gun. Lilah wouldn't become another Mrs. Peiffer, felled by Emery's dirty tricks and insider knowledge. She tugged at the collar of the polyester pajamas her mom had bought at Nordstrom Rack. The rash spreading on her neck was one of virtue.

• • •

The next morning, Lilah had a tension headache that woke her up well before her alarm. She tiptoed to Annie's room, where the lights were already on to better peruse the Harvard course catalog.

"Have you heard anything yet?" Lilah whispered.

"Don't worry," Annie said. "You did the right thing."

"I know it was the right thing," Lilah snapped. "Sorry. I didn't get any sleep."

"Relax," Annie said. "Dean Andrews will announce it at Chapel like he always does."

"What if she doesn't get kicked out?"

"Then she has to live with soul-crushing guilt. But if anyone's up to it, she is."

"Wait—you think there's a chance she'll stay? Did you see her or something?"

In Lilah's mind, expulsion was a sure thing. Annie had acted so certain the night before that her blasé response felt like a bait and switch.

"I don't know how these things work," Annie said. "Maybe she gets immunity or something. Everything's different for legacy kids."

Lilah's heart dropped.

"This is exactly why I should email the admissions people at Penn. Derrymore can't just sweep this under the rug."

"I wouldn't do that," Annie said.

"Because I'll look bad? Don't worry—I'll send it anonymously."

"No because … you already got her kicked out. Isn't that enough?"

It would be classic Emery to twist something where she was so obviously in the wrong into a disaster for Lilah. Even though Emery could never come back from one set down on the court, Lilah had seen her do it in every other arena because the Hoopers knew every backdoor and side door and had done every bouncer some life-debt-sized favor. Emery had inherited every trick in the book, joker cards, secret weapons, and cheat codes. She was born knowing loopholes Lilah would never hear about. Emery's entire life was con-structed on top of a storehouse overflowing with Get Out of Jail Free cards, and she didn't have an emergency $20 bill hidden in her shoe, she had a blank check.

"Penn should know that she lied," Lilah said. "Emery said she started *Interrogate* and she's never written a single word. It's a lie."

"You said you were first chair violin and nothing happened to you."

CHAPTER 47

Linear algebra. English. Chapel. Mandarin. Lunch. History. Physics. Tennis. Dinner.

She couldn't wait for Chapel. Lilah went to see Dean Andrews first thing. Once he confirmed that Emery had been removed from the premises her nerves would settle. But he wasn't in his office. The drama was unfolding at a bad time: a math test followed by an in-class essay meant Lilah couldn't afford to be distracted. Every time someone walked by the classroom, Lilah peered through the glass panels flanking the door to see who it was.

Annie sent a text between first and second periods:

What did he say about the letter

Lilah replied:

Wasn't in. Did u see her/hear anything?

Nothing. She's gone.

Lilah wrote a rushed essay about agency and taking responsibility for your actions: Persephone had been careless to eat pomegranate seeds in the underworld (the goddess had only herself to blame) and finished with ten minutes to spare. She jogged to Dean Andrews' office hoping to catch him before Chapel, but the office door was still shut.

Lilah headed toward Chapel with a clear plan in her mind: she'd waylay Dean Andrews. She'd go up to the lectern and force him to read the homecoming note right then and there. He might be irritated by her aggressive approach but she was within her rights to advocate for herself—especially given that she was the precise type of student whose well-being consistently fell through the cracks at Derrymore.

Her lungs were pumping pure indignation as she took her seat in Chapel. She scanned the pews for signs of Emery, whose assigned seat was empty. Noah was looking around nervously (was he paler than usual?) and when Candace stooped down to whisper something in his ear, he nodded gravely. All signs pointed to expulsion.

One minute before the hour and still no Emery—the only explanation was that justice had been served. Lilah glanced down the aisle one more time and caught Candace's eye. Perfunctory smiles were exchanged—then Lilah noticed that Candace was wearing the burgundy hoodie. Her mind raced to make sense of how it had come into Candace's possession as teachers called for quiet and Dean Andrews introduced Devin, who played a five-minute song on a lap steel guitar. After the twangy performance, the dean adjusted the podium mic before clearing his throat.

"We have quite an exciting announcement today. One of the things we are constantly striving to improve ..."

Maybe she was mistaken about the hoodie. She was being paranoid. Lilah looked over her shoulder at Candace and confirmed that she wasn't hallucinating: the golden fur inside the wine-colored hood was unmistakable. It was the same color as Candace's hair. Maybe Candace had plucked it from the restored loot before Emery returned. It had been sitting alluringly on the top of the pile. Stealing wasn't beyond Candace. Lilah's whole body buzzed—it didn't seem possible that she could wait until the end of the hour to get the news she was waiting for, but what choice did she have?

Maybe Emery bequeathed it all to Candace as a parting gift. It wasn't unthinkable that she would jettison the entire load—she wanted no memory of Derrymore or the wrongs she had committed. Candace probably had the periwinkle sweater, too. If Dean Andrews would just get to the disciplinary announcements, everything would be okay.

He gesticulated and emphasized the words "equality," "resources," and "accessibility." He said "benefactor" about fifteen times, then segued into something about a new college counseling center equipped with year-round staff expressly appointed to help rising seniors put together their applications over the summer months.

"We realize that Derrymore still has a ways to go in making the college counseling experience the best it can be for all of our students—no matter what kind of financial background you come from. For this reason, we're thrilled that a generous alumnus has stepped up to help Derrymore reach the heights we know we are capable of and funded this worthwhile initiative. What we have in store will all but guarantee that Derrymore continues to have one of the most successful matriculation records of any secondary school in the world.

"I'm going to step aside and allow someone else to introduce the man of the hour. Who more fitting than his daughter,
in our senior class? An outstanding Derrymorian in her own
right: Miss Emery Hooper."

He lowered the mic slightly and Emery appeared on stage,
the periwinkle sweater draped over her shoulders.

"Thank you, Dean Andrews."

Emery hadn't been in her normal seat because she was
sitting in the first pew with her father. Lilah had been checking behind her, but she should have known to look for Emery
in the front.

"I know from personal experience how much pressure ..."

A prickling started in Lilah's armpits and she began to
perspire profusely. She had read that stress sweat smelled
worse than workout sweat and she clamped her arms down
to her sides. Annie leaned forward conspicuously to get
Lilah's attention. When they made eye contact, Annie
mouthed *ohmygod* then sat back. Lilah was in a daze as Emery
hugged her father, who had come up to the podium.

"Thanks for the great intro, Emmy. It's always an honor to
be invited back to the campus where I formed my most
enduring friendships ..."

There were no expulsions. Mr. Hooper dismissed them
from Chapel ten minutes early. Lilah shuffled out of the
building in disbelief. What had gone wrong? What would
Emery do to her? No one could prove the cover of *Interrogate*
was an illustration of her. Emery didn't *own* periwinkle. Lilah
gasped—the Chinese class essays. Why had she told Emery
that she'd enlisted her parents to write them? There could be
no more vindictive enemy than a slighted Hooper. Emery had

told many high-spirited stories about her father's putting right to wrongs that were often not-quite-fully-wrongs. It wasn't really cheating, Lilah insisted to herself. It wasn't the same as stealing someone's life story.

Did Dean Andrews expect Lilah to keep quiet and know her place? Once he saw the note, he'd understand she was ready to fight back. She patted the folder in her tote bag. It had been wise to keep the note all these years.

Annie shoved her way through the crowd and whispered into Lilah's ear, "Her speech was so bad."

Before Lilah could respond, a woman in a pussy-bow blouse and a pencil skirt stopped in front of her.

"Ms. Chang? I'm Mrs. Brandt-Elliot, assistant to the headmaster. Can you follow me please?"

Lilah's limbs were leaden but she allowed herself to be led away from the chapel. Mrs. Brandt-Elliot spared Lilah the burden of talking by keeping up a stream of comments about how lovely Derrymore was in the fall and how the weather would be just perfect for the bonfire.

Lilah nodded distractedly while her heart beat in the out-of-control way it did before violin recitals. She prepared herself for the worst: the cover of *Interrogate* constituted bullying and Emery had gone to the headmaster, not in anger, but in tears. Emery had convinced him that Lilah had caused irreparable emotional damage and Mr. Hooper demanded action. Remember: it had taken all of one day for the Hoopers to expunge Mrs. Peiffer from Derrymore.

It wasn't Lilah's style to go in guns blazing. That's why the maneuver with Dean Andrews had failed. But if they were going to drag Lilah down, she'd take Emery with her.

She'd let the headmaster say his piece, but he'd be dumb-struck when she calmly presented the homecoming note. *Don't panic*—she forced herself to take slow breaths. At most, her Mandarin infractions were commensurate with Emery's crimes. They couldn't punish Lilah without punishing Emery, too.

The headmaster's office was on the second floor of a Queen Anne–style house that Lilah had never been invited to. The first floor was dedicated to an event space and a conference room, with floors buffed to shine. She followed Mrs. Brandt-Elliot up a grand staircase and down a carpeted hallway. The office was tasteful and modest—deep shelves filled with books (about the school or by Derrymore authors) and a slim desk with a modest sitting area for visitors—not what Lilah had expected for the headmaster. It made sense, though. Headmaster Runciter was rarely on campus. He was known to be a very talented fundraiser and spent most of the school year touring major cities to hobnob with donors.

Mrs. Brandt-Elliot surprised Lilah by sitting behind the desk. She told Lilah the headmaster would be ready for her soon. A moment later, a door Lilah had not noticed opened and she realized the error she had made.

"Lilah Chang, it's a pleasure," the headmaster said, extending his hand.

Her last name was extra foreign coming out of his mouth—an offensive sound that he had to warp his tongue to pronounce. It reminded her of the gym teacher in middle school who would always sing *Chang, Chang, Chang* to the tune of "Chain of Fools" when he saw her. (It was that much worse because he had a good voice.)

"Marjorie, will you grab me a coffee and anything Lilah might want?" the headmaster said, still wringing her hand.

"I'm fine," Lilah said, embarrassed by her clammy grasp. "Thank you."

"Come on in," the headmaster said, and stepped back from the doorway with a flourish.

The first thing Lilah noticed was the vaulted ceiling. Buttresses soared above them. Casement windows looked out onto the Isle and there was a huge fireplace with ancient sconces on either side. The headmaster sat behind his desk and crossed his ankle over his knee, indicating to the chairs across from him.

"Please have a seat," he said.

The fabric of the upholstered chair itched Lilah's thighs and she adjusted her microfloral Forever21 dress.

Though she was intimidated by the office, the view of the Isle took her breath away. She stared.

"Beautiful, isn't it?" he said. "If I ever need inspiration I just look outside my window: *The isle is full of noises, Sounds, and sweet airs, that give delight and hurt not.* I also see a funny thing or two, as you can imagine."

The headmaster laughed on cue and Lilah's nerves rattled. She clasped her hands in her lap and dug her fingernails into her palm.

"I'm sure you're wondering why you're here. Why did Marjorie ambush you at Chapel?"

He explained that he knew she was applying for scholarships and wanted to help. He, the headmaster of Derrymore, wanted to write a personal letter of recommendation attesting to Lilah's excellence as a student and an activist. He held up the Money Edition of *Interrogate* and said it was his favorite publication on campus, even though he had been EIC of *The Derry* back in his day.

"How does that sound?"

Lilah's heart was pounding in her ears. During the walk over, she had devised a thousand scenarios—but this one exceeded her imagination.

"You're going to write a letter of rec for me?"

"I've already written up a draft."

He handed it to her over the enormous Edwardian desk.

Lilah didn't need to see that he had called her "one of the most outstanding students in a high-achieving class" to understand how meaningful such an endorsement would be.

"Do you think this is something you'd want in your file?" he asked, grinning. "For your applications?"

Her eyes flicked nervously from his fixed smile to the Derrymore letterhead with the embossed crest in red and the headmaster's signature in ink above his title.

"And don't worry," he added, "I'll pass it on to Tanya. She'll have a final look. But at a glance, is there anything I've missed?"

Lilah skimmed the letter, barely able to focus her eyes. Since she had never interacted with Headmaster Runciter before, someone had obviously clued him into her entire Derrymore career.

"Wow. This is—" Lilah's voice got caught in her throat and she swallowed hard. "Sorry. Thank you so much. It makes me sound so much better than—"

"It's just the truth," the headmaster said. "Excellence speaks for itself."

Lilah laughed nervously.

She glanced at the copy of *Interrogate*. It seemed impossible that he wouldn't ask her a single question about it, and that he hadn't brought up Emery's name or mentioned the conversation with Dean Andrews.

"Did I leave anything out?" he asked.

Was Lilah supposed to mention the vast scope of things he had omitted? Was it her duty to bring up the situation that Headmaster Runciter had clearly been informed of and jeopardize the offer he was making her? Did he know about her Mandarin essays?

He gestured to the letter. "Take your time reading it over. Make sure I didn't miss anything."

Lilah read it again. The backs of her thighs were sweating against the woolen fabric. He was a good writer. The letter had warmth and personality—it sounded like he really knew her.

"It's wonderful," she said.

The tack Derrymore was taking was the opposite of what she'd expected: they weren't trying to scare her into submission, which also meant there was no way to take Emery down with her, because both of them were getting off the hook. It was shaking out in the one way Lilah had never imagined: zero consequences, double rewards.

"Um. I don't mean to be difficult—but there's one thing missing. It's just that, this season, I'm captain of the tennis team."

He jotted a note on his desk blotter.

"Of course. Can't forget that. I'll update this and make sure the *whole business* is taken care of swiftly."

She handed the letter back to him with trembling hands.

Once it was back in his possession, the headmaster's smile dropped.

"Now that that's squared away—is there anything further we need to discuss?"

The question grazed the fourth wall. His gaze wouldn't release hers. It was Lilah's chance to denounce Emery Hooper on the record. The folder was sitting in the bag at her feet. It wasn't too late. All she had to do was reach down and place the note on his desk. She didn't even have to explain it. If her voice failed and the shaking of her hands became uncontrollable, she could point to the context document. Now was the moment to demonstrate she couldn't be bought, that she would never trade her integrity for a favor from a powerful man, that life was about more than—

"No," she managed. "That's it. That's everything. Thank you for the letter."

His smile returned. "Thank *you* for your contributions to Derrymore. I'm thrilled to see what you'll go on to accomplish. Let Marjorie know what class we stole you from and she'll make sure your tardy is excused."

Lilah pushed her chair back.

"So we're done here," the headmaster said in a tone that was open to interpretation.

It could've been a question if Lilah wanted it to be, but she let it pass as a statement and exited the office on wobbly legs. The secretary was waiting for her. Marjorie heard everything that went on in the headmaster's office.

"I got you a soda," Mrs. Brandt-Elliot said and extended a can of Diet Coke. "I know they're terrible for you but every girl has a sweet tooth. Now, what class are you heading to?"

When Lilah started down the hallway, she heard male voices coming up the staircase. Suddenly, Dean Andrews and Mr. Hooper were approaching.

"The trustees couldn't be more excited about this," Dean Andrews said. "The kids, too."

"It'll be *interesting* to hear Gordie's estimate for when we can break ground. The squash courts took so long I figured Emery would be graduated by the time they were ready."

Dean Andrews laughed and made a joke about refunding Mr. Hooper for every day the project ran late.

As they passed by, Mr. Hooper flashed Lilah an anodyne smile and greeted Marjorie familiarly. The smile held not one ounce of recognition. Lilah's gaze lingered on the man who had taught Emery that a conscience was something you could overcome with enough determination.

"Gordon's ready for you," Marjorie said. "You can head right in."

"Perfect," Mr. Hooper said, and he entered the headmaster's office with the ease of someone who never wonders if they're welcome.

Once the door shut, Dean Andrews addressed Lilah.

"Before you run off to class," he said, smiling so his eyes crinkled, "I wanted to check in. Everything seems like it's been sorted out."

The urge to blurt out that she had an incriminating letter surfaced, but that wasn't how this game was played. Lilah had shaken the headmaster's hand and agreed to play defense. She nodded and wished she could press the icy can against her burning forehead.

"I'm glad we were able to help you out," Dean Andrews said. "Headmaster Runciter's letter will be quite a boost. Where are you planning to apply?"

"UNC," Lilah said. Her mouth was dry. "Chapel Hill."

The dean shook his head ruefully.

"We're going to *take care* of you," he said, lowering his voice. "Aim higher. I bet your parents would love if you put your eggs in the Harvard ED basket. And if there's anything else we can do to help, just name it."

He had already taken a few steps down the stairs when Lilah said, "So a new building is all it takes?"

"I didn't catch that—sorry?"

Dean Andrews turned to face her.

"A new college counseling center," Lilah said, pressing the can of Coke against her bare thigh so it burned. "That's what it takes to avoid the one-strike policy."

"Huh? *Oh.*" Confusion left the dean's face and he shook his head slowly from side to side. He cleared his throat and placed his hand on the banister of the staircase. "Look. An initiative at the scale of the Hooper Center takes years of planning. It's been in the works for over three years. *Three years.*" His eyes bored into hers. "So don't worry. This had nothing to do with you."

EPILOGUE

For the first time in Derrymore history, Commencement took place on the Isle. It was canopied and beautiful with red and black pennants hung between the ancient lindens. The Green would never see another graduation ceremony—it was already on its way to becoming the Hooper Center, which had broken ground (on schedule) in early May.

Emery posed in her white dress beside Candace, then Noah, then Errol, then Candace again while her mother jostled with the others to get the best shot.

"Let's get one of the future roommates!" her mother said.

Riley dutifully stepped up and put her arm around Emery's shoulder.

"Smile! Say *Penn '15!*"

Errol, who was smoking a cigar, had already exhausted the pen15 jokes, but Riley still pinched Emery's arm and stifled a giggle. Every time someone congratulated her, Emery felt a wave of nausea. *Penn 15 Penn 15 Penn 15*—the drone of it was a reminder that she'd let fate take the wheel. But it wasn't succumbing if it was preordained, right? We don't hold Oedipus in contempt. We pity him.

Riley was going to Wharton. She had been deferred in the winter, but her acceptance arrived punctually in spring. Her father had gone to Williams and her mother had attended

Smith—Emery was dying to know who Riley's family knew at Wharton, but the information wasn't volunteered. (That Riley was admitted on merit was never entertained.)

They would be roommates in Riepe. Their neighbors would be Riley's cousin's best friend from Horace Mann and Emery's tennis camp friend who went to Harvard-Westlake. Their world would expand, but only ever along one axis.

"Girls and Noah," Emery's mom directed the next shot.

"Mom, can we take a break?" Emery complained. "You already got hundreds. I'm so thirsty."

"I want to get some with your teachers, too," Mrs. Hooper said. "Okay fine—take five minutes. But don't stray."

The graduates dropped their aching smiles and searched the crowd for the Derrymore videographer. He was recording the quadruplets under a shady tree at the edge of the Isle. At the 10th reunion, it was a Derrymore tradition to screen the Commencement Farewell Video. The time capsule was a way to entice alumni to return to campus for a glimpse of their former selves (and the opportunity to make their first sizable contributions).

"What are you going to answer?" Riley asked.

The videographer's question was the same every year: Who will you be in ten years?

I'll be a mom of twins and pregnant with my third.

I'll be an entrepreneur with my own line of going-out tops.

I'm probably going to work for my family's company.

While Emery was half listening to her friends rehearse their prophecies, someone took hold of her arm.

"Em-lee!"

Suddenly she was face-to-face with Mr. and Mrs. Chang.

• • •

Annie said she would be an orthopedic surgeon in ten years. Cassie would be pursuing a doctorate in something. Jenny provided a non-answer because she still wasn't sure what she wanted to study in college, and she needed to figure it out so she could support her parents in their old age to pay them back for all they'd sacrificed on her behalf. Lilah was in the middle of answering that she might be a journalist when she caught sight of her mom's hands gripping Emery's upper arm.

She froze in the middle of her sentence.

"Why don't you start over?" the videographer asked, wiping sweat from his forehead.

Lilah's eyes were glued to the scene. What was her mom saying? Would Emery reveal everything? Lilah hadn't told her parents a single thing about the fraudulent essay or trying to get Emery expelled, but they knew all about the head-master's letter of recommendation.

When they asked how such a boon had fallen into Lilah's lap, she gave all the credit to *Interrogate*: Headmaster Runciter admired it so much that a letter of rec was the least he could do. The magazine had been a constant point of tension—Lilah's mom had nagged her to give it up and disparaged it at every opportunity—so the lie came to her instinctively.

Mrs. Chang never apologized, but she quit harping on it.

"Who will you be in ten years?" the videographer prompted impatiently.

"Sorry—uh. Hopefully, I'll be a journalist. Thanks."

Lilah watched her mother fawn over Emery, certain that

Penn was the topic of discussion. Throughout senior year, Lilah had given her parents brief, unprompted updates on Emery to save herself the agony of explaining what had really happened. It was easiest to lie and pretend everything was normal.

Emery's body language was stiff and uneasy. In horror, Lilah realized the Hoopers were standing a few feet away. It was only a matter of seconds until they swept in and attacked her parents. *Get away from our precious daughter who has never done a single thing wrong in her life,* Lilah imagined them saying.

Lilah was sweating through her cheap eyelet dress. Her friends had sighted her parents and figured out the cause of her distress.

"Are they confronting her?" Jenny asked.

"I never told them what happened," Lilah said.

"*What?*" Annie said. "You didn't tell them she stole your life for her essay?"

"They wouldn't be mad about that," Lilah said. "Or sympathetic to me. My mom always says rich kids have different rules."

"Not if they're stealing *from you,*" Annie said.

Lilah shook her head.

"That doesn't matter to my mom. She would be mad at me for ruining things with Emery. Whenever she tried to make me quit *Interrogate* she'd say even though I was wasting my time and their money, at least I got that one thing out of Derrymore. Oh no—"

Now her dad was talking to Emery.

• • •

Emery's heart dropped when she saw the familiar Asian faces.

Mrs. Chang was chattering excitedly and it took Emery a few seconds to determine it was friendly, not aggressive. Anger and enthusiasm were the same frequency for Lilah's mom.

"Such long time, no see!"

Mr. Chang nodded meaningfully in agreement but—as usual—said nothing.

Emery was too agitated to make a graceful exit. There was no way to slip out when Mrs. Chang was clapping and butchering the pronunciation of "Pennsylvania."

"You're doing so well—always, always doing so well," Mrs. Chang said, unaware that Emery had not uttered a single word of thanks. "Thank you for influence Lilah and being good role model for her. She needs someone so good like you."

Emery swept the Isle and the stillness of four white-clad figures caught her eye. Lilah had clocked the meeting and she was watching with a level of stress that Emery could detect from fifty feet away.

Mrs. Chang was saying something about Lilah taking the train from Georgetown to visit Emery in Philadelphia: "Tickets are not so expensive if you buy advanced."

Emery was still rooted to the spot where the Changs had intercepted her when Mr. Chang stepped forward, shook Emery's hand, and readied himself to say something. Mrs. Chang could be fake, but Mr. Chang might be the one to cut straight to her conscience.

He took a long pause as he gathered his thoughts and Emery felt her breathing go shallow. She had half a thought to rip her hand from his grasp and flee, but he was pressing something into her palm: a red envelope, thick with cash.

"Congratulations," he said, five distinct syllables, with more feeling than she had ever heard him use before. He spoke the next words slowly: "You have a lucky life."

ACKNOWLEDGMENTS

The thank-yous begin with Mark, who replies within the minute and is reachable in every time zone. Your calm voice of reason has been my lodestar through the twelve labors of this book. Katherine—thank you for opening my cold email. I had mentally shelved this book when you came to its rescue. For your time and effort, thank you, Michael and Olivia at Trident; Allison, Jacob, Renata, and the 8NP team; Sam, Zoey, and the Zando team; the MetroPR team, and Vi-An Nguyen for the cover and Derrymore crest. Your commitment to doing right by this book was second to none.

To my teachers: Mrs. Gallagher at PDS. Taije Silverman at Penn. Benjamin Taylor at TNS. Some of my favorite years were spent at The Lawrenceville School but in writing this book I realized that worshipping institutions is dumb. Credit is due to the teachers who taught me to read, write, and live a meaningful life: Mr. Robbins, JRob, Dr. Cunningham, and Dr. Williams. Every page of this book was informed by what I learned around your Harkness tables.

All the places I wrote and revised this manuscript: the Nantucket Atheneum, Handlebar, Jefferson Market NYPL, the Penn Club, Moshava (shoutout to Jamali), and the Kimmel Harding Nelson Center for the Arts.

To Chrispy and Pan. To my essay students. To Grace, my

TikTok tutor. To the Susmans, for your hospitality and the beautiful backdrop of my author photo. To my thesis group, Luksa Saluk.

To Michelle, Taylor, Julie, Emilia, Chiara, Zach, Evan, Randall, Jack, and Luke—friends of the highest order. I will never skewer you in a vicious satire.

Most people are lucky to have one soulmate. I have two.

Jerry: You're the CC fajool of my dreams. I can't imagine a better way to spend my life than FTTin' it away. With you, every day is BXHPBSM and every night is zoom in on FNU. (It's your fault my acknowledgments look like yearbook shoutouts from a bfr high schooler.) Thank you for giving me more material than I will ever be able to use in one lifetime. I love you so much iclwou. I will *definitely* skewer you in a vicious satire (T and I are already workshopping the title).

Tal: Everything I do is dedicated to you—every word, every grin, every meltdown—and this book is no different. I am first and foremost an author of love letters to you (and I am second, Sanibel R. Lazar). Thank you for my new last name, for eating the large oysters that freak me out, for performing *Barry Lyndon* to make me laugh. When I think of this book, I will always remember how you believed in it from the very, very beginning. Everything I've ever wanted, I've found in you. I love you too much.

Photo credit: Tal Lazar

ABOUT THE AUTHOR

Sanibel is a writer of Korean-Taiwanese descent. She grew up in Princeton, New Jersey, and studied classics at the University of Pennsylvania before getting her MFA at The New School. Her essays have appeared in *New York* magazine, *ELLE*, *Air Mail*, and *Literary Hub*. At The Lawrenceville School, Sanibel did not graduate cum laude but she did get voted "sassiest." She lives with her husband in Greenwich Village. *To Have and Have More* is her first book.